ROOMMATE

ROOMMATE

SARINA BOWEN

TUXBURY PUBLISHING LLC

Editing by Edie Danford. Proofreading by Claudia F. Stahl. Cover photo by Wander
Aguiar.

RODERICK

Sometimes adulting just sucks.

These are my thoughts as I drive my rickety Volkswagen Bug up my parents' gravel driveway. I haven't been here for most of a decade, and I'm bracing myself in every possible way. Anything could have happened during the intervening years. They could have moved away. (Although that's unlikely.) They could have gotten divorced. (Also hard to picture.)

Conceivably, one or both could be dead.

I don't even know how I'll feel if that last thing has happened. My parents and I didn't part on good terms, to put it lightly. But people can change their ways.

Not all of them do, though.

At first glance, my parents' property looks exactly the same. The little one-story house is still clad in cheap vinyl siding, and its shade of ochre-yellow is just how I remember it.

The tall pines have been carefully pruned of their dead lower branches, which argues for the continued existence of my father, who always enjoyed firing up his chainsaw to tidy things up. Also, Dad's old ride-on mower is visible inside the garage.

He's still around, then. I feel a little hit of relief, which makes no sense. The man will probably shut the door in my face when he sees who's come to visit. This is going to end badly. I'm already ninety-nine percent sure.

Still, I need to ask for their help. After paying for the gas to drive up from Nashville, I have less than four hundred dollars to my name. And no job. If they turn me away, I'm sleeping in my car again tonight.

It won't kill me, but it's not ideal.

Parking in front of the garage, I get out and almost bleep the locks. I'm so used to parking in Nashville. I haven't lived under these tall pines for eight years.

Back then, I couldn't wait to leave this place. I had my reasons, and some of them were solid. And I used to hate the trees and the winding country roads as much as I hated my parents' attitude.

I still hate the things my parents said to my teenage self. But Vermont looks better to me than it ever did before. I'm ready to live somewhere without smog and traffic. I miss the smell of woodsmoke in the nighttime air, and the sight of the sun setting over the Green Mountains.

Maybe it's weird to feel nostalgia for a place that wasn't good to me. But I'm in the mood to give Vermont a second chance. I'm hoping it gives me a second chance, too. And I'm about to find out if driving eleven hundred miles was a good idea or just plain stupid.

As I approach the house, the front door is already opening. My dad stands on the other side of the screen door, TV remote in his hand, staring at me like he's seen a ghost.

"Hi," I say carefully.

"Roddy," he whispers. He makes no move to open the screen door, but then, neither do I. Maybe we both need a minute to get over our mutual shock.

He looks older. It startles me to catalog all the gray in his hair and the new wrinkles around his eyes.

I'm pretty sure that I don't look like the skinny eighteen-year-old I used to be, either. So he's staring back at me trying to get over that, too.

2

"You're back?" he asks, still befuddled.

"Well…" I let out a nervous chuckle. "I've been living in Nashville. And yesterday I just got in my car and drove up here without a plan. It took me two days."

I won't tell him why I left Nashville. He won't want to hear about the awful way my relationship ended. Hell, he won't want to hear about my relationship at all.

"So," I continue. "I'm happy to be back in Vermont. But I'm kind of starting over. And I was wondering if…"

"Ralph?" my mother's voice calls from deeper inside the small house.

I have very little time to prepare before she appears behind him. She's drying her hands on a dish towel, her hair in a messy bun.

My heart gives a little squeeze of familiarity before I can steel myself.

"Roderick," she whispers, her eyes popping wide. "Oh, honey. What's happened?"

"Well, not much," I stammer. "I just needed to get out of Nashville and start over. So I was thinking of doing that here."

"Here?" She squeezes the dish towel, her eyes alight.

"Perhaps," I say, trying to sound like it isn't my only option in the whole world. But if I step over the threshold and stay with them, it has to be because I'm invited. I won't live with their disdain. Sleeping in the car would be better.

"You want to stay here," my father clarifies. He's still holding that TV remote. And he still hasn't opened the screen door.

It's not a good sign.

"Just for a little while," I say. "Until I find a job and a place of my own. I'm a baker."

"You…what?" my mother asks. "Like, cakes?"

"Bread, mostly. I went to culinary school. I specialize in bread-baking."

My father squints at me, and that's another clue this isn't going to work. "Culinary school," he echoes. There's dismissal in

3

his voice. *Baking is not a real man's job.* I might as well have said that I'm a ballet dancer, or that I star in a drag show. My father's ideas of what a man should do with his life are straight out of the fifties.

"No more guitar?" my mother asks. She's hoping I've grown out of being the queer little music nerd my father couldn't tolerate. She's trying to sway him.

"No guitar," I agree, although it kills me a little to imply that I somehow got with Dad's program and outgrew music. The truth is that I accidentally left my guitar behind in Nashville.

I did outgrow musicians, though. But that's another long story.

"If you stay…" My father purses his lips. "It's our house, our rules."

I swallow hard. "I'm a great house guest. I even cook. And clean up."

My mother makes a happy sound and reaches for the latch on the screen door. She even elbows my father a little to shift him out of the way.

He doesn't move, though. He's still staring at me like I'm a puzzle he's trying to figure out. "But you're not… You won't…" He falters.

"I won't what?" I ask, already knowing where this is going.

Dad can't even spit out the loathsome words. "You have a girl-friend?" he asks.

Coward. I shake my head. "I don't have anybody. That's why I'm standing on your front steps. I had to leave a bad relationship with nothing but my clothes and a box of books. But I still date men, if that's what you're asking. I'm still gay."

My mother lets out a sound of dismay. And the way my father's face shutters, I know I came here for nothing.

"You haven't been to church," my father says, as if that isn't a non-sequitur. But to him I suppose it isn't.

"Not lately," I admit. "My life blew up, Dad. I have nowhere to go. I'm asking to stay in my old room for a couple of weeks until I can regroup. And I'd help out around here, of course."

There is a terrible silence while we stare at each other. And then he slowly shakes his head. "Not until you ask God's forgiveness."

It's really astonishing that you can storm out of a house at eighteen in the middle of a shouting match, and then pick right up again in the same place eight years later. We're still trapped in the same dialogue we'd had my entire last year of high school.

"I am humble before the Lord," I say quietly. "But I will not apologize to Him for who I love, or who I am."

My father gives me a disgusted look, as if I just announced my committed worship of Satan. He folds his arms across his chest. The posture is clear. *Go away. You are no longer my son.*

Message received. I feel a flash of the old hurt, but it's followed swiftly by exhaustion. My anger is muted by two days behind the wheel of my car and by already having years of living with his rejection.

Still, I look him right in the eye. *You arrogant fuck. Who says you can judge me?*

My mother sniffs, and I know she's crying. Mom wants me to come inside. But she doesn't want it enough to stand up to him.

That's when I finally realize I'm done here. Probably forever. There is nothing left to do but turn around and leave.

I take one last look at him. But there is no softness there. No affection for the kid he used to love, although I've always been me. I'm the same boy who caught all those baseballs with him in the various yards around the country where we lived when he was in the Air Force. I'm the same son who mowed the lawn and got up early to go fishing, because I craved his attention.

He doesn't even blink. His rejection is unmoving.

So I turn around and make myself walk away.

The sound of the heavy wood door shutting behind me comes even more suddenly than I expect it to. And I have the sudden, terrible urge to spin around and hurl myself at that fucking door.

Open up, you cowardly fuck! I might scream. Part of me wants to make a big scene, the way I used to when he lectured me during my senior year of high school.

But the other half of me is already numb. I drove all the way to Vermont thinking I might have a chance. *When God closes a door, he opens a window.* It's the worst kind of cliché, but I wanted it to be true. All the way here I wondered if my breakup was some kind of sign that I was meant to live my life elsewhere. I thought maybe I was sent home again for a reason.

Apparently not, though. This week, when God closes a door, he also engages the deadbolt.

I go back to my car and start the engine again. Might as well have left her running. I do a three-point turn without looking at the house, yellowed pine needles crackling under my tires. It's time to form a Plan B. So I point my car toward the center of Colebury.

I'll bet my father is already watching the playoff game again. Maybe he's treated himself to a second beer, just to wash away the disturbing intrusion of his queer son during the fifth inning.

And my mother is crying into a hand towel in the bathroom. Quietly. So she doesn't make a fuss.

I can't think about them right now. I have more practical problems—like how to get a job immediately. And where to sleep tonight. Best-case scenario—there is magically a job opening at the King Arthur Flour Bakery, where I began my career. But even if they hire me tomorrow, it will be at least two weeks until I could expect to be paid.

I have to figure out how to stay alive for several weeks on a few hundred dollars.

As I drive into town, I notice that my gas tank is almost empty. There goes twenty-five bucks. I drive slowly anyway, taking in the sights, wondering what's changed. Just before the turn into Colebury, I spot a couple of new businesses. There's a bar called the Gin Mill with lots of cars in the parking lot. That place looks like a good time, but I don't have money to spend, not even on a single beer.

In the same lot, though, there's another business that's even more interesting to me. The Busy Bean. A coffee shop. It's closed now, but I make a note to pay it a visit soon. If it's a big coffee shop, they might be able to use a baker, one who doesn't mind pouring coffee, too.

Beggars can't be choosers. And since I'm *this* close to becoming an actual beggar, I have to keep my options open.

I gun the engine, climbing the hill toward the town square. The houses look a little better maintained than the last time I was here. It's a warm autumn night, and there are people standing outside the old diner, chatting. That place has shined itself up, too. When did Colebury get cute? I'm stunned at how cheerful it looks, with window boxes on the store fronts and every street lamp lit.

My nostalgia bubbles up inside me again like yeast. This is my hometown, even if I never felt welcome here before. I was born here. And even if I spent most of my first eighteen years living on various military bases around the world, I finished high school here, too.

And I like the look of the place, damn it. I feel the pull.

Wouldn't it be funny if I settled down in Colebury right under the noses of my parents? I want to see the look on my father's face when I walk into the diner holding hands with my future boyfriend.

Now there's a happy thought I'll need to revisit when I'm trying to fall asleep in the passenger seat later.

Behind the old diner, I see something that's actually useful to me. A gym. TRY A WEEK ON US, reads a sign in the window.

It's the first lucky break of the day. Or maybe the month, if I'm honest. If the gym has even a half-decent locker room, I can shower there every night. I'll need to look professional while I'm job hunting.

I park my car and get out. *Come on, Colebury. Don't let me down.*

7

KIERAN

I'm leaning against my car in the parking lot at the gym. I'm aware that just standing around outside the gym defeats the whole purpose of being here, but I'm on the phone, listening to my older brother plead with me to do his chores at home.

"Come on, this is my opportunity to make an extra hundred bucks. You can come into the Gin Mill and I'll buy you a beer."

"How can I come in and drink beer if I'm moving the cows for you?" I ask. People always tell me that I have a grumpy voice. But lately it's extra grumpy when I talk to Kyle.

"Come later," he says. "After chores."

Only Kyle would pretend that's a workable plan. He expects me to abandon my workout, drive forty minutes home, move the cows' grazing fence before it gets dark, and then finish the other farm chores.

Then drive forty minutes back for a free beer? Ridiculous.

And here's the shitty thing—Kyle gets *paid* by our dad for farming. But I don't. "You have two jobs, and Kyle does most of the ranch work," he'd said last year when he'd finally added Kyle to the payroll.

That would make sense if only it were true. But Dad's back problems started getting worse right after that, so I've been pitching in three nights a week. "Let me get this straight. I'm doing your chores for free so that you can earn money elsewhere?"

"Please?" he begs. "What if I paid you twenty bucks? It's only a two-hour gig, but Alec says the beer-industry people are big tippers."

I look forlornly toward the gym. If I'd gotten here ten minutes earlier I would have been inside already, unreachable. I do everything that's asked of me. *Everything.* And nobody really appreciates it.

"Tell me this—what are your plans for the rest of the week?" I demand. He's terrible at planning. And I need him to use his head for once, before I lose mine.

"Well, tomorrow I promised Dad I'd take him to the newest *Robot Wars* movie in Montpelier…"

While he talks, my attention is snagged by a man who's just climbed out of a bright blue Volkswagen Bug. He's reading the sign on the door of the gym. I can't see his face, because he's turned to the side. But I get a good look at his muscular shoulders, which are straining his black T-shirt. And his forearms have terrific muscle definition…

"Kieran?" my brother prompts. "Did you get that?"

No, I was just admiring a dude. I close my eyes and try to forget the hot guy across the parking lot. This is the extent of my sex life —admiring men, and then feeling confused about it. I spent the first twenty years of my life thinking that attractive men were interesting to me only because I admired them as people and wanted to be like them.

But that was only half right. Lately it's gotten harder to ignore the fact that I also want to be *under* them. Or over them. Or even side by side.

Just as I'm having this bold thought, the guy reaches for the door to the gym. And he turns his body in a way that lets me see his face…

That's when everything goes a little haywire. Because I recognize that face. It's been years since I've seen it, though. And I'd bet every dollar in my wallet that he doesn't even know my name.

Thank God.

My face flushes hot and my body runs cold. It doesn't matter that he didn't look my way before disappearing into the gym, or that there would be no way that he would remember me the way I remember him. I still feel a flash of utter shame.

"...so that's why I'll need your help the next few nights," my brother is saying.

"The next few nights," I echo stupidly.

"Look, I know it's a lot. But this thing with Dad's back is a bummer, and there's really no way we can get through the next month without a lot of extra hassle."

I must still be experiencing an adrenaline rush, because I suddenly snap. "Hassle for *who*? You want to pull a shift at the bar, where you can earn extra money and hit on women. And tomorrow you want to go to the movies, but it's with Dad so you think that excuses your lack of planning. And I zoned out for that last thing you said, but I'm sure it doesn't matter. Because unless you said you're going to save babies from a burning building, I can't understand why you think it's okay to bail on me three or four nights in a row."

There is a deep, stunned silence after I deliver this tirade. I never go off on Kyle, although maybe it's time I did. My life is ridiculous. I work like a dog, and I never complain. I never do a thing for myself, and all I wanted tonight was a goddamn workout.

"Well," he says a moment later. Then he clears his throat. "Tell me how you really feel."

I feel like a dick, that's how I feel. A wave of cold remorse washes over me.

"I won't take the bartending shift," Kyle says. Then he hangs up on me for the first time in his life.

Standing here in the gym parking lot, I'm breathing a little too fast and my heart is hammering. I can't believe I snapped like that. Yes, it's time to stop doing everything my family expects. Standing up for myself is a fine idea. But I didn't have to be a dick about it.

And Roderick Waites is back in town.

My gaze travels back to the gym door. He's still in there. Which means that I just blew up at my brother for nothing, because I'm not going into that gym.

My thumbs are tapping out a text to Kyle before I can even think twice about it. *Take that bartending shift,* I say. *It's fine. I'm on my way home to move the cows.*

By the time I get into my truck and start the engine, he's already replied.

Dude. Are you sure? You just lost your shit at me.

I'm sure. But tonight when you get home we have to make a plan for the rest of the week. Because I'm not doing all your chores again tomorrow just so you can go to the movies.

Fine, he replies. *Thanks. Later!*

I back out of the parking spot and turn the truck toward home. I suppose I could take my dad to the movies tomorrow. But Dad wouldn't want my company, he wants Kyle's. The privilege of being Dad's favorite is lost on my goof of a brother. Kyle is incapable of imagining that life doesn't fart rainbows on everyone the way it does on him.

Something's got to give, I tell myself as I put some miles between Colebury and home. This isn't the first time I've wanted to break out of my rut. I'm twenty-five years old and still live at home. My family is a minefield, yet they depend on me for farm labor.

And—worst of all—I still care too much about what other people think. Case in point: I just ran away from the gym, because of a guy who won't even remember me. That's ridiculous.

But at least I realize that. It's a start.

———

Back at home, I do all the chores and then some.

First I put the cows in the north pasture. Moving cows is easy enough in good weather. It only requires me to move the portable fence and wave them through the opening. "Go on, enjoy," I say as they file past me eagerly. Our herd is grass fed, and they don't need to be asked twice. The long, seedy grass and corn stalks I'm offering are like a recently freshened, all-you-can-eat buffet.

Let's face it—the cows are easier to handle than any of my family members. They go where they're needed, no questions asked. But my dog—Rexie—gives the cows a nice loud *woof* just to pretend he's working hard.

Rexie and Kyle have a lot in common, honestly. They're both a little ridiculous. They both have an inflated sense of their own usefulness. And I love them both in spite of it.

After the cow parade, I close up the fence and turn the electricity on. Since it's October, darkness is falling fast. In another couple of weeks we'll have to set our clocks back, and then it will be pitch dark before five. I'm already squinting as I check the hens' nesting boxes for eggs, and topping up their water, and I have to turn on my head lamp to connect up their electric fence.

Most of our farming income is made on grass-fed beef. We also grow some corn and organic oats as feed crops. By this time of year, all the crop work should already be done, but Kyle and I still have to bale the oat straw. It would have been done weeks ago, if it weren't for my dad's back pain getting worse.

I make a mental note to remind my brother to make the baling a priority. Again. After that, I spend forty-five minutes raking cow shit out of the lower farmyard in the dark.

It's boring drudge work, and my mind starts to wander. And, fuck, it wanders right to Roderick Waites—the guy who climbed out of a blue Volkswagen and right back into my brain.

I wish I could say I haven't thought about him since high school, but that would be a lie. And if I were a more spiritual person, I'd probably interpret Roderick's reappearance in town as a sign. A wakeup call.

Nobody knows all the tangled things in my brain, but for a

split second when I was a teenager, Roderick came close to learning one of my biggest secrets.

The first time I saw him on his knees in front of another guy, it was an accident.

It was autumn then, too. I'd been at a high school football game. It was chilly that night and, last second before leaving for the game, I'd grabbed my dad's jacket from the hook by the door. After shoving my hands into the pockets while standing on the windy sidelines, I'd found a flask of whiskey. My father must have last worn the jacket when he was sitting out in the deer blind with his pals. *Bonus.*

But, of course, I'd had to sneak around to find a place to take a taste.

Leaving the crowd and the game, I ducked inside the door to the school's gym. Under the cover of the bleachers, I drew out my dad's flask, and unscrewed the top. Just as I raised it to my lips, I froze at the sound of whispered voices. Whoever was speaking had entered the gym at the other end of the bleachers.

Their shadowy figures weren't easily visible. But I guessed it was a couple looking for a little privacy for a make-out session. And since a couple sneaking off together wasn't a threat to me, I stood my ground.

I took a swallow of my father's hooch. My first sip wasn't life-changing—it burned going down and made my eyes water—it's what happened next that changed everything.

After screwing the lid on the flask and pocketing it, I ducked out of the gym and into the hallway. Feeling nosy, I walked toward the gym's other entrance, noiseless in my Nikes. When I reached the door, I eased into a position that allowed me to spy on the couple I'd heard whispering to each other. They were silent now, and I wanted to know why.

When I saw who it was, I swear my heart almost stopped. A varsity soccer player—Jared Harvey—stood beneath the bleachers, bracing his hands on a tread overhead. Roderick Waites knelt in front of him, unzipping Jared's jeans.

You can bet I didn't even blink for the next five minutes. I was riveted by the tension in Jared's body. The muscles in his arms bulged as he held on to the tread, his chest rapidly rising and falling as he watched Roderick tug down his underwear and free his cock.

"Suck it, man," Jared bit out.

Roderick didn't hesitate. He grabbed the base of Jared's dick in one hand and eagerly took the tip into his mouth. Jared made a strangled sound and tipped his head back in pleasure.

I could barely breathe as Roderick hollowed out his cheeks and sucked. And I became lightheaded when he began to bob up and down.

"*Ungh*!" Jared grunted. "Goddamn. Faster."

Instead, Roderick slowed his pace, looking up at Jared with luminous eyes. And, damn, the sounds he made—the smack and slurp made my teenage brain melt.

Jared's hold on the tread got shaky and, at last, Roderick picked up the pace. Jared gasped, one of his big hands falling to land in Roderick's hair. Roderick glanced up at him again, and the eye contact seemed to burn Jared. He yanked his hand back and looked away.

I saw Roderick reach up and tug Jared's balls with his free hand. No, I *felt* it. I was suddenly, painfully aware of my own arousal, of being so hard that my jeans were uncomfortable.

Jared cursed and shuddered, every muscle locking. His face slackened with release, and Roderick's throat worked as he swallowed. It was the most erotic thing I'd ever seen in my seventeen years. My heart was thumping and blood pounded in my ears.

And other places.

Self-preservation finally kicking in, I backed away from the doorway and ducked into the men's room across the hall.

In the mirror, my face had been flushed, my eyes hooded and dark. I'd looked like a man who'd seen his dirtiest fantasies brought to life. Because I had.

For days afterward I don't think I had a single rational

thought. Both Roderick and Jared were seniors—a grade above me—and it was a good thing we didn't share any classes. I probably would have burst into flames, if I had to speak to either of them. I spent a lot of time thinking about what I saw, and wondering if they were gay.

The weird thing was that I had all those thoughts about them without considering why I was so obsessed. That would take a few more years.

But the story doesn't end there. Two weeks later there was another home football game. As I sat in the bleachers with my brother and our friends, I saw Jared get up and head toward the school. Roderick's dark head passed by the side of the bleachers a minute later.

I'm sure you know what I did next.

"Taking a leak. Back in a few," I muttered to my friends. Then I snuck into the school building and tiptoed down the dark hallway again. I have never felt so much shame as I crept toward the gym. What the hell did it mean that I wanted to watch this?

But curiosity was burning me up inside. Would it be Jared on his knees this time? Or would they do something totally different?

I'm sure I shivered with anticipation as I slowly peered around the gym's door. The picture was the same. Roderick sucking off Jared. Jared gasping and writhing and desperate. I watched every second that I dared.

And that wasn't the last time either. It took a couple more secret trips to the gym before I learned my lesson. I'd known I needed to stop watching, but I just couldn't stay away. Also, it was the final home game of the season, and what was one more sin among so many?

That last time was different. From his usual spot on the floor, Roderick used one of his hands to unzip his own fly, and he stroked himself while he sucked off his friend. I was dying slowly in my hideout, my eyes glued to his hand on his cock. Jared was almost ready to blow, and so was I—hands free.

But that didn't happen. Because Roderick's gaze shifted in the dark.

He lifted those blue eyes and looked right at me. And his expression told me that he'd known I was there. He'd known it all along.

You would've thought I'd turn around to run, but I froze, my shame complete. And then? He stared at me while he came all over his hand.

God. Even now—years later—the memory gets me hard. The sheer nerve of those boys getting off on school property. They were living, and I was watching.

But *man* did I like watching.

A sharp whistle from the farmhouse breaks my reverie. It's my mother calling me in to dinner. I hang up the rake on the side of the barn, adjust my jeans, and head toward the house.

Eight years later I'm still thinking about Roderick Waites. And I'm still keeping secrets, still doing exactly what everyone expects of me.

Nothing has changed, really. Nothing at all.

KIERAN

As I kick off my boots in the mudroom, I take a deep breath and try to rearrange my thoughts. I've lived here my whole life, but lately the place really brings me down. "Hey, Ma," I say, after entering the kitchen. "How are you doing?"

"Okay," she says from the stove. Then she drops her voice. "But your father is a bear today. And there's something we need to talk about at dinner."

"Okay. Sure," I agree. Although my father is a bear almost all the time, and we both know it. "Are we making some sandwiches?"

"No, I cooked!" she says. "Chicken casserole."

"Great," I say, mostly meaning it.

My mom's cooking is bland, and that dish is particularly taste-less. She'd never been a great cook, but when her doctor suggested she cut down on the sodium, the menu took a turn for the worse. Chicken casserole with no salt? Trust me, you don't want any. Even Rexie prefers his kibble to mom's casserole.

I'll eat it anyway, though, because I'm hungry, and it's free. For a few years now, I've been saving up to rent a place of my own. My dream is to live in town.

My pile of cash is pretty tall at this point, so when Dad is back to work again, I can start looking for something cheap. There's even a chance that I'll rent a house in Colebury from Zara, my boss at the coffee shop. She's probably losing her next-door tenant next month. "He was offered a job in another state," she'd said. "If they leave, I'll rent the house to you on the cheap, if you can help me with the yard work and the snow removal this winter." And then she'd named a price that fit my budget, especially if I got a roommate.

Man, I would shovel *acres* of snow to have a place of my own.

Meanwhile, I set the same kitchen table I've set my whole life. It's square, with a joint right down the center. My mother and I always sit on one side, and my father and Kyle sit on the other. It's a damn metaphor if I ever saw one.

"How was the desk job today?" my father asks as he shuffles into the room and pulls out the chair on his side. He says *desk job* the way some people say *acupuncture*. Like only a crazy person would get a job at an office.

"Fine. Busy." I stick to one word answers with him. We have so little in common and don't see eye to eye on anything.

"If they're so busy, why don't they take you full time?" Dad sits down gingerly, accepting a plate from my mother, looking down at the beige blob of food on it with a grimace.

Please don't critique the food, I privately beg him. I can tolerate my dad's ire toward me, but when he picks on my mother, I tend to lose my cool.

"I mean, how can you learn the ad business if you're only there four afternoons a week?" he asks, picking up his fork with a wary glance at his dinner.

"I learn plenty," I say mildly. The truth is that I haven't said much about my job in Burlington. Nor have I said a word about the college course I'm hoping to take this spring. He won't approve. And there's no law that says I have to explain myself to him.

I'm just going to do my own thing and give the bare minimum

amount of information to anyone who asks. That's how you keep the peace in this house.

"You didn't go to the gym?" my mother asks, just to keep the conversation flowing.

A wave of discomfort rolls through me, because the question makes me think of Roderick. Again. I wonder if I'll ever be able to think of that guy and not feel embarrassed. "I almost made it to the gym. But Kyle called me and sent me home to do his chores instead."

"It is his night, isn't it?" my mother asks. "Where is that boy?"

"Tending bar for a couple hours, for extra cash." I shovel in some more of my mother's casserole and chew so I won't say what I'm thinking.

"It's good to earn extra cash," my father says, excusing Kyle. "We're going to have a tough season around here."

"Why?" I set down my fork. "Did we lose an animal?"

"No." He shakes his head.

That's when the kitchen door opens and Kyle steps through, grinning. "Am I just in time for dinner?"

"Yes you are!" my father says, smiling for the first time, because his eldest—his boy—is home.

"It's my super power." Kyle hangs his coat on a hook.

"Sally, get him a plate," my dad says.

My mom gets up and makes Kyle a plate, while my brother slides into his chair. He plops twenty bucks on the table in front of me. "Thanks for your help."

"Sure," I grunt, wishing I'd never made a big deal about it in the first place. I tuck the bill into my pocket anyway. My rent fund can use it.

Mom sets a plate in front of my brother, and then takes her seat again. "Since Kyle's home, we might as well talk about this winter." My father's scowl tells me I won't like whatever she's about to say. "Your father is having back surgery. Soon. He's going to be out of commission for months."

"Weeks," my father corrects gruffly.

19

She rolls her eyes. "It's a spinal fusion. Major surgery, with a long recovery time."

Spinal fusion. Yeesh. I'll be googling that later, but it already sounds dreadful. I feel a rare pang of sympathy for Dad. But when I look up at him, the steely look in his eyes asks for no pity.

"Okay," I say, draining my glass. "You know Kyle and I will pitch in." I give my brother a sideways glance.

"Yeah, we've got this," he says. "It's good that you're doing this before calving and planting."

"That's the idea," my mother says. "It's going to be a rough time for a little while. But I knew you'd both pitch in. It's the Shipley way."

"Right," I say, trying to keep the bitterness out of my voice. "I can give you weekend afternoons and Mondays. I don't go to the office on Mondays."

"What if you found a job closer to home instead?" my father asks.

Wait, what? "You think that's so easy to do?"

"It has to be easier than driving clear across Vermont to work that desk job. And you're pouring coffee in the mornings. Seems like you could save yourself a lot of trouble and take a job at the hardware store in town."

"So you'd have me quit the Busy Bean and bail on Audrey and Zara? Is that the Shipley way?" The Bean is owned by Audrey Shipley, my cousin's wife. If my mom was gonna pull the family card, it seemed worth mentioning.

My father shrugs, as if I'm being ridiculous. "Audrey can find someone else to sell muffins, no?"

"How about you let *me* figure out the best way to get paid?" I ask, and each word is a little chip of ice. The undertone is perfectly clear, too—if *he's* not paying me, then he can shut the hell up. "I just offered you every spare hour of my week. Is that not good enough?"

"It's great," Kyle says quickly. "We'll figure this thing out, right?"

"Right. But you'll have to be thoughtful about your schedule. Baling those oats is a two-man job, so you're going to have to make yourself available when I'm off work."

"No problem," he says.

"That means baling and handling the fences even when there's football on TV."

"I know. *Jesus*." Kyle gives me a grumpy look, too.

But I already know how this is going to play out—a long, cold season doing farm work after putting in a full day at my other two jobs.

"If we all pull together, it will be okay," my mother says.

"That's right," Kyle echoes. "And cold drinks when the work is done. That's the Shipley way."

He makes it sound so simple. Meanwhile, I'm sitting across the table, trying not to scream.

In this house, *that's* the Shipley way.

RODERICK

I pass a difficult night in the passenger seat of my car.

In the first place, it's harder to find a safe place to park than you'd think. Being invisible isn't easy. I'm afraid to lurk where the cops might notice me. I suppose I could google *homeless shelters in Vermont* and find one.

But I don't want to. When I was eighteen, I spent some time in homeless shelters. I'd rather not repeat that experience. I am never going to be that terrified teenager again. I don't want to go back to that defeated mental state. I don't want to even say the word *homeless*. I'm just between houses at present. At least this time I have a car. I'm locked in and safe.

That's what I'm trying to tell myself, anyway. But sleep is fitful. Every little sound wakes me up. I'm parked behind a dumpster in back of a karate dojo. I keep expecting to see a police cruiser pull up with its lights flashing.

Also, my legs are numb, and whenever I try to roll over, I smack my knee against the door.

I doze fitfully. At some point during the darkest part of the night, my thoughts turn to my ex, Brian. He's asleep in our bed right now, sprawled out and comfortable. *His* bed. It was never really ours. I spent three years loving him on his terms. Hiding our relationship in public. Feeding on the scraps of attention he was willing to give.

On some level I always knew he wasn't capable of loving me back, even though he would sometimes tell me he did. But just as often he'd push me away. He'd "forget" about our plans, or change his mind at the last minute. He did these things just to keep me on edge—to prove that I wasn't really necessary in his life.

Eventually I got clingy and threw down an ultimatum, which he pretended to consider. But then? He cheated just to make sure I knew he was in charge.

That's the Cliffs Notes. And now I'm sleeping in my car, because he froze me out of our bank account the minute I left town. At a gas station in Massachusetts I realized he'd canceled my credit cards, too.

Forget my numb ass—it's hard to sleep when you're questioning all your life choices.

Dawn comes eventually. I blink my bleary eyes and make a plan. First I'll hit the Colebury Diner for a cheap plate of eggs. Then I'll brush my teeth and wash my face in the men's room.

It's a thirty minute drive to Norwich, where I did a one-month internship at King Arthur Flour after culinary school. I'll get there by eight a.m., when they take their first break. My old boss is still listed on the website. I'll dazzle him with my recent experience, and he'll offer me a job on the spot.

And if that doesn't work, I'll cruise by every bakery in Vermont. Something will work.

Two hours later, I leave the fancy new King Arthur facility feeling discouraged. Gone is the cozy, undersized kitchen where I learned to bake sourdough. The new gleaming commercial space was as unfamiliar as the faces in it. My former boss has moved into management and works in a different building now.

"I'll give you a great recommendation, Rod," he'd said when I called the number they'd given me at the new bake shop. "Go ahead and fill out an application. But I know the baker gets several applications each week."

"Great, I'll do that," I'd said, my heart sinking.

"Come back next month if you're still looking. They always need seasonal help in the retail store."

"Will do. Thanks." I'd filled that application out, which took five minutes.

But now I climb back into my car again and crank the engine. I have never felt so untethered from the world as I do right now. I have no address. No job. And no real friends, either, because they're all coworkers at the job I left behind in Tennessee, or—worse—pals of Brian's.

The scary truth is that if I disappeared from this earth today, nobody would notice, or come looking for me.

Also, I need coffee. Nobody should be expected to solve his not-quite-midlife crisis while under-caffeinated, right?

So I point my car back toward Colebury. *Chin up*, I coach myself. I can't expect my problems to be solved within the first hour of job hunting. I'm the kind of guy who always has to hustle for everything he gets. King Arthur is the biggest bakery in the area, but it's not the only one that could hire me.

I hope.

It's still midmorning when I reach the Busy Bean. When I step out of my car, I smell good coffee brewing. The scent of a strong brew on the piney Vermont air is like a siren's song to me. I approach the door, already filling up with hope. *Come on, Vermont. Give me something to believe in.*

The first thing I notice is the acoustic guitar music humming off the wide-plank floorboards. The scent of coffee is stronger, too. And the place is *adorable*. It's full of mismatched furniture upholstered in dark colors and animal prints. There are snarky sayings chalked onto the ceiling's wide support beams. One verse in particular catches my eye:

Roses are red
Violets are blue
I love my coffee
And if you talk to me before I drink it I will cut you

I let out a happy snort. Is it possible that I've found my people?

Cautiously, I approach the bakery case. I hope it's not full of underbaked institutional cookies and rubbery bagels.

But, nope! It's full of homemade pastries. They're simple— mostly muffins and scones—but they look too good to have been dropped off by a food distributor's truck. My stomach rumbles as I take in the offerings.

"Can I help you?" This question comes from a tall woman with dark, wavy hair. "I recommend the lemon muffins, because my partner just made them, and if you don't have a couple, I'm probably going eat some more of them."

"I would love a couple of muffins," I say. Not only am I legitimately starving, but it makes opening up the conversation that much easier. "And a small coffee, black." I pull out my wallet. Just because I'm broke doesn't mean I can survive this day without more caffeine.

"Dark roast or breakfast blend?"

"Dark roast. Breakfast blend is for sissies."

The dark-haired beauty laughs. "That will be four fifty."

That's pretty cheap, honestly. I push a five-dollar bill toward her. After she makes my change, I drop the bomb. "Listen, if there's any chance you are hiring, can I leave my name? I'm a baker by training. But I make a mean espresso, too."

The woman's hands freeze on the cash drawer. "You're a *baker*," she says slowly. "Are you looking for part time or full time?"

"Well, full time. But right this second I'm not picky. If I don't find what I'm looking for, I'll have to piece together a couple of jobs."

"Did he say full time?" asks another voice. A sunny-haired woman appears suddenly in the doorway behind the counter.

"He did."

The blonde emerges from the kitchen, dusting flour off her hands. "So I guess we're talking about this now?" She steps out where I can see her. She's a little thing and appears to be pregnant.

"So..." I'm not even sure what to say. "You might be looking to hire some help?"

"We really need to," the dark-haired one says. "But we've been putting it off. I'm Zara Rossi by the way."

"Nice to meet you, Zara. I'm Roderick."

"And I'm Audrey Shipley," says the cute blonde.

"Oh, the Shipleys." That familiar name perks me up. "I remember your family. They were always winning awards at school and running things at church." Everybody loved the Shipleys. And there were a lot of them.

"Well, I wasn't enough of an overachiever to be born a Shipley," Audrey says. "I had to marry one."

"Whatever works," I say, and she laughs.

"Do you both run this place?" I ask, trying to get a feel for whom to impress.

"Yep!" Audrey says, buzzing around behind the counter, straightening the empty cups. She reminds me of a jolly bumble bee. "We're partners."

"Oh," I say slowly, not quite sure what she means by that.

Zara laughs, and it's a rich, full sound. "Not *life* partners. We just own the business together."

"Okay." I let out a nervous chuckle. "Sorry for jumping to conclusions. Tell me what you are looking for."

"We need somebody full time. Somebody reliable, with good references," Zara says immediately.

"I can be all of those things," I promise. "I once did a summer internship with the guys down at King Arthur Flour. That was a few years ago, but they'll still vouch for me. Lately, I've been working in a big Nashville bakery. I have references there, too."

Zara nods. "So you're from Vermont originally?"

"Sort of? I was an Air Force brat. I was born here, but then we moved away. We came back my last two years of high school."

"You went to high school in Colebury, right?" Zara asks. "I thought you looked a little familiar."

"And you just moved back home?" Audrey adds.

"Yeah," I say, trying not to look uncertain. "I want to stay in Vermont, but only if I find a job." The truth is I don't know how much time I can give myself to look for work. The safest thing would be to get right back in the car and try to get my old job back in Nashville.

"Why did you leave Tennessee?" Zara asks.

Tell the truth, or lie? It's not an easy decision. "I got out of a bad relationship. Seemed like driving out of state was the only way to fix it." That's understating things somewhat, but they don't need all the gory details.

"Don't *grill* him," Audrey yelps.

Zara laughs. "I managed a bar for five years. Grilling people is how you weed out all the nutters." She gives me a sheepish smile. "Sorry. But it is."

"Oh, I'm sure," I say, hoping to sound agreeable.

"Well, fine," Audrey says. "Zara is the businessperson. She keeps me from fucking up."

I bark out a laugh because it seems wrong to see such a sweet-looking human dropping f-bombs.

"But let me tell you a little more about the Busy Bean. We've been open for about a year. It's just been Zara and me and a part-time employee. But he can't give us any more hours, and we need someone full time. I'm having a baby this winter." She pats her belly. "And Zara has a lot going on in her life, too. We need full-time help, but we've been putting it off because we're cheap."

"You do your own baking, right?" I tear apart one of the muffins Zara served me and toss a bite into my mouth. "Wow. Good lemon flavor."

"Thanks!" Audrey beams. "We do all our own pastries. But we buy our bagels."

"I can make your bagels," I say, putting another bite of muffin into my mouth. "Easy peasy."

"But would you have to start at four in the morning?" Audrey asks. "That's why we don't make bread."

"Nah. Now, baguettes need a four a.m. start time. But bagels and pretzels don't need that kind of double rise. I'd use a sourdough starter for flavor, but the rise would come from instant yeast. One rise time. Boil 'em up and bake for twenty minutes."

"Pretzels?" Audrey asks with a dreamy sigh. "That sounds amazing."

"You could try me out for a probationary couple of days, and I'll show you," I promise. "How's your oven?"

"It's all right," Audrey says. "Nothing fancy like they have at King Arthur."

"You don't need a fancy oven to make small breads and rolls," I say quickly. "The giant oven is necessary for crusty boules and baguettes. In a smaller oven you can bake rolls, bagels, freeform pizza, pretzels, popovers…"

"Pizza!" Audrey yelps. "Now I want pizza."

"You were just telling me that you had to watch the carbs," Zara says. "That's why we agreed to have chicken salad salad for lunch."

"Plus it's fun to say chicken salad salad," Audrey points out.

"So that's chicken salad—"

"On salad!" both women say at once.

I have a feeling this would be a fun workplace. Besides, if the Shipleys run it, the place is bound to do well.

"Can I have those references?" Zara asks. "I'll call them today, and then if you were serious about working a couple of days as a trial, I think we should do that."

"Sure! Let me grab my résumé out of my car," I say. "One sec."

I run outside, where I grab a folder. By the time I get back inside, Zara and Audrey are having an intense, whispered discussion. "Hours, pay, benefits," Zara is saying. "We don't have any of that stuff nailed down."

"We can do some research," Audrey says. "It's time, right? I'll ask May about the legal stuff."

"Okay, sure." Zara turns to give me a smile. "I thought we'd procrastinate a little longer, but then you walked in. Maybe it was meant to be."

I hope she's right. Because if there's someplace in this world that I'm meant to be, I haven't found it yet.

KIERAN

Sometimes fate just slaps you in the face.

I hear these words, and my face prickles with awareness. Because fate is definitely smacking me around today.

After seeing Roderick at the gym yesterday, I wasn't even surprised when he walked into the Busy Bean this morning. If I came back to Colebury after a long absence, I'd check out the cute new coffee shop, too.

But now he wants to work here? Fuck my life.

I steal a glance around the doorframe just to confirm what I already know—he's getting in good with Zara and Audrey. They're all smiling at each other like a bunch of BFFs.

Is there any way this ends well? Maybe he's a horrible baker. Maybe he'll burn everything and give the customers food poisoning.

And I'm obviously a terrible person, or I wouldn't be thinking like this.

The urge to walk out the door right now is powerful. But that's not what a man does. I take Audrey's cookies out of the oven and move them to a cooling rack, so they won't burn.

I can't believe Audrey actually abandoned a batch of cookies in the oven. She got distracted by all this talk of new employees. If

I'm honest, she gets distracted a lot lately. She calls it "pregnancy brain."

The truth is that Zara and Audrey really do need a full-time employee. I can't give them any more hours, and when Audrey has that baby, she's going to need to take some time off. This past summer, Audrey went on a ten-day honeymoon, and it nearly killed Zara.

But Jesus Christ, does it have to be *him*?

"Let's give you the nickel tour," Audrey says. "Our Italian espresso machine isn't fully automatic. Have you used one of these before?"

"Absolutely. I put myself through cooking school while working at a Starbucks."

"Not the evil empire!" Audrey yelps.

"Sorry. That's who was hiring."

All three of them laugh, as if Roderick's worked here for years. It's obvious that Audrey loves him, and Zara is getting there. He's really working hard out there.

I wish he weren't so charming. This is bad. Bad, bad, bad.

I peer out the kitchen door again, getting another glimpse of Roderick's dark hair and bright blue eyes. At eighteen, he was attractive, so it's not exactly a surprise to note that eight years later he's devastating. The men must fall at his feet. Or women. I guess I really have no idea. Sometimes the company we keep at eighteen doesn't reflect who we really are.

Ask me how I know.

"And there's just the one grinder?" he asks, gesturing with a muscular arm.

"Yep," Zara agrees. "We don't serve flavored coffees, so we don't have to clean it out all day long."

"Gotcha."

And then the inevitable happens. Roderick turns his chin a notch and glances in my direction. And I handle it all wrong. Instead of stepping out to greet him, I duck back into the kitchen and out of sight. Eavesdropping was a stupid thing to do.

Fuck.

"Hey—who's the Peeping Tom?" I hear Roderick ask.

All my blood stops circulating.

"What?" Zara asks, and I can hear her walking this way.

"The spy in the kitchen," Roderick says with a chuckle.

I have all of about two seconds to panic before they file into the kitchen. I throw the cookie dough mixing bowl into the sink and blast the water as Zara introduces Roderick to my back. "This is Kieran Shipley, who's only with us in the mornings. Kieran—this is Roderick, who might be working with us."

"Nice to meet you, Kieran," Roderick says.

"Same," I grumble over the water's spray. I turn my chin a fraction to nod at him.

But somehow it's enough. The smile falls right off Roderick's face as his eyes widen. "Oh," he says stupidly, recognition settling into his expression.

And now I know that Roderick has a killer memory to go along with his killer body. It's just my luck that the dude remembers my face. I didn't think he would. The high school gym thing happened seven or eight years ago, in some seriously bad lighting.

But he's blinking at me with curiosity in his eyes.

And he called me a Peeping Tom just now. Which, I guess, I am.

Jesus Christ. There is no end to the humiliations that life doles out. I turn back to the dishes in the sink and get to work, Roderick's gaze burning a hole in my back.

RODERICK

Kieran Shipley. All these years later, I finally know his name. We weren't in the same class at school. We never spoke. But of course I remember him. Who could forget?

At eighteen, I thought of myself as a wild man and a party animal. I wasn't afraid of anything. My plan was to become a famous guitar player and screw the world's most attractive men after each concert.

Sexual encounters beneath the bleachers were my idea of a raucous good time. And if a younger guy wanted to watch, the more the merrier.

From the look on his face, though, Kieran Shipley doesn't share my fond memories. He has daggers in his eyes as he turns back to his work.

So this is a setback. Twenty-six-year-old me needs a job. Badly. I wonder if Kieran is going to screw this up for me. He's a Shipley, too, like Audrey.

"Can we call you after we get a chance to sort ourselves out?" Zara asks. "Audrey and I need to huddle up and figure out if we're ready to hire a full-timer."

"Of course!" I say, snapping out of my funk. "You have my

résumé, with the references on the back. Just holler if you have any questions."

I shake everyone's hand, except for Kieran's. He's too busy scrubbing a pan like he's trying to teach it a lesson.

Then I get back into my car and continue my job search.

At seven o'clock that evening, my unemployed butt is running a quick three miles on the treadmill at the gym. I've had no calls from Zara, or from anyone else.

I spent the afternoon trying to put in applications at bakeries and restaurants around the area. I visited Price Chopper and also the Colebury Diner. Nobody needs a baker.

That's the curse of a small town—a tiny labor market.

I suppose I could go back to Nashville. My boss would take me back. But Nashville isn't really my home. It was Brian Aimsley's. And since I never want to see him again, I can't make myself go back.

The treadmill keeps me at a steady pace, and my feet slap against the belt as I try to burn off another wave of fear and anger. For the last three years I gave my whole soul to Brian. The more I think about it, the worse I feel.

Our Nashville friends were really *his* friends. Our social life happened on his schedule. He's a musician who frequently tours, so I'd stack up my work hours for the times when he was gone, making myself available when he was home.

I was so accommodating. And he gave so little back.

There's sweat dripping off my body now, so I hit the stop button and slow my paces. When I step off the treadmill, the floor does that thing where it feels like I'm still in motion. Teetering, I grab my phone and peek at the messages, because hope springs eternal. And—boom! There's a text from an unknown 802 number.

Roderick—can you come to the Busy Bean tomorrow morning

at seven? We discussed it and we want to do a trial period. If tomorrow is bad, let us know when you can come. —Zara.

Hot damn. I didn't think I'd get this chance. But I sure am happy about it. Tomorrow at seven I'll bring out my A-game in the kitchen. I will bake perfect bagels. I will dazzle with pizzas and pastries. I will scrub the floor if they ask me to. And I will charm the heck out of them while I'm doing it.

And somehow I'll make friends with Kieran Shipley. Not that it will be easy. If only I hadn't said, "Who's the Peeping Tom?" I hadn't been referring to high school—my word choice was just a shitty coincidence. He must know that, right?

The only things I know about him are that he's smoking hot and he used to enjoy watching me blow another guy under the bleachers. I spotted him that first time, and then he kept coming back.

Maybe he's in the closet and thinks I'm going to out him. But Kieran has nothing to fear from me. Unless he's afraid of excellent bagels.

That night—after another shower at the gym, and a takeout sandwich—I park my car behind a yarn shop that's on a curve in the road. The parking spot isn't visible from neighboring properties, and the sign in the window says they open tomorrow at ten a.m.

I still don't feel safe. Once again I spend the night squirming around in the passenger seat, waiting for a psycho to bash in my windshield with an ax and murder me. Anxious thoughts chase through my brain at dizzying speed.

On the plus side, it's no problem showing up for work before dawn. I can't wait to get out of this car. At six a.m. I'm brushing my teeth with bottled water and tidying up my hair with a wet comb. By six thirty, I'm rolling into the Busy Bean parking lot.

I'm so early that I have to tap on the kitchen window to let

Audrey know that I'm here. She opens the door with, "Morning, sunshine. There's no coffee yet, but we can fix that soon."

"I'd be happy to make it," I offer. Although I haven't eaten much these past few days, and my stomach is too empty for coffee.

Being broke is the worst. I just need a little bit of luck to come my way before I can stop feeling like a homeless loser.

"Grab an apron," Audrey says, pointing to the clean ones on a hook. "I'm making biscotti."

"How can I help?"

"Sliver these almonds?" She tosses me a bag.

"No problem." I wash my hands and get to work.

We work together for a while in companionable silence. We finish the biscotti and then move on to two kinds of muffins—corn and pear ginger. "The pears are from Zara's family's orchard," she says. "We use local food as often as we can."

"Is there locally grown flour?"

She shakes her head. "Not often. But we can use local butter and milk, and fruit, obviously. My husband's family has a big apple orchard, so I make a lot of tarts."

My stomach rumbles loudly, and Audrey laughs. "Somebody likes apple tarts."

"Love them," I say mildly. My poverty is not her problem, and complaining about my hunger doesn't make me a better job prospect. "I remember the Shipley orchard. They used to hire teenagers in the fall. And there were bonfire parties."

"We still have those parties. There's one in a couple weeks. But the youngest Shipleys are out of high school."

"Cool. Hey, can I ask a favor? My sourdough starter needs feeding, and I didn't have time this morning. Could I feed it a cup of your flour?"

"Of course! Show me your ways."

"Awesome. One sec." I dash out to my car to get the jar, leaving my crusty measuring cup behind. Even if I can't feed myself very well right now, I've still fed my sourdough starter every night and every morning. I'm using a five-pound bag of the cheapest white flour from the store, but I won't let him die.

"So let's see how you do this," Audrey says when I return.

I set the jar down on the counter and screw off the top. "Audrey, I'd like to introduce you to William Butler Yeast."

She snorts. "You named your starter?"

"Everybody names his starter. What *did* they teach you in cooking school?"

She watches with a smile while I remove two thirds of the stringy, bubbly batter from the jar. A sourdough starter is just three things: flour, water, and the millions of natural yeasts living in the mixture. Every day you have to remove two thirds of its bulk and then replace it with fresh flour and water, so that the yeasts have enough to eat.

"Don't you have to weigh it?" Audrey asks. "I thought there was some precision involved."

"You're supposed to," I admit. "But I've kept William in this jar for so long that I can just eyeball it now." The discarded starter goes into a metal mixing bowl that I've grabbed off a shelf. Then, into William's jar, I add a half cup of water and nearly a cup of flour. I stir the sticky mass together with a wooden spoon and close the jar again.

"So that's how the magic happens?" She lifts the mixing bowl and takes a sniff. "I'm getting... bananas. And a whiff of alcohol."

"Right, I smell that banana ester, too. And alcohol is a byproduct. I let it go a little too long between feedings." That's what living in your car will do for you. "So there's extra alcohol present. William eats twice a day to stay at peak performance."

"Can we make something with this?" she asks.

"Sure!" This is just what I need—to put my hands in some dough and make the kitchen smell like fresh bread. When I'm baking in a warm kitchen, that's when I know everything is okay. "Do you have any yeast, though? If we wanted to do a bread that's entirely leavened by sourdough, it won't be ready until evening. When I'm making a strict sourdough, I start it the night before."

"Probably?" Audrey goes to the refrigerator and roots around. "I have this. I don't know if it's your brand." She hands me a package of Red Star.

"Perfect. Let's make some pretzels." I open the yeast and sprinkle about a teaspoon over my sourdough starter. "All we need is flour and water and maybe a dollop of honey or some sugar."

"Not a problem," Audrey says. "Let's see your magic."

If I had magic, I wouldn't be broke right now. But did I mention that I'm a natural showman? "Get ready to be dazzled, Audrey. We're eating well this morning." I dip the metal scoop into the flour and get started on a batch of pretzels.

KIERAN

I unlock the front door of the bakery and step inside. The air already smells like pumpkin muffins and coffee. Shrugging off my coat, I'm just about to call out a greeting when a baritone voice sings out a line from "Royals" by Lorde.

I freeze in place, listening to the next line and the finger-snapping that goes along with it.

"You are way too good at this!" I hear Audrey say with a giggle.

"Sing the high part. We'll rock it together."

Roderick. He's here.

The two of them keep singing, and I have déjà vu. Because once again, I'm standing frozen in place, eavesdropping on Roderick like a creeper. Audrey was right. He is way too good at this. His voice is like a soulful liquid pouring through me, leaving goosebumps behind.

It's seven o'clock in the morning, but I am vividly awake and wondering how I'm supposed to work elbow to elbow with this guy. He's back. And I am not ready.

They sing the whole damn song before I snap out of it and hang my jacket on a hook.

"Is that you, Kieran?" Audrey calls.

"Yeah," I rasp awkwardly. "Morning."

"I'm covered in cream-cheese frosting!" Audrey calls. "Want a pumpkin muffin? Although you should know there are bagels, and they are spectacular."

"Good tip," I mumble as my heart sinks.

If Roderick made spectacular bagels, he's probably here to stay. This is terrible. Working at the Busy Bean isn't my life's goal. I started here to help my cousin's wife, and to save up for my own place. But it's comfortable, or at least it used to be. Now I have to work with *him*? Not possible.

―――――

Sure enough, Roderick comes out of the kitchen ten minutes later to work the morning rush with me. "Just tell me if I screw something up," he says in a chipper voice. "Okay?"

I jerk my chin in a nod, avoiding eye contact. What is he thinking right now? *Oh right. Now it's time to serve coffee with the creep who used to watch me blow guys under the bleachers.*

I want to die. Preferably quickly.

Unfortunately, the next few hours move at a snail's pace. Ordinarily I'm a perfectly competent barista, quick, but bad at small talk.

Today I am all thumbs. Whenever Roderick stands close to me, I lose my train of thought. He smells like baked goods and citrus. Sometimes he hums a bit of a tune under his breath, and the notes bounce like rubber balls inside my chest.

And every time I catch myself paying too much attention to him, I become a little more of a self-conscious wreck. Each order takes twice as long to fill as it should.

Still, I hold it all together until Roderick suggests that we work assembly-line style to clear out the line. "Do you want to fill the orders or work the register?"

"Fill the orders," I grunt. Because I'm better at coffee than people.

On the one hand, this new arrangement is a relief because it keeps Roderick out of my personal space. I no longer have to take so much care to avoid bumping into him. But now I have a new problem. Roderick jots the orders on the cups, and he has terrible handwriting. So, and this is an introvert's nightmare, I have to ask him questions.

"Dark soul? Dark scar?" I guess, squinting at a cup.

"Dark roast with a scone," Roderick says with a flinch. "Sorry. I'll do better."

Of course that says *scone*. My face reddens as I dive into the pastry case. He's more careful on the next few cups. But then the Retired Teachers Knitting Club descends on the Busy Bean, and the line grows long again.

"You guys okay out here?" Audrey asks, dropping a fresh tray of muffins into the case.

"No problem," Roderick says with a quick smile, although his blue eyes flash with panic.

A busy shop doesn't rattle me, so long as I don't have to make small talk with anyone. Maybe that's why I don't ask him what the next few scribbles say. I start guessing instead. It goes fine, until I fill an order that asks for "BB and BCH", and I serve up a breakfast blend with a buttered chive biscuit.

One minute later though, Mrs. DeAngelo, my third-grade teacher, is standing in front of me yelling. "Coffee? I asked for a Berry Buster Tea. And this biscuit looks good, but it is not the bagel with cream cheese I ordered." Naturally, Audrey sticks her head out of the kitchen just then, a question on her face.

"Sorry, Mrs. DeAngelo," I stammer. "Let me fix that." I take the coffee out of her hand and look for the tea bags.

"Oh, shit. Sorry," Roderick says. "Sorry. I didn't realize I was that hard to understand."

"S'okay," I mutter. Everyone is staring at me, which is my least favorite thing in the whole entire world.

"You could have asked," Roderick says under his breath, reaching for a bagel while I make Mrs. DeAngelo's tea.

Yeah, I could have. But talking to you is like crossing a bed of hot lava.

"It's a shame that you're still so distracted," Mrs. DeAngelo says loudly to the whole planet. "Always doodling in class instead of listening."

Roderick cringes on my behalf and hastily spreads cream cheese on the old bat's bagel. Then finally, we're rid of her.

"Sorry about the terrible penmanship," Roderick whispers. "If my teacher ever showed up, she'd have plenty to say about that."

I only grunt in response, wondering how it could be only ten in the morning. Four more hours of this? I don't think I can take it. Mrs. DeAngelo was right, anyway. I can't concentrate this morning to save my life. Roderick wipes down the counter, humming under his breath, and the rich sound climbs right under my skin and vibrates through my consciousness.

I glance at the time. It's only advanced a minute since the last time I looked, and I let out a sigh.

RODERICK

As the day wears on, I charm Audrey by keeping the customers happy. And when Zara comes in at noon, I charm her with my baking success. "We had to save you a bagel and a pretzel to try because we sold the rest," I tell her.

"Someone bought a dozen pretzels for her office after tasting them," Audrey chirps. "She said it wouldn't be right to keep them to herself."

But the one person I cannot charm is Kieran Shipley. He avoids eye contact with me, even when I'm being super friendly.

I don't take it personally, of course. He must be worried about our high school encounters. Maybe he thinks I'll tell his family that...

Okay, I don't have the first clue what he's worried I'll say. He obviously remembers me, and not in a good way. But I can't tell if his chilly attitude is because he's embarrassed, or becaue he's a jerk. Either way, I don't have any fucks to give about shit that happened in high school.

Maybe if I could get him alone for a minute, we could talk it out, though. Clear the whole thing up.

But Kieran leaves for the day before I get my chance. And then Audrey asks me to come back tomorrow and open the coffee shop with Zara. "We both want a chance to get to know you," Audrey says.

"Excellent!" I say with a bright smile. "Sounds great."

I sleep like shit that night in my car. You'd think being halfway to getting a job would've relaxed me, but instead, I lie there in the cold car and think of all the ways I could still screw it up.

If they run a credit check on me, will the bank say that my credit cards have just been canceled? Is that how credit checks work?

My bigger fear is that they'll ask Kieran whether or not they should hire me, and he'll talk them out of it. Kieran is one of those people who listens more than he talks. He can probably smell my desperation.

And he's family. Audrey is married to Kieran's cousin. "They're a big, close-knit family," she'd said as we chatted.

I'm doomed. And doomed people sleep poorly.

The result is that I'm bleary the next morning when I report for duty with Zara. The bagels and pretzels turn out great, but I'm sluggish behind the counter. I need more calories, too, but I don't want to stop to take a break.

When Kieran shows up for work after the breakfast rush, Zara declares that she's taking a break to check in on her daughter. "Can you bake another batch of muffins and some cookies for this afternoon?"

"Of course!" I say brightly, relieved to give up counter duty.

I can almost feel Kieran rolling his eyes. He's not buying what I have to sell. He steps up to the counter, and I go into the kitchen, retreating to our separate corners like fighters between rounds. I put the muffins into the oven and wait.

I'm having a happy dream. The best kind of dream.

I'm in a gleaming restaurant kitchen, cooking a meal for the actor Henry Cavill. And he's *flirting* with me. But I can't tell if he's flirting for real or just being friendly. As I set a plate down in front of him, I'm trying to decide whether or not to slip him my phone number.

"You're really cute," he says. "But it's too bad we knew each other in high school. That ruins everything."

"Why?" I ask Dream Cavill. But he can't answer me, because the oven timer starts ringing loudly. I look around but can't find it.

A few seconds into its persistent beeping, I startle awake and realize that pesty sound is not part of the dream, but real. With a gasp, I yank my head from my hands and rise from my stool so quickly that I sway on my feet.

I lurch over to the oven and check the pumpkin muffins. They'll need another two minutes, so I close the oven door and shake my bleary head. Finally, I stop the timer's infernal noise. I spot Kieran in the doorway, frowning at me. He's the only witness to this shit show.

I haven't even been offered the job yet, but I've already fallen asleep on it. This is not good.

"Sorry," I try to say, but it comes out as a croak. I clear my throat and try again. "I was just..." The sentence peters out, because there's no excuse that I can offer. Sleeping in my car is killing me. I look like death this morning and am now capable of slipping into REM sleep while the muffins bake. It's unprofessional, and I really hope Kieran doesn't mention it to Zara and Audrey.

He probably will, though.

Kieran disappears without a word, which is just as well, I guess. Zara will be back any moment. I take out the muffins and set them on a rack to cool. Then I stir up a batch of oatmeal cookies with raisins.

Ten minutes later, as I'm dropping cookie dough onto a tray,

Kieran enters the kitchen. He places a mug of steaming coffee on the worktable beside me and disappears before I can say anything.

It's a pretty helpful gesture considering that Kieran hates me. Every friendly thing I say to him goes wrong somehow, and when we worked the counter together yesterday, it had seemed like I couldn't stop bumping into him. Maybe he's just clumsy, but it was probably my fault.

And although he likely brought me the coffee so I wouldn't burn the place down by accident, I should still thank him.

I don't get my chance until that afternoon. Zara retreats into the little office to order some supplies. The shop is in a rare lull, the only customers outside on the patio, wearing their coats in the weak October sunshine.

"Can I talk to you for a sec?" I ask Kieran.

"Why." His forehead wrinkles. The dude does *not* want to talk.

But I plow ahead. "Just thought I'd introduce myself properly, because I hope we're going to be working together."

"Nice to meet you," he grits out.

"Yeah. I can tell you're thrilled." I chuckle. "Look, we obviously went to the same high school—"

"It was a long time ago. I don't even remember." He shuts me down with a few quick words. Then he swallows hard, betraying his discomfort.

And that's when I get angry. Can we really not get past my teenage stupidity?

"Yeah, okay," I say slowly. I cross my arms in front of my chest to show him that his brusque tone doesn't scare me. Although I have to lift my chin to look him in the eye. He's probably got four inches on me, as well as bulging biceps that I can't help but admire. It's too bad Kieran Shipley wants nothing to do with me, because the man is as hot as he is grumpy.

And now I'm staring.

"I guess I must be thinking of somebody else," I say so slowly that it sounds like a tease. "Pity, though. Because once upon a time I really enjoyed putting on a show for that other guy. Whoever he was. And I'm pretty sure he enjoyed it, too."

And then—because self-preservation was never my strong suit —I give him a sleazy wink, turn on my heel, and disappear into the kitchen. But not before I glimpse a flash of red on his face.

I just made him angry. Awesome. I must not want to buy decent food or sleep in a real bed after all.

Nice going, Roddy. You're fucking everything up again.

But if Kieran Shipley can't deal with me, maybe this job was never meant to be.

KIERAN

Longest. Week. Ever.

Every time I turn around, Roderick is there. I'm in hell, and I'm behaving like a teenage prick. And I feel like one, too. But I cannot have a casual chat about high school with Roderick. Not within earshot of customers or Zara. That'd be like turning my soul inside out.

He's Mr. Charming, with that easy smile. *Hey, about high school…* Like that's an easy conversation.

I'm in knots over it. And every time I catch a glimpse of his smile, I can picture him putting his mouth to other uses. He knows something about me that nobody else suspects—I watched him because I *liked* it. He knows something about me that I haven't managed to tell a soul.

Including myself.

When Zara gets off the phone, my torture ends. "You can call it a day, Roddy," she says.

He has a nickname already? That can't be good.

"Audrey and I are going to have a chat about what we need in terms of hours. And we'll be in touch. Here—I'm going to pay you in cash for these two days of work."

Paying him in cash is good, right? It means he's not actually on the payroll. Maybe they aren't hiring him. Maybe I don't have to feel exposed every time I set foot in this place.

My relief is short-lived. Audrey buzzes through the door a little later, and the two of them go into the kitchen to talk, while I serve the afternoon crowd.

As I'm cleaning up the coffee bar, I overhear them.

"So… Who's going to tell Kieran?" Zara says. "I'll flip you for it."

My heart dives into my stomach as Audrey says, "You tell him. I'll watch."

"Tell me what?" I ask, sticking my head into the kitchen.

They both startle. "Um…" Audrey smiles.

"We hired Roderick," Zara says.

"What?" I shouldn't be surprised, but I'm still miserable. "He couldn't possibly be the best choice." There's no way I can see his face every day and not think about the way I shamelessly and repeatedly invaded his privacy when I was a teenager. Or why.

Audrey and Zara exchange a glance.

"Buddy," Audrey says slowly. "Why don't you like this guy?"

"He's a dick," I say immediately. And then I feel a new crushing wave of shame. Because what I mean to say is, *I saw his dick. And I liked it.*

"Based on what, though? How do you know him?"

Shit.

"High school, right?" Zara offers.

"Yeah," I grumble.

"So…" Audrey offers me the plate of muffins that they've been chowing. But I shake my head. "Is he *still* a dick? I mean, I don't want to hire a dick. But is he presently a dick, or might he have outgrown it?"

I grind my teeth. "I dunno. I have to wipe down the machines and get going."

It's a chickenshit move, but I need a minute to wrap my head around this new development. The only person who ever glimpsed my hidden truths has invaded my life. It's not his fault, but I want him gone.

I clock out. As I climb into my truck and head for Burlington and my second job, I'm as stressed out as I've ever been. *He's a dick*, I'd told Audrey and Zara. I don't even know the guy. And Zara and Audrey need a new employee.

I'd slandered him for no reason. Shame burns hotly inside me. I'd talked smack about a person I didn't even know, only because I didn't want to confront myself. That's not the guy I am—is it?

Also, I have this nagging feeling that Roderick really needs the job. If that's the case, then I've done something incredibly evil.

I park behind the advertising agency and go inside, heading straight to my desk, even before saying hello to Mr. Pratt, the owner. I sit down in my fancy ergonomic chair and dial my cousin's wife's phone.

"Hey!" Audrey says when she picks up. "Everything okay?" It's unusual for me to call her after hours.

"Yeah," I say slowly. "Look. What I said earlier?"

"You mean about Roderick?"

"Right." Jesus, I don't even like saying his name aloud. "It was just a stupid thing in high school. Nothing to worry about."

She's silent for a moment. "Are you sure? I trust your opinion."

"I'm sure." My voice is gravel. "It's nothing. Just high school crap. Ancient history. I mean—I wouldn't want to hire the high school version of *me*, even."

"Oh, I would," Audrey says easily. "You're a little too serious, maybe, but you're a solid guy. I'll bet you were always like that. From birth." She laughs.

"Um, thanks?" She's right. I *am* too serious. People say that all the time. It's just that I don't know how to be anything else.

"Thanks for telling me," Audrey says. "I feel better about him now."

"Yeah…" I sigh. "Forget I even said anything."

"All right. Will I see you at Thursday Dinner?"

"I don't think so," I admit. "My dad's surgery is that day."

"Oh! Of course. Let me know if you need me to adjust the schedule."

"No, it's fine. And he'll be okay." There's really no reason why she should be stressed out over the old grump. Enough people are busy worrying about him already. "See you tomorrow?"

"Of course! Be well!"

I hang up the phone feeling slightly better about myself.

Just slightly.

Mr. Pratt ambles over. "Top of the morning to you!"

"Likewise." That's our little joke. He lets me work from two or three in the afternoon until I'm done, which is always somewhere between six and nine at night.

It's a strange arrangement, but Pratt needs me. He isn't an artist. His specialty is writing snappy copy. He used to have a business partner who did all the art, but that guy retired to Florida.

These days, Mr. Pratt has his lazy son Deacon working here during the day. And he has me here, from late afternoon into the evening, to do all the art that Deacon can't manage and to fix all the messes that Deacon makes.

It's not a terrific situation. But the pay isn't too bad, the hours are flexible, and I'm getting paid to make art. Most weeknights I do my thing and leave the Photoshop files for Mr. Pratt to inspect in the morning.

"So, I love what you did with the vinyl records." Pratt holds up a printout of some work I did last night. "Very slick placement of the text on version three."

"Thank you." I always create several versions of each draft, which is easy enough to do digitally.

"I'm not sold on version one, though." He holds up another printout. The design looks horrible, because someone has completely fucked up my lettering. And by "someone" I mean Deacon Pratt.

"Yeah," I say slowly. "I wanted that text in charcoal. And that typeface is too vintage for this brand, I think. That's not the one I used."

He frowns. "Switch it back, would you?"

"Sure," I say, holding back a sigh. "What else do you have for me?"

"A few logo ideas for Winooski River Savings. Let me grab 'em." He goes back to his desk while I fire up Photoshop on the computer.

In spite of the Pratt family dynamic, I do love this job. I've been taking online design courses, and I hope to take a real class at Moo U next year. If I could make a real living in graphic design someday, that would be amazing. My family doesn't know any of this, though. They think I'm selling advertising, and I haven't bothered to correct them.

Keeping my work a secret isn't a normal thing to do. I realize this. But I started keeping secrets when I was a teenager, and I've never learned how to stop. And I also don't see the point of telling everyone what's in my heart. I don't want to listen to their opinions about it.

Who's got time for that?

"Let's see," Mr. Pratt says, flipping through his notebook. "Their old logo was circular, see?" He holds up a page with a familiar image on it. "I'd like you to keep the paddles and the canoe from their old logo. But I think it should be brighter somehow. Bolder."

I consider the old logo for a moment. "I'm glad they're updating this. Sketch art doesn't really say *bank* to me. But neither does a canoe…"

This is a tricky design problem. My favorite kind.

"What do you think we should try?"

He says *we*. But he means me. "Let me play with the shape of the boat and the paddle, and see what I can do. I think if we put a wave form under it—like river rapids—it could be splashier."

"Good, good!" he says, passing me the page. "Try that."

And I get to work.

Four hours later, I lock the place up and stagger out to my car. Working two jobs is no picnic, but it's very good for my bank account. At least I'd told Kyle that all the farming work was his tonight. No exceptions.

It's a long drive home. On the way, I stop in Colebury to buy a burrito and wolf it down. It's dark when I hit the two-lane highway toward Hardwick. The shops are all shuttered, and there's no traffic, but I go slow, because the cops love to use this stretch as a speed trap.

That's how I happen to spot the blue Volkswagen parked behind the pet-grooming place. I notice it because of the blue glow coming from somebody's phone on the passenger side of the car.

Roderick. What's he doing in there?

I look away, because I can't afford to think about blue Volkswagens or the people who drive them.

RODERICK

I got the job! Full time, too.

But it's too soon to celebrate, because I'm curled up on the backseat of my car, uncomfortable as hell. My hip fell asleep about seven seconds after I lay down. It's already numb, and the pins and needles sure to be next.

I'll try to sleep for an hour or two here, before giving up to sit in the passenger seat. Up there I'll be uncomfortable in fresh and interesting ways—my feet will fall asleep and my ass will go numb.

But everything is going to be fine, because Audrey and Zara hired me, and I'm earning a living wage. Zara paid me in cash for my two trial days, so I can keep eating while I wait for the payroll to kick in. I'll need to pay for a gym membership, too. There are only three days left of my trial period. I've quickly become their best customer, thanks to the hot showers, the complimentary shampoo, and fresh towels.

It's cold in the car tonight. I have one of my ex's sleeping bags piled on top of my body. It's the only thing of his that I swiped. Brian liked camping, and I went along with it because I liked keeping Brian happy. But after my homeless stint at eighteen, sleeping outside won't ever seem fun to me again.

Tomorrow night it's supposed to dip below freezing. It's not clear how long it will take until I can find somewhere to live. Most businesses run their payroll at least a week in arrears. That means a paycheck next Friday at the earliest. And I still won't have enough money to rent an apartment.

I need to find somebody who's looking for a roommate. I peeked at Craigslist, but the offerings were thin. The cheapest rental apartments I found on the web start at eight hundred dollars. Theoretically I could afford that, except I don't know if I could pass a landlord's credit check. Before I lived with Brian, I had some hard years. And also, landlords sometimes ask for first and last month's rent and a security deposit. Under those conditions, I'd be sleeping in my car for weeks.

So I need a room someplace where they aren't too concerned with the rules. A house shared with college students, maybe. I'd be a good roommate. *Neat freak will make you sourdough waffles once a week on his day off. Gay AF. Quiet because he has no friends.*

These are the things I think about while I slowly fall asleep in the refrigerator chill of my tiny German car.

The next few days are exhausting but glorious.

At first, Zara and Audrey don't change their schedules. One of them is always present when I show up at six to help them start the day.

My bones ache from sleeping in the cold car, but I always feel better after the first hour in the kitchen. My new bosses like to play music while we bake muffins and start the coffee. The smell of pastries in the oven is like therapy to me. And since Zara and Audrey have given me free rein to test my own recipes, I'm up to my elbows in bread dough at least once each morning.

Push and turn. Push and turn. Kneading a loaf has always centered me. When I can bake, everything is right with the world. The yeasty smell of dough soothes me.

Meanwhile, I make it my business to learn everything I can about the coffee shop. I master their espresso machine and figure out when all the deliveries happen. Their cash register system is nothing too complicated.

"I've got this," I tell Audrey on Wednesday. "You can let me open up the place tomorrow if you want to start sleeping in sometimes."

Her smile is a mile wide. "We are *thrilled* by this idea, trust me. But Kieran's dad just had surgery, so he's not coming in for a couple days. After we get through that, I promise Zara and I will let you open for us. We can't wait."

"Awesome," I say.

"Listen, about Kieran…"

I turn down the music—we're rocking out to an old Violent Femmes album this morning—and wait for Audrey to continue. I'm desperately curious about Kieran, to be honest. He's working that whole strong-and-silent-type thing. Those brown eyes. Those strong shoulders. If I spotted him in a gay bar, I'd be all over that.

"He's kind of quiet," Audrey says.

"You don't say."

Audrey laughs. "It's just the way he's made. I mean—he's the best kind of guy in the world. He'll do anything for his family. But he's not a charmer. Zara and I don't like to leave him alone with the customers for too long. He isn't rude or anything, he just has RGF."

"Resting…grouch face?

"Exactly!" Audrey giggles. "My whole point is this—don't take it personally. People sometimes get the impression that Kieran doesn't like them. But that's not the case."

"Gotcha," I say. But I'm really thinking, *Oh, honey. You have no idea how much he wants me gone.* "Is his dad going to be okay?"

"Yeah," Audrey says as she hands me a bag of coffee beans to pour into the grinder. "It's back surgery, which sounds dreadful. But it's not the sort of thing that kills you."

I stay quiet, hoping she'll keep talking about Kieran. My

curiosity runs deep. What's the other job he runs off to every afternoon? Is he single? Does he date men? Women? Both?

But Audrey doesn't elaborate. "I'm going to flip the sign, okay?"

"You go, girl."

She unlocks the front door, flips the sign from CLOSED to OPEN, and hangs the Open flag outdoors.

I hope we have a flood of customers and sell every last one of the onion bialys that come out of the oven. I need the Busy Bean to be the most profitable business on the planet.

And I need that paycheck.

Kieran reappears after a couple days. He's taciturn behind the coffee bar, serving customers promptly but silently. He doesn't have much to say to me either, but I'm not offended.

"Are you sure six work days a week isn't too many?" Zara asks while pondering her new work schedule. She has me baking alone in the kitchen on three mornings and coming in later on three more.

"It's all good. I need the hours," I assure her. *That's what happens when you walk away from your life with nothing.*

"Okey dokey," she says.

My first morning opening the kitchen alone is on a Saturday. And it's Kieran who's scheduled to show up at eight. I hear him walk in the front door, whistling. "Hello?" he calls out.

"Hey," I reply. "It's only me back here."

There's a pause. I wonder if he'll even respond. Would he really ignore me completely? "Oh. Hey," he says a beat later. "Morning."

I go back to work shaping the bagels I'm making, but he doesn't appear in the kitchen. I hear the sound of chairs moving around on the wood floors as he checks the front of the house.

Then it gets quiet.

I have a tray of muffins to bring up front, so I step out of the kitchen. At first I don't spot Kieran, but then I realize he's standing on a stool behind the counter, his hand raised as he sketches something on the signboard.

Taking another step, I see the blackboard wall has been swept clean, and Kieran is drawing a new design. In multicolored chalk he's fashioned a big turkey—a tom with a colorful spread of tail feathers. There's a speech bubble beside his beak that says, *Life is short. Eat dessert first.*

"Wow. Do you draw everything on the displays in here?"

Kieran startles. For a second his balance goes haywire, and he comes close to falling off the stool. "Shit," he curses under his breath. He puts a hand to the wall to steady himself. Luckily, only the chalk falls down.

"S-sorry," I sputter.

"No problem," he says, but his eyes close briefly, displaying his irritation.

"That's a killer drawing," I say, even though he probably doesn't care what I think. "I assumed Zara did all the art and wrote all the notes. Because the quotes around here are so..."

"Snarky," Kieran offers.

"Yeah." They really are.

He jerks a thumb at the talking turkey. "I just channel my inner Zara when I'm changing up the weekly wisdom."

I snort. It's the first funny thing I've heard Kieran say. He doesn't talk to me, and he isn't chatty with the customers, but sometimes I've heard him and Audrey laughing together, so I know he's capable of joy.

He's still Mr. Enigma. I wish I could say that I didn't care, or that I haven't been watching him, but that would be a lie. I'm definitely tuned in to the Kieran channel, even if the signal is sometimes hard to make out.

"So, uh, is your dad okay now?" I ask, hoping to keep the conversation alive.

He makes a face and then climbs down from the stool. "He'll

be fine. And he's cranky as ever." He bends down, and I absolutely *do not* check out his ass as he retrieves the chalk off the floor. It's in two pieces.

Kieran lays the broken pieces carefully in a tray of chalk on the counter. Even the tray is beautiful, with at least two dozen colors, each of them long and perfect. Except the salmon piece, which is now a glaring imperfection among the carefully kept rainbow.

"Oh man," I say. "I'm sorry."

"Why?"

I nod at the chalk. "It was perfect before."

Kieran looks down at the tray and shrugs. "Perfect-looking art supplies don't stay that way very long. Unless you don't use 'em. And then what's the point?" He turns to me and removes the tray of muffins out of my hands, and I realize I'm still standing here holding them like a dummy.

He slides the tray onto the counter and then uses tongs to arrange half a dozen muffins on a plate.

Meanwhile, I'm watching his back muscles flex, because Kieran is hot, and I have no shame. A man is the very last thing in the world that I need right now, but nobody ever said I was smart. If I were better at self-preservation, I wouldn't be in this mess.

"You want to make yourself useful and unlock the front door?" he asks without a glance in my direction.

"Yeah, sure," I say, snapping out of it. I hope Kieran doesn't tell Zara that I'm a slacker. "I've got a couple more things to finish up in the kitchen, and then I'll help you with the morning rush."

Kieran says nothing. He readies the counter for our first customers and ignores me.

On my way back into the kitchen, I allow myself one quick glance at his biceps straining the sleeves of his T-shirt. Because I never did have any self-control.

Zara comes in three hours later, beaming. "Check it out!" she says. "I slept until seven and played with my kid. And the customers still got served."

"And the building is still standing," I add from behind the counter. I'm wiping down the espresso machine because we're experiencing a midmorning lull.

"Anything to report?" she asks, hanging her jacket on a hook.

"Nope," Kieran says. He's eating one of my bagels slathered with cream cheese.

Zara points at him. "You want to take off? I know things are still nuts at your house."

"Sure," he says, then crams the last bite into his mouth. "Thanks."

"Dude," Zara says. "Where's my bagel? Tell me you still have sesame."

"I saved you some in back," I promise her. "Sesame and poppyseed."

"Score," she says. Then she snaps her fingers. "Kieran, wait!"

He stops halfway to the door.

"Look." She grabs something out of the pocket of her hanging jacket—a key ring. "It happened. They're gone."

He stands very still. "Really. You're kidding."

"Nope. But they paid me for next month, too, so it's hard to even be angry. So? Are you in? No pressure."

"Heck yes."

"Heads up." She tosses the keys, and Kieran grabs them out of the air. "It's yours whenever you're ready, but your lease doesn't start until December first, since the other guys paid for November."

"Whoa, thanks." Kieran stares at the keys in his hand as if she's given him a treasure. "I'm not sure when I can actually use these."

"Doesn't matter. It's something to look forward to, right?"

"You have no idea," is his answer. Then he actually smiles, and it transforms his face. Damn, that smile is potent. "I'll need furniture. Guess I'd better get on that."

"And kitchen stuff. Towels. Sheets. It's endless," Zara says. "But who doesn't love to shop?"

"Me," Kieran says with a gruff chuckle. "I better post my listing, too. So I can pay for all of it."

"For a roommate?" Zara asks.

"Yeah." Kieran pockets the keys. "Lots to do. Later! Thanks, Zara."

He's almost at the door when Zara says exactly the wrong thing. "Hey, maybe you don't have to hit up Craigslist." She turns to me. "Roderick, are you looking for a place to live? Where are you staying, anyway?"

Kieran's gaze flies to mine, panic in his eyes.

"Oh no, I'm all set," I say quickly. "I'm staying with my parents for a while to save money."

Kieran blinks, relaxing.

"Okay," Zara says, nodding twice, as if she realizes she's overstepped. "Put me to work Roddy. What needs doing?"

"We should make some cookies for the afternoon crowd. You want to bake or serve?"

Kieran slips out while we're discussing it. I don't even see him go.

A rented room is something I need very badly, but I am way too proud to say so.

KIERAN

With Zara's keys in my pocket, I feel like a new man. This is it. The rest of my life starts now.

I drive home, thinking optimistic thoughts. I need to order a bed to be delivered to the new place. I'll do that right away, even if I'm not ready to move.

If you have a bed, it's official, right? Everything else can come later.

Since it's Saturday, I don't have to go to my Burlington job. Kyle and I have plans to bale the oat straw, but it's not even noon, so we've got five hours of daylight left.

While we're out there, I'll tell Kyle that I'm moving out. He can get used to the idea while I'm still here, working hard while my dad heals up from his surgery.

But eventually I'll be a free man—free to live somewhere else and let Kyle take on most of the farm labor with dad.

And free to figure a few other things out, too.

I bump along our dirt road with the music blaring, feeling optimistic. And I just ate the chewiest, most amazing sesame bagel I ever tasted in my life. Even if part of me still hopes Roderick will turn tail and leave town again, I will miss that man's baking.

When I park my car outside the farmhouse, though, reality sets in. Kyle's pickup isn't here, and neither is my parents' truck.

Inside, I find my dad in his easy chair, looking uncomfortable. Actually, uncomfortable doesn't even cover it. His lips are white with pain. "You okay?"

"Do I look okay?" he snaps. "Is your mother back yet?"

"No," I say slowly. "Where'd she go?"

"Grocery store," he grunts.

"You want help getting out of that chair?"

His lip curls with the horror of needing help performing such a simple task. I can see him wrestling with his choices—remain in pain, or accept help from his least favorite son?

"Yeah," he eventually grunts. As if it kills him to ask me for help.

I reach down and offer him my hand, which he grasps with both of his. Then he pulls himself up with a weary groan.

"Doctor said a straight-backed chair would be better than that recliner," I remind him.

"Not deaf. I heard him."

Right. "Where's Kyle?" I ask as my dad eases past me, walking like a ninety-five-year-old.

"Dunno. Not my job to keep track of him."

So I guess it's mine. I take out my phone and shoot off a text to my brother. *Can we bale straw today?*

His response comes quickly enough. *I'll start it tomorrow. Where are you?*

Watching college football with Griff on his lunch break.

I feel a sharp, irrational pang at being left out of these plans. I'm usually at work right now, though, and not free to hang out in the middle of a Saturday. They wouldn't expect me to be available.

It would have been nice to be asked, though.

With nothing else to do, I go outside and collect eggs from the chickens. Rexie barks hello, trotting across the meadow to see me.

And the hens cluster around me like groupies at a rock concert. At least the animals are happy to see me.

Since I'm here, and it's a nice dry day, I decide to bale some of the oat straw myself, even though it's really a job for two. But then I discover that I can't, because we're out of diesel for the tractor, and Kyle has driven the truck with the tank on it to Griff's.

I shouldn't be so annoyed, but I am anyway.

Kyle, please get some diesel and come home. It's the perfect day for baling.

Griff wants me to press some cider, comes his response.

My blood pressure spikes, because Griff will pay Kyle for his hours, so of course Kyle wants to stay. But didn't we just talk about this? Kyle's double-dipping can't happen on my dime, and I've already pitched in too many hours this month.

I don't think Kyle realizes that Dad's back may never be a hundred percent again. It's going to be a rude surprise when I'm not around to pick up the slack anymore.

Look, I'm available now, I reply. *I would have gotten started alone. But the diesel tank is with you.*

Fine, he replies a minute later. *On my way.* I can almost hear him grumbling, like I'm inconveniencing him right now.

While I'm waiting, I move the chicken tractor and take care of some other chores. On a farm, there's always something more to do. Clock-out time comes only when it's too dark to see.

Kyle drives up eventually. He's remembered to get the diesel on his way home, so at least I don't have to go to jail for murder. "Hey," my brother says, jumping out of the truck, his movements brisk. Again, it's obvious he's mad at me for interrupting his Saturday.

He won't stay mad, though. Kyle doesn't hold a grudge. He's an easygoing guy. He sees no evil and takes no sides. Still, it's frustrating to me that he never notices all the tension and the crosswinds in our family. I feel like I have to carry that burden alone.

It's easier to be Kyle than to be me, and I envy him more than he will ever know.

After we gas up the tractor, we hitch up the baler and drive it out to the field. "You want to bale or toss?"

He shrugs.

"I'll toss," I say, taking the harder job.

"Okay," Kyle says easily. Then he climbs back onto the tractor, and off he goes.

I move my pickup truck into the field and wait a moment until the baler poops out a few square bales. Then I start heaving them into my pickup truck.

It's repetitious, and the truck needs to be constantly moved. But the physical activity starts to work its magic on me. When I'm moving, my mind becomes calmer.

Kyle and I have always been farm boys, unafraid of hard work. My brother may be flaky, but once you get him started on a task, there's no one better to have on your team. When I was a little boy, I thought my father and my big brother were everything. I was never happier than when we were all outside together, working shoulder to shoulder.

Those were the days when I was ignorant of the shadowy corners of my parents' marriage and too young to notice that my dad would never love me as much as Kyle. I thought Kyle's status was due to birth order. He was the bigger brother and therefore more admirable. And therefore I was always trying to compete. I worked my skinny little butt off so I could wield a hammer like Kyle or lift a fifty-pound bag of chicken feed. There was only the fresh air and the sunshine and my zeal to do the work of real men.

I just assumed I was every bit as deserving of my father's love as Kyle was, and that I'd get my share eventually.

Spoiler alert: I never did.

Meanwhile, I developed interests that nobody else in the family shared. Although I didn't know anyone else who could draw, I did so obsessively. My father's green John Deere was one of the first things I drew, and it became the subject of hundreds of pictures. I used up every green crayon in the house, and when they were gone, my mother joked that I'd have to start drawing Kubotas, because they're orange. So I did. Problem solved.

Art was something that was only mine. Kyle couldn't compete. And I needed that, because my desperation to be Dad's other sidekick wasn't working out so well. I didn't know why.

Until one ugly day when I was fourteen, and I overheard my family's big doozy of a secret—that I was the kid nobody had wanted.

It was a hard thing to hear at fourteen, but many things in my life made more sense after that.

Kyle and I bale oats until we can't see the field anymore. He shuts off the tractor and climbs down to stand beside me, where I'm sweating in spite of the October chill. "That's better than half of it," he says. "Are we gonna bale the rest tomorrow? Or were you thinking of grazing it?"

I consider the question. "Safer to bale it, unless it rains before we can do it. It's in really good shape right now, and if we get early snow you'll be hating life."

"Cool. We'll bale it, then."

This whole exchange bothers me, though. I'm not the one who should be figuring this stuff out. "Hey Kyle?"

"Yeah?"

"You need to know that I'm moving out at the end of the month."

"What?" My brother gapes at me. Even in the dark I can tell that it never occurred to him that this was a thing I might do. "Where would you go?"

"I rented the house next door to Zara."

"Why, bro? Here you've got free rent."

"It was never free," I remind him. "Twenty hours of farm work a week."

"But—" Kyle gulps. "You still have to pitch in while dad is laid up. You can't just bail on me."

"Like I'd *do* that?" My voice actually cracks in surprise. "You'll have me until all the harvest stuff is done. But you need to understand that Dad isn't going to have a miraculous recovery. He's had disc trouble for thirty years. I don't think he'll ever throw bales of hay around again."

"Nobody said that," Kyle insists. "He's having all this surgery so that he can get better."

"He's having all this surgery so that he doesn't get worse," I argue. "The real blessing here is that you don't seem to have inherited it. Keep your back strong just to be sure, okay?"

Kyle squints at me. "You too, right?"

"Right," I say quickly. "But I'm not the one who needs to do farm work forevermore. This is your spread."

"And yours," he adds, still not getting the message.

"It was never mine."

"Bullshit. That's the dumbest thing I ever heard. Just because you and Dad argue sometimes doesn't mean he's cutting you out of the will or some shit."

I want to shake Kyle and scream, *Pay attention!*

Then again, it's not my brother's fault. He can't see what I see, because he doesn't have all the information. "I'm not Dad's choice. It's nice of you to pretend otherwise, but it isn't helpful right now. This is your farm, and he needs you to step up and take over. Either you do that, or he'll reinjure himself. You know it's true."

"Fuck." Kyle shoves a bale of straw further onto the truck and then looks around, like he's seeing our darkened farm for the first time. "I'm a good worker. But I'm shit at the business stuff. I'm no good at planning."

At least he realizes this. "All you need is some focus. Channel your inner Griffin." Our apple-farming cousin is a savvy businessman. "Hell—ask Griff to help you. You know he would."

"But you won't," Kyle grumbles.

That's right, and it gives me a pang of guilt. Except I know better than to help, because Kyle would just let me do everything. "I'm busy making other plans. New house, new classes in the spring." I'm finally taking control of my life. And that means weaning Kyle off of my assistance.

"Just don't move out," Kyle says, as if this were a negotiation. "I'll step up. I'll plan everything. But you should really stay here."

"It's a done deal. Sorry." Just saying those words is a big deal for me. I'm no longer caving to everyone's expectations.

Kyle's face creases in frustration. He kicks the last bale of straw over and then stalks off without me.

I suppose I could walk off without finishing the job, too. Just to prove a point. But I squat down and grab the last bale, heave it into the truck, and then drive it back to the barn.

KIERAN

My mother has made dinner by the time I get back to the house. It's lasagna, which is one of her better dishes. It's edible, anyway.

We eat in the same tense silence I've always known. Usually it's my dad who's stewing in his resentments, but tonight Kyle is also adding to the stony vibe in the room.

For the first time, though, I know I'm here by choice. The keys to Zara's rental house are burning a hole in my pocket. Soon I'll be sitting in my own space, eating food of my own choosing. It won't be good food—I don't know how to cook, and I can't afford to eat take-out every night—but it will be all mine.

"You boys get all the oat straw in?" Dad asks, interrupting my thoughts.

"Not all of it," Kyle says.

"Kieran could have started earlier," says the old man.

"We were out of diesel," I say.

"Could have gotten the diesel yourself."

Kyle has the decency to cringe.

I shove another bite of lasagna into my mouth, and the noodles are tougher than they should be. I'm going to learn to cook for real, I decide. *Everything* is going to change. I look down at the cow-shaped salt and pepper shakers on the table. I made them for my mother in art class when I was fifteen. She loved them and filled them immediately, standing them in a place of honor in the center of the table.

My father had said they were silly and asked her to keep the old ones out. To this day, there are two competing sets on the table.

I've always accepted his disapproval quietly. I never really had a choice. But now I do, and it's dawning on me that I could move to my new place right now. The only inconvenience would be commuting back to the farm for chores.

Sitting here at the silent dinner table, once again in the shadow of my father's disapproval, I'm beginning to think my sanity should rate higher than convenience. I clear my throat. "Got some news to share."

It's rare that I start dinnertime conversations, so the scraping of plates pauses, and everyone stares at me.

"I'm moving out, into a place I rented. Tonight," I hear myself add. And why not? I'll still have to drive between Hardwick and Colebury, but this way I'd be commuting to do farm work instead of coffee-shop work.

For a second my parents just blink at me. Kyle scowls.

"Honey!" my mother gasps. "What brought this on?"

Just everything. "I've been saving up," I say. "And this will make my Busy Bean commute a whole lot easier."

Kyle shoves another bite of food in his mouth, glowering.

He won't stay mad, I remind myself. And he doesn't pay attention, so he doesn't realize how unhappy I've been.

"Waste of money," my father mutters.

"No, it isn't," I say. "I've been meaning to get my own place for a while, now. Zara's tenant fell through on the place she rents out, and she made me a deal I couldn't refuse."

"A house? You don't have furniture," my mother points out.

"That's true," I admit. "But everyone starts somewhere."

"You can take your bedroom furniture," Mom offers.

"Like hell," my father says. "What if we have a guest?"

The rest of us stare. Nobody can even remember the last time we had a guest. My mother's sister comes once a year and stays in a motel.

"Don't worry about it. I have money," I say. I don't want my old twin bed anyway. I want to start fresh.

Kyle avoids my eyes.

I finish my dinner in a few quick bites. "I'd better get my clothes together. Thanks for dinner, Mom. Excuse me."

"You can borrow my big suitcase," she offers.

"Thanks."

Fifteen minutes later I'm sliding that suitcase into the back of my truck. I have barely anything to move into a house. Clothes and toiletries. A box of my favorite books. Art supplies. My sleeping bag and camping mattress.

My mother comes outside carrying a very ugly lamp. I assume she's dug it out of the cellar, because it's only vaguely familiar.

"Thanks."

"I don't want you sitting in the dark." She chews her lip.

"I'll be fine. Hey, Mom? Could I take my desk? From my room?"

"That old thing? You go ahead. Kyle!" she shouts, and I spot my brother slinking off toward Dad's truck.

"Kyle! Help Kieran with the desk."

My brother is silent as he follows me one more time up the little staircase to our rooms. He waits while I remove a few things from the desktop, and then grasps one end of it. But then he lets go and stands tall again. "Why are you doing this?" he asks suddenly. "This is ridiculous."

Of course he thinks so. Because he doesn't pay attention.

"It's not ridiculous. I'm moving out because I want to. It will be easier this way. You'll see. More room." *Less tension.*

"This is still your farm," Kyle says. "It will always be your farm, even if I end up running it."

That's just about the most generous thing he's ever said to me. "I appreciate that," I say quietly. "But I have other interests, too.

And it's only Colebury, dude. I'm not moving to Europe." Although sometimes I wish I could.

"Yeah, but you're leaving me alone with this shit."

Now it's my turn to gape. I take in Kyle's pissed-off face, his dark brown Shipley eyes that we don't happen to share. "I'm not *ditching* you. Jesus. But I'm not planning on becoming a full-time farmer, Kyle, and I never will. I have other things to do, so I'm going to go do them."

Even though my brother is a dunderhead, and I'm sometimes angry at him, I experience a familiar moment of compassion towards him. He looks absolutely bereft. *Don't go*, his eyes say.

Men don't voice these things aloud, though. So Kyle gives a bewildered shrug.

"I'll come out Monday for chores," I say. "And if you decide to bale the rest of the straw, let me know and I'll arrange it so we can do that together."

"All right." His voice is thick. He finally lifts his end of the desk and waits for me to do the same.

We maneuver the wooden desk down the stairs and outside while Mom holds the door. We lift it into the truck's bed, and I shut the tailgate with a satisfying clunk.

"That's it, I guess," he says as the dog trots up.

Rex sits down and whines at my feet, licking his chops, and looking nervous. It's a little unusual for me to load up the truck and drive away at night. He can tell that something different is happening.

"You're coming with me, boy?"

He beats his tail against the gravel drive.

"Okay, man. Let's get your dish and your leash. You can try out city living."

Rex is a free-range mutt. We think he may be a pit bull and Labrador mix. He grew up running around our fifty-acre farm, but Rexie has slept in my room every night for ten years, since the neighbor gave him to me as a puppy. My rental house has a yard, and I'd been hoping it would be enough space for an aging farm dog. Colebury isn't exactly a city, and he might even love it there. If he doesn't, I'll make the difficult decision to bring him back out here to stay with Kyle.

Kyle and I walk back to the house once again. My mother is fretfully swiping a sponge on the table, and my dad is seated in the same chair that was killing him earlier. I lean down to pick up Rex's water bowl and food dish.

"What are you doing?" my father asks.

"Rex will need these," I say quietly.

"You can't take Rex," my father growls. "He's our dog."

I freeze on the way to the sink, where I'd meant to empty out the water bowl. "He's mine. He always has been."

"I've fed that dog for ten years," my father storms.

"*Dad*," Kyle says, shock in his voice. "Rexie loves Kieran."

"Don't take the *dog*," my father rants. "He keeps the raccoons away from the chickens. And he chases off the deer. He's part of the family. We can't do without him. *Please*."

I'm just standing here holding two dog dishes, not sure what to do. He has a point about the predators. But there's so much more to this story. He's willing to fight for a ten-year-old mutt who farts loudly during dinner. He'll even say *please*.

He didn't beg for me to stick around, though. No tears for me.

With my heart in my throat, I set the bowls back down on the floor. "Fine," I say under my breath. "I see how it is."

My mother twists the sponge, looking between me and my father, wondering if he'll relent.

But nope.

I shove my hands in my pockets and stride right out of there.

Kyle follows me again, the screen door banging behind him. "Kieran," he says, hurrying to catch up. "He didn't mean it like it sounded."

I don't even bother to argue. Rex is waiting patiently by my truck for me, and his tail thumps as I approach. "You're going to have to hold him."

Kyle curses under his breath. "Maybe we can find another farm dog for dad."

"Maybe." I kneel down in front of Rexie. "Stay here, man. I'll see you for chores on Monday." I stroke him between the ears, and his tail thumps faster. "Be a good boy." When I stand and open my truck's door, he tries to follow me.

Kyle lunges forward and hooks two fingers in his collar. "Come on, Rex. Let him go."

I climb into the truck and start it, banging the door shut. Kyle holds the dog back, and they both look at me with sad eyes while I drive away.

I drive toward Colebury feeling torn up inside. I'm ready to live my own life, but I guess I wasn't totally ready to hear what everyone else thinks of it.

It's only seven thirty, and I realize that some of the big box stores outside of Montpelier will still be open. As soon as I get to a hilltop—where the cell service is better—I pull over and take out my phone. I find a mattress store that closes at eight, and I call them.

"Look, if you tell me what you're looking for, and you're willing to plunk down your credit card number, my guys can load a couple of choices onto the truck and drive 'em to your house tonight. You'll choose a mattress on the truck, and they'll carry the winner inside. What size? And what's your budget?"

"King-sized," I say immediately. What's the point of moving out of your tiny childhood bedroom with a cramped twin bed if you can't have something better?

Maybe all my choices will prove ridiculous. But at least they're mine.

He gives me a brief education on mattress pricing, because I know nothing. And we settle on a couple of lower-range choices. "You need sheets?" he asks me.

"I need everything."

He laughs, but it's true.

After we hang up, I lead-foot it to Colebury to pick up a few things at CVS. I need toilet paper, soap, shampoo, paper towels. Dish soap. Laundry soap.

I've spent eight hundred dollars in the last hour, and it's terrifying. I'd better post a listing for a roommate immediately.

Driving out of the CVS, I still have a half hour until the mattress company is due to show up. So I roll slowly toward central Colebury, where the commercial strip gives way to my new neighborhood on the village green.

It's quiet now, because it's a weeknight, and the temperature is plunging. As I roll past the yarn shop, there's a familiar car that's visible only for a moment as the road bends.

A blue Volkswagen Beetle. And if I'm not mistaken, there was a light's soft glow inside it again.

I finish the route home, feeling unsettled. Roderick wouldn't be sleeping in his car, right? He said he was staying with his parents.

It's not really my problem either way. It's got nothing to do with me.

The Colebury diner comes into view, its too-bright lights cheerful in the dark, and beyond it, the town green. It's one-way around the green, so I follow the streets alongside it until I get to my house.

Mine. What a crazy concept.

I pull into my empty driveway and park as close to the garage door as possible. Then I hope out of my truck, feeling like a kid on Christmas. The backdoor opens onto the driveway, and I unlock it in a hurry.

It's quiet inside, and cold, too. Zara has the thermostat turned low. The place is perfectly empty, and I walk through every echoing room with a smile on my face. There's a downstairs bedroom next to a bathroom with a big tub in it. That's the room I'll rent out.

Upstairs there're two more bedrooms. One will be my room, and the other will be my studio. I'll find someone to help me carry the desk upstairs, and I'll put it near a window.

Then I'll paint again for the first time in years.

As promised, the delivery guys drive up to the house at eight thirty. I'm waiting on the porch, watching snowflakes fall—something that was not in the forecast.

"Are you Kieran?" the driver asks, hopping out. "Let's do this."

Although I feel ridiculous lying down on a plastic-covered mattress on the back of a truck, I shop carefully. Ten minutes later I've chosen the firmest of the three mattresses he brought.

It takes all three of us to struggle the thing upstairs and into the back bedroom of the dark house.

"Better turn the heat up, dude." The driver chuckles as we flop the mattress onto the bare floor. "It's gonna snow tonight."

My first thought is that I hope the rest of the oats don't get too wet.

My second thought is that my desk is getting snowed on in the back of the truck. I'll have to pull into the garage to keep it dry until I can get someone to help me carry it inside.

"Thanks for your help, guys." I tip them fifty bucks.

"Pleasure doing business with you," they say on their way out.

And then I'm completely alone in my own pad, with my brand new king-sized mattress. It takes me a while to put the new mattress pad and sheets on it. But eventually I'm lying there under my sleeping-bag-as-duvet, enjoying the silence.

Although I know it will be difficult to fall asleep. I wish Rexie was here. I wonder whose room he's chosen to sleep in tonight. Kyle's probably. That traitor.

I'm not really drowsy, so I open my laptop and take a peek at the real estate on Craig's List. There's a section for "rooms available," and I need to know what kinds of things people put in their listings.

I read through them, and then make the mistake of glancing under the "looking for housing" heading. Right away, the newest listing catches my eye. *Single guy looking to rent a room, hopefully close to Colebury. New in town, but with references. Employed full time with an early morning job. (But I will leave silently.) Clean and quiet. Gay AF. Available as soon as my first paycheck clears next Friday.*

Roderick. It has to be him. He'd told us that he had a place to stay. But it's not true, is it? Ten bucks says that right now he's sitting in his Volkswagen behind the yarn store.

I close my laptop and put it on the floor. My new bedroom is at the back of the house, away from the streetlights, but the darkness won't help me sleep tonight, not now that I suspect Roderick is sleeping in his car. It's snowing, for fuck's sake.

He's homeless. And, damn, I'm an asshole. I could have cost him his good, full-time job at the Busy Bean, just because I was uncomfortable with something I'd done in high school.

I roll over. My bed is comfortable, but the house is too quiet. Every creak of the roof and tick of the heating system seems to echo inside my head. I always wanted to live alone, where I'd have space to breathe. I thought it would be easier to be myself.

There's plenty of space here now, isn't there? And yet I'm the same screwed up person I was when I was living in the cramped little room in my parents' house.

Go figure.

RODERICK

I have a job with nice people who do good work.

I get to bake things for a living.

Everything is going to be fine.

These are the blessings I repeat to myself as the temperature drops. There are snowflakes falling on my windshield now, too. I can't even see properly out the windows.

I close my eyes and picture a comfortable bed, with a fluffy comforter and smooth sheets. But that only makes me think of our bed in Nashville, where Brian is probably right this moment. What's in his head? I'd like to think he's lying there missing me, but I know better. Because I hadn't just caught him cheating, I'd caught him balls deep in a female fan, backstage at a concert he'd known I was attending.

When I'd walked into his dressing room, he hadn't even stopped the world's oldest activity. He just looked over his shoulder at me with a red, angry face. I'd walked out, knowing he'd punished me on purpose.

We'd had an argument that afternoon. I'd pressed him to consider coming out.

"You know I can't," he'd said.

"Why not? You have all the money you'll ever need."

"It's not just the money. It's my career."

"You're letting the fans rule your life."

"And you're a needy little fuck."

I am, in fact, a needy little fuck. I need people to treat me like I matter, even when I haven't stood up for myself.

I'd already spent way too many months of my life expecting Brian to change for me. I'd known I was pushing him to the breaking point, but I hadn't been able to stop myself.

"We've been hiding ourselves for three years already," I'd told him. "Like assholes. How does this end?"

He'd answered that question quite effectively a few hours later. He hadn't even had the decency to break up with me. He left me to gather up the tiny scraps of my remaining pride and make the decision myself.

Brian is probably relieved, spread-eagle in our old bed, snoring happily right now. Meanwhile, I lie freezing in a car, a few miles from my childhood bedroom. It was my choice to come here. I should have called my parents before I pointed the car north, but I thought it would be harder to say no to me in person.

Not so much, though. My parents are also toasty in a comfortable bed, unburdened by thoughts of me. I'll bet they forgot about me as soon as my car left their driveway.

I pinch my eyes closed against the unwelcome heat of sudden tears. Men aren't supposed to cry. It's part of the bro code. I press my thumb and forefinger into the corners of my eyes and take a deep breath.

A car approaches, the low rumble of an engine accompanied by tires crunching on the gravel parking lot. Twin headlight beams flash, and I forget to breathe as a car door opens and footsteps approach.

Knuckles rap on the front windshield, and my heart crawls into my mouth.

"Hey, Roderick?" says a low voice. "You in there?"

I let out a gasp. Who's this intruder who knows my name?

"Roderick," he repeats. "Come on, man. Show me that you're alive."

I'm startled to realize that the voice belongs to Kieran Shipley.

"Dude." He knocks again. "You're in the back, right? Come on. It's cold out here."

"You're cold?" I sputter, throwing off the sleeping bag. "Don't let me inconvenience you."

"Hey." He tries the door handle, but of course it's locked. "I wasn't talking about me. I mean it's too cold to sleep out here."

Isn't this just mortifying? "I'll be fine. Move along now. There's nothing to see here."

I hear a loud thunk, and wonder for a moment if Kieran punched my car. But then I sit up and realize that sound was his forehead hitting the roof. His big farm-boy body has knocked the snow off one window, and is now bent into a defeated posture against my car.

"Get out," he says. "Come on. Take this address, okay? I have an extra room to rent. And I have enough on my conscience already. If you croak out here, I will lose my shit."

With a groan, I open the door and climb out, wrapping my stolen sleeping bag around me. "Let me get this straight. You want me to come home with you because it'll help you sleep better."

The moonlight reflects off the light carpet of snow. He blinks, his handsome brow wrinkled with tension. "Something like that. But you'll sleep better, too, right? Win-win."

"I don't like owing people. You don't even like me."

"Don't even know you," he growls in that abrupt way that Kieran says so many things. He squints at me. "What's wrong? Did something happen?"

"No! Nothing!" I bark, swatting at my face. I must look like I've been crying. I have never been more embarrassed than I am right now. "Go home, Kieran. You don't want me for a roommate. You don't even want me in the same area code."

He flinches. "Wasn't ever about you, though."

"It never is," I hiss, because I'm so tired of men who can't sort out their shit. I was an excellent companion to Brian, who wanted me desperately about half the time and then couldn't stand the sight of me the other half.

"Look, you should have just told one of us you were sleeping in your car."

"It's not your problem," I argue.

Kieran blinks. "Doesn't mean we wouldn't care."

And now I feel like a heel. "It's *embarrassing*, okay? I didn't plan on leaving Nashville as quickly as I did. And I drove up here hoping to crash at my parents' place. But they shut the door in my face. It's not the kind of story that's fun to tell."

His big eyebrows furrow. "Why'd they do that?"

"It's the gay thing." I make sure to keep eye contact while I say it, because I never let anyone know how much it bothers me. "They're not into it."

"Oh." He sighs. "Parents are the worst."

"Yeah." An awkward silence falls between us. I shiver against the snow falling in my face.

"Here," Kieran says. He pulls an old business card out of his pocket and hands it to me. It's from a barbershop, but he's scrawled an address on the back. "It's the white house right on the Colebury green. You can't miss it. I'll leave the side door open. Take the downstairs bedroom. There's nothing in it, but it's heated."

"You can't leave your door unlocked."

He rolls his eyes. "Better lock it after you come in, then."

At that, he walks across the lot, climbs into a pickup that's almost as old as my car, and drives away.

I let out a shout of frustration that dies quickly in the nighttime void and then get back in my car. There's snow in my hair now. I sit for a moment, stubborn and shivering.

He probably hopes I won't actually show up. He did his part, right? He gave me the option, so now he can feel okay about it.

Then again, he drove over here at eleven at night to offer me a room in his house.

I ponder my choices for a little while longer. I can either sit here feeling cold and miserable all night. Or I can go someplace I'm not wanted.

It's really freaking cold in my car, so in the end, it's an easy decision. I'm clinging to the bottom rung of my own life, and Kieran Shipley—Lord knows why—just offered me a hand up.

I'd be an idiot not to take it.

Even so, it takes me another half hour to get up the courage to drive into the center of town and pull into the driveway of a pretty white house right on the town green. I double and then triple check the address before I walk up to the side door and try the knob.

It's unlocked.

I take a deep breath and then push the door open. "Hello?" I call out, and the sound of my own voice echoes. "This had better be Kieran's house. Either that, or I'm about to be arrested for trespassing. And I don't have bail money."

I hear what may possibly be a distant snort of laughter. And then quiet footsteps begin to pace down the dark stairs.

Kieran comes into view bit by bit. First the plaid pajama pants on long legs. And then those abs and a broad chest covered by a T-shirt that stretches tautly across all those muscles. But the darkness—or maybe it's the late hour—softens him. "Hey," he says quietly.

"Hey," I grunt, sounding grumpy in spite of my gratitude. "I, uh, know it's late. You're going to be dead in the morning."

"And you're not?"

I shake my head. "If I can lie flat for five hours, it will be the best night of sleep I've had in a week. But are you sure about this?"

"Of course," he whispers. "Let me give you the nickel tour."

I follow him through the darkened rooms, where the street-lights from outside show me enough to get the lay of the land. The kitchen has been recently updated, but everything else is old school—in a good way. The ceilings are high, and there are original moldings and traditional wood floors.

"Nice house," I say, giving a low whistle.

"I know." He runs one hand through tousled hair. "It's a lot nicer than I'd be renting without the insider's price from Zara. I figured I'd rent out this downstairs bedroom." He gestures toward the darkened doorway at the back. "That way we'd have separate bathrooms."

"Good plan," I agree. Lord knows I'm not strong enough to resist a glimpse of his naked body as he steps out of the shower.

I *want* a glimpse, of course. Because I'm still breathing.

This is probably a terrible idea, but not terrible enough for me to sleep in my car if I don't have to.

"Upstairs there's another two bedrooms and a bathroom. And an attic I haven't ventured into. So I'd have more space than you. But I also agreed to do some maintenance for Zara. And a few other things."

"Cool." I wave a hand to indicate that square footage is not exactly important to me. "How much is the rent?"

"Your part would be six-fifty a month, plus utilities. I have no idea how much heat and electric will cost, though."

"That's all?" I'm stunned. "That's cheap."

"Well, it's exactly half the rent. That's why I wasn't gonna find two roommates. Didn't seem necessary."

"Wow, okay." I brush past Kieran and walk down the hallway into the empty bedroom, where there's a window seat that looks out into the backyard. It's a terrific little room, in a kickass house.

"Zara gave me a deal because she wants some help while Dave is away, and she wanted to rent to somebody she knows."

"Yeah." I clear my throat. "Look. I don't want you to turn away somebody you'd rather have as a roommate just because

I'm strapped. I don't want charity. You weren't so happy to see me roll back into town."

"Yeah." He winces. "Let's just forget about that."

"You never said why, though," I press.

"Seriously?" He folds burly arms over his chest. "It's not that hard to figure out."

"Because of high school," I guess.

"Yes, Captain Obvious. But that's, uh, water under the bridge. I haven't been a stalker since then."

I actually grin. "You weren't a stalker. You were a voyeur. It's different."

"Look," Kieran grunts. "You want the room or not? My only condition is that we never speak of this again."

"Okay." I bite back my smile. "Sorry. It's just that you're the only one who doesn't like that memory. I kind of like voyeurs. I don't have very many hang-ups…" I catch the look on his face, and raise two hands in supplication. "Right. Never mind. We won't speak of it again."

"Thank you."

"It's just stupid high school shit, anyway," I add. "Lord knows I don't want to be held accountable for anything I did as a teenager. Or, hell, my early twenties. Okay—one of these days I'm going to stop making stupid decisions. Any second now." I laugh, and Kieran smiles so quickly that I might have imagined it.

We end up eyeing each other for a quiet moment. And suddenly I become all too aware that I'm alone with a hot farmer boy at midnight in an empty house. His eyes are beautiful, but they're the kind that see more than they give away. I have no idea what this man is thinking. And if he has his way, I never will.

"What else do you need from me?" I blurt out. "What about a security deposit? I'd need to get a real paycheck before I can give that to you. If that's a deal-killer, I'll understand."

"Nah." Kieran shakes his head. "Zara didn't charge me one, so it would be a dick move if I asked that of you."

"Oh," I say slowly. "Did, uh, Zara make you rent me the room? Because if she did, we can just say I wasn't interested…"

"No." He frowns. "She has no idea. And our rent isn't due until December first, anyway."

"Okay," I gulp. "Unless you change your mind before then, you've got yourself a roommate." I reach out a hand to him.

Kieran actually hesitates for a fractional second before reaching out to shake. When our palms meet, a flash of heat washes across my skin. His fingers close over mine, and I'm far too conscious of how close we're standing together in what is going to be our house.

If this is what it will feel like to live with Kieran, I'm so very screwed. "I'll bring in my sleeping bag, then."

"I've got a camping mattress you can borrow until you get a real bed." He yawns and stretches, and his T-shirt rides up a few crucial inches, so I check out his abs.

Rein it in, Roddy, I coach myself. *Or you'll be back on the street before you know it.*

Kieran doesn't notice, though. He lumbers upstairs to get the camping mattress, while I dart outside to get a few of my things.

After I come back into the house, I close the door behind me and lock it tightly. Then I let out a big sigh of relief. I'm still dangling over the abyss, but someone just threw me a lifeline.

Thank you, Vermont. This place isn't half bad.

That night I lie down in a quiet room and stretch my toes all the way to the bottom of the sleeping bag. I have five straight hours of the best sleep I've had in ages, and when my alarm goes off, I wash up in a warm bathroom and then drive to work.

The commute takes literally three minutes. I've never had it so easy.

Zara and I make two dozen gorgeous bagels and a slew of muffins and pastries. When Kieran comes in to work behind the counter, I fix him a pumpernickel bagel with smoked salmon and cream cheese and carry the plate out front. "This is for you. Thanks for everything."

He blinks. Then he takes the plate and licks his lips. "Thank you. And you're welcome. I'll start the coffee before I eat this."

"Good plan."

As I return to the kitchen, I catch Zara watching us. "What's up with Kieran? Anything wrong?"

"Not a thing," I say, carrying some dishes to the sink. "I, uh, asked him to rent a room to me, and I guess I'm your tenant now, too."

"Oh," she says, obviously startled. "That's nice."

She has no idea.

When I get off work at three, Kieran is off to one of his other jobs. The dude works hard. So I'm left to my own devices, exploring his house in the daylight.

I don't go upstairs, because I won't invade his privacy. But I poke around the empty living room, taking in the inlaid details in the wood floor, and admiring the view of the town green from the front window. Colebury isn't a fancy town, but this is the nicest part of it. Most of the houses around the square have been recently upgraded. My parents' church is visible on the opposite side of the green. Once a week they'll be a quarter mile away, I suppose, praying for my soul.

Or not. I wonder if they think of me at all.

On this depressing thought, I continue my investigation of the house. The dining room is beautiful, with built-in china cabinets in the corners. It lacks a table and chairs, but nobody's perfect.

In the kitchen, I open all the cabinets and drawers, finding them empty. So I go out to my car and fetch the very few items that I brought with me from Nashville. I've got my favorite mixing bowl, a single All-Clad skillet, a kitchen scale, my lucky saucepan, and my knives.

A cook never goes anywhere without his knives. I left my whole life behind in Nashville, including my guitar, but somehow I had enough clarity to take my favorite kitchen essentials. I wasn't about to walk away without my five-hundred-dollar set of Wüsthofs. They're worth more than the guitar, anyway.

I tuck all these items away, which only takes a few minutes. And then I wonder if Kieran would want me to stock up on a few more things that every kitchen needs. Would he be grateful? Or would he think I'm dominating his space?

I ponder the question for a minute or two. But, fuck it. This kitchen is empty and sad, and cooking is my area of expertise. I grab my car keys and the wallet that contains all the money I have in the world.

And I head for the store.

Maybe I go a little crazy at the grocery store, but a guy needs to eat, right? When I get busy cooking in Kieran's kitchen, I feel happier than I've been in a long time. I rub spices all over a pork loin and set it to roast in my skillet, leaving my saucepan free for a nice batch of applesauce.

It isn't until I hear Kieran walk in the door at seven thirty that I notice there's flour on the countertop and steam on the window-panes. I've made myself at home before he's had a chance to do the same.

Hastily, I start cleaning up. But there he is in the doorway, holding—

"Is that a pre-made sandwich from a convenience store?" I ask, unable to keep the horror out of my voice.

He looks down at the plastic wedge in his hand, as if he's not quite sure how it got there. "I decided not to stay for dinner at my folks', but then I didn't have a better plan."

"Well, I made a pork tenderloin and applesauce. Then I realized I don't, uh, have any plates. So I had to make some rolls to eat it on."

"It smells so—" He sniffs the air. "Wow. Really good."

Even this small crumb of praise makes me grow taller. "Then let's eat. You can save that for tomorrow." I grab the plastic sandwich container out of his hand, open up the refrigerator, and chuck it inside.

Kieran catches the fridge's door before it closes. "Holy cow. You did some shopping."

"Well, I guess I did." I let out a nervous chuckle at all the food I've crammed in there. A gallon of milk, because it's cheapest that way. Apples, winter squash—because it's cheap. Butter. A few condiments for cooking. Blocks of cheese, because it's an inexpensive protein, and some of them were on sale. My sourdough starter. "Look, I can keep all of this on two shelves and give you the other two. I don't need to hog the space."

He shrugs. "There's plenty of room. And I don't know how to cook. Like, at all. Do you think you might…"

I wait.

"Never mind." He shakes his head.

"I might what?" I prod.

He puts his phone onto the countertop charger and avoids my gaze. "I want to learn how to cook a little," he says. "I can't afford to eat out every night. Could you, uh, recommend a book you like?"

"You can't learn from a book," I tell him. "It's all about technique. I'll teach you to cook. It's the least I could do." I move closer to him, because this idea excites me. Cooking is fun when there's someone to feed.

Those brown eyes widen. "Really?"

"Sure. No problem. Cooking is like breathing to me. It's the only thing I've ever learned how to do more quickly than other people seem to."

That, and blowjobs.

"I'd appreciate it," he says, jamming his hands in his pockets. He leans back a fraction of an inch, and I realize I've invaded his personal space. I do that to everybody when I get jazzed up about something.

I take a healthy step backwards. "Let's eat this food before my rolls burn." I open the oven and carefully remove the stainless steel lid to my skillet, which I've repurposed as a baking sheet. There are four large rolls ringing the handle.

The skillet itself is on the bottom rack, the roast browning nicely in the pan.

"Whoa," Kieran says. "That's impressive."

"It's a twelve-dollar roast and a dollar's worth of flour. This is why I never eat take-out food. Oh, and—" I lift the lid of the saucepan, and the scent of apples rises into the air. "Apples are cheap this time of year."

He snorts. "They're free if you're cousins with Griffin Shipley. I eat so many of them in the fall that I might be fifty percent apple."

The other fifty percent is beefcake. I keep that idea to myself. But Kieran Shipley is so attractive that my slutty little mind can't stop noticing him.

I give myself a mental slap and then ask a nosy question. "Audrey lives at the orchard?" I'm super curious about my new bosses. I pluck the rolls off the skillet's lid and drop them onto the countertop to cool. Then I pull the skillet from the oven, setting it in on the stovetop to rest the roast before I slice it.

"Yup, they have a big spread. The orchard is their main business, but there's also a small dairy. Griffin makes hard cider, and that's turning into his biggest moneymaker."

"Cool." I can't imagine the luxury of growing your own food. And getting Kieran talking makes me feel like I've won a prize. "Would it be weird to put applesauce inside the sandwich? Because we don't have silverware, either."

He shrugs. "You don't have to feed me at all. But that sounds pretty good to me."

"Awesome. Give me ten minutes to assemble this, and I will blow your mind with my pork loin."

Wait, did that come out sounding dirty?

"Thanks," he says simply. And then he goes upstairs to change.

KIERAN

I thought that having Roderick as a roommate would be super weird. But it turns out that when your life is hellaciously busy, you don't have time to feel weird. After our awkward dinner at the kitchen counter, I don't see much of him for a while.

The next two weeks are a blur of coffeemaking, Photoshop, and driving to Hardwick for farm labor. Every night I stop at a store on my way home to pick up things I need for the house. I buy a set of plain white plates and bowls. I buy towels and more sheets. A king-sized quilt and blanket.

I buy a couch that's discounted by half because one of its feet is missing. That's an easy fix, because we have all kinds of wood scraps in the barn. It only takes me a few minutes to find one that's the right thickness, and to cut it to size. Nobody looks at a couch's feet, anyway.

Climbing into bed every night knowing Roderick's in the house hasn't been as strange as I'd thought it would be, either. His light is usually off by the time I stagger upstairs after another busy day.

Roderick still sleeps on a sleeping bag in the middle of his empty room. The only thing between him and the wood floor is the camping mattress I lent him. He seems perfectly happy with this arrangement, though. In fact, he looks much better rested than he used to. The circles under his eyes are gone, and he doesn't fall asleep at work anymore.

And I've been grateful he's kept his promise not to mention the high school incident again.

One Friday night I come home from the ad agency to find Roderick reading a book on my new couch. "Hey!" he says, slapping the book shut. "I was waiting for you. It's time for your first cooking lesson."

It's embarrassing how much I like hearing that he was waiting for me. "What's on the menu?" I ask, tossing my coat onto a doorknob. I really need to hang some hooks in the entryway. Soon.

"Roast chicken with herbed butter and garlic," he says.

"That sounds…complicated." Maybe this wasn't such a great idea.

"I know!" he says, leaping up and looking gleeful. "It's not, though. That's why I chose this recipe. Come on." He practically gallops into the kitchen.

There's a whole chicken lying there in the center of his skillet, and some other ingredients on the counter.

He lifts a sprig of an herb off the counter. "This is…"

"Rosemary," I say.

"And…"

"Parsley," I say, beating him to the punch again. "I grew up with farmers. And even if my mom can't figure out how to put flavor in food, my Aunt Ruth sure can."

"Well." Roderick sniffs. "I guess you're going to do just fine. See this butter? I left it out on the counter to soften." He pokes the stick, and his finger leaves an indent. "Open that sucker up and dump it in a bowl."

I follow this simple instruction, and then he hands me a fancy chef's knife. "Now you're going to learn how to get the skin off of garlic quickly." He puts a clove of garlic on a cutting board that I've never seen before. It must be a new acquisition. "Smack it with the side of the knife. Go on."

Whap. I smack the garlic, and now it's flattened.

"Nice!" He chuckles. "Now take the skin off. That's easy when you've crushed it a little."

He's right. I flick the skin out of the way.

"Slice it thinly, okay? Then overchop it in the other direction."

I slice the garlic into fine slices, but then I'm stuck. "What does overchop mean?"

"Like this," he says. He actually reaches around my body and pivots the knife, and my concentration goes haywire. I'm too focused on the heat of his chest at my side and the brush of his thumb on my hand. "Okay, a little finer," he says.

I squint down at the garlic and give it a few clumsy chops, but my attention is still on him. He's standing so close to me that I feel a puff of his breath when he talks. And I like it way too much.

"Good enough," he says. "Now do another one."

I force myself to concentrate. The minced garlic gets tossed on top of the butter, along with parsley and rosemary that I chop, too. Then Roderick hands me a wooden spoon and has me mash it all together.

"Time to preheat the oven," he says. "Use four twenty-five. Four fifty is even better, but sometimes it makes the house too smoky. Always cook a chicken hot and fast," he says with a chuckle. "What's good for sex is also good for roasting chicken."

Now my neck and face are on *fire*.

"Last step," he says. "Using your hands, you're going to shove half of that butter under the chicken skin, over the meat."

"What about the other half," I ask, my face still red.

"We'll freeze it for next time." He grabs a piece of waxed paper and plops half the butter onto it. He shapes it into a log and rolls it up before I can blink.

I get to work buttering the chicken, but I might have gotten more of it on me than on the bird.

"It's a messy job," he concedes.

"Not nearly as messy as gutting and plucking the chicken," I point out.

"You've done that?" he yelps.

"Many times. Next time you need a chicken, give me three days' notice, and I'll bring you a really fresh one and show you how."

He puts a hand on my back, and I feel the warmth through my T-shirt. "I think I'm happy to let the store handle that for me, farmer boy." That hand disappears, but I can still feel it after it's gone. "Last step," he says, grabbing a cardboard container of kosher salt. "Salt and pepper the fuck out of everything. That's a technical term. Memorize it."

I laugh again. That's twice in one day.

We let the bird roast for an hour. I shower and call my brother, then Roderick makes rice.

"For brown rice or basmati, try two cups of water to one of rice. That usually works." He lifts the lid off the saucepan of rice, and a homey scent fills the air.

"That smells delicious."

"I just threw in some turmeric and cumin." He shrugs. "We ought to have a vegetable, too. But we're out of pans, and we're out of time. So maybe I'll tackle that at your next lesson."

"Good plan."

He opens the oven door, and the chicken is gorgeous, like something on a magazine cover—golden brown and sizzling everywhere.

"Jesus," I murmur.

"I know, I'm hungry, too," he agrees. "Move your big self out of the way so I can get this." With a dish towel in each hand—my mother gave me those from her stash—he lifts the skillet onto the stovetop. "It has to rest for five or ten minutes, then we feast."

I can barely stand the wait. But when I finally get my first bite, it's *delicious*.

"Your cooking rocks," Roderick says, biting into a thigh. We're standing at the counter side by side, because there's no table.

"Don't flatter me, it's your recipe," I say, nudging him with my elbow. I have that happy glow you get from eating something amazing. The garlic and butter have turned an ordinary thing extraordinary. "But what I don't understand is this—if cooking is so easy, why do so many people do it badly?"

"I've always wondered the same thing," he says, licking his fingers.

The sight of his tongue reminds me of something else, and I look away. *Jesus.* Even if Roderick has been good about not bringing it up, the memory is obviously still there, lurking in my psyche.

And I have no idea how to make it go away.

RODERICK

November rolls on. Before the end of the month, I leave my rent check on the counter when I leave for work at five a.m. It's money well spent. Every morning I wake up in a snug house instead of in my car. And I sleep soundly at night knowing that the door is locked and that there's a burly farm boy somewhere in the house.

I'm a pack animal. I'm not cut out to live alone.

Also, I'm already deeply in love with Kieran's house. The living room has a high ceiling and shiny wood floors. It has the old bones of a home that's been standing for a century. I love the creaky built-in cabinets in the dining room we don't use. And the ornate staircase spindles.

Little by little, we're furnishing the place. Kieran shops at stores and online. One morning when I wake up, I find a large, creamy rug in the center of the living room. I lie down in the center of it and decide I approve.

For my part, I've been haunting the thrift shops in Montpelier, slowly furnishing the kitchen with my finds. I've bought coffee mugs with roosters on them and a shiny copper teakettle.

One Saturday I swing by a church rummage sale and hit the motherlode: egg cups, serving spoons, a two-dollar cast-iron griddle with the tags still on it. And those are just the bigger purchases.

On Monday, for the first time ever, neither Kieran nor I has a shift at the coffee shop. That's the day that Zara and Audrey have claimed to work together. "We'll get a chance to start the week and talk. Just the two of us," Audrey had said.

I wake up at six thirty, though, because I've trained myself to be awake in the morning. I run out for groceries, because it's time for Kieran's next cooking lesson.

He comes downstairs at eight, wearing flannel pants, a snug-fitting waffle-weave shirt and sleep-tousled hair. As usual, I experience a rush of affection for the hot farm boy who rescued me off the streets.

I don't gush about my gratitude, though, because it's clear that Kieran doesn't know what to do with praise. And my exuberance generally makes him a little uncomfortable. So I try to rein myself in whenever we're together.

Still, I can't stop wondering how good it would feel to be grabbed up in those strong arms and hugged. Or, say, pinned to the bed while he fucks me. I'm not picky.

"You didn't have to do that," is the first thing Kieran says to me this morning.

"Um, what?" I'm still distracted by my morning sex fantasy, and by the way his hair is grown out and starting to curl. I want to sift my fingers through it.

"The soap dish in my bathroom," he clarifies.

"Oh!" I wave a hand to dismiss this bit of nonsense. "Lucky find." The dish is made from a single piece of waxed, carved wood. It reminded me of Kieran.

"I can pay you back," he says.

"Sure, man. If you really want to, I'll take your twenty-five cents."

"Wait, what?"

"Church rummage sale. But look! I also got this…" I grab his muscular wrist and tug him over to the stove where my new Dutch oven waits. "It's the best that four bucks can buy."

"Wow." He chuckles. "What are you going to make in that?"

"Not me, you. I shopped for your next lesson."

"I want to pay for the groceries," he says immediately.

"Fine. I still have the slip somewhere. Today you're making pulled pork. The cooking time is five hours, so you'd better get started. Here." I hand him a mixing bowl. "Two tablespoons of brown sugar. And a quarter cup of paprika. You're making a dry rub."

He blinks at me with sleepy eyes. "Before coffee?"

His expression is so unguarded and sweet that I just want to give him a hug. But I've learned that Kieran is not a toucher. When I sometimes slip up and pat his arm, he always grows still and wary.

I grab the stove-top espresso maker—another thrift-store find —and fill it with water. "I'll caffeinate you. But you're rubbing that butt."

He blinks. "Sorry?"

"Pork butt. Also called shoulder or picnic roast, depending on where you are in the country. Preheat the oven to two seventy-five."

"Isn't that kind of low?"

"Yep! Low and slow. Just how I like my..." I break off laughing, because Kieran's face is reddening already, and I haven't even made the joke yet. "Never mind. We don't have a slow cooker, so we're using the oven. Real pulled pork is made in a smoker, but this will still be super good. If you ever get started."

Kieran finally takes the hint and preheats the oven.

After I bully him into stirring six spices together, and rubbing the mixture all over four giant chunks of pork, he scatters a few quartered onions in the bottom of the pan and lays the spiced meat on top of it.

"There you go!" I cheer. "Put that puppy in the oven. Good. Now I'm going to make us some yeasted pancakes." I set my new griddle on the stovetop. "We can't smell pulled pork all day on empty stomachs."

Kieran watches me stir together the batter I left overnight on the counter. "Can't you make pancakes a little simpler than that?" He's leaning against the counter, sipping the coffee I made for him. As he lifts the cup, I admire the dark hair on his tanned forearms and sigh inside.

"Sure. These are better, though. More flavor." I whisk together the batter, and then turn on the burners under the griddle.

Kieran drains his coffee. "What's that noise?"

"Hmm?"

"That weird little chirp. From your phone."

I glance at the counter where my phone is charging. "You don't know that sound, huh?" *Fascinating*.

"No?"

I grin. "That's the sound Grindr makes when someone messages you."

"Oh." He looks into his empty mug.

"It's another clue," I add. Kieran doesn't seem to date men or women, but there are times when I'm sure he's checking me out. Then again, I'm sort of vain. And Kieran is the hardest man to read on earth.

"To what?"

"To *you*. If you don't know the sound of Grindr, it's a clue. I've been trying to figure you out."

When he speaks, it's not to tell me to fuck off and mind my own business. "If you do, let me know," he says. Then he goes upstairs until I call him back down again to eat pancakes.

After breakfast, Kieran leaves to do chores at his parents' farm. He reappears at suppertime, when the house smells like heaven.

"Wow," he says, tossing his coat onto a hook he installed this week. "That smells amazing. Did it work?"

"It always works," I say, swirling the wine in my half-empty glass. I splurged on a cheap pinot noir, which I've been sipping while I wait for him to reappear. "I pulled it out three hours ago. You check it, okay? Use the tongs."

In the kitchen I watch as he lifts the pot and pokes the meat. "It's falling apart. I just want to dive in head first."

"You will," I promise. "But my rolls are in the oven for another fifteen minutes, okay? Turn on the burner and we'll heat this up. I'll call you when it's time."

"Awesome. Right back," he says, then disappears upstairs.

When the bread is done and steaming up the kitchen, I call up the stairs. "Kieran?"

There is no response.

After a second try, I climb the stairs slowly. This is Kieran's private domain, and I don't want to invade it. On the other hand, there's pulled pork waiting.

When I reach his room, I realize why he can't hear me. He's facing his desk, painting away on a giant, propped-up pad of watercolor paper, earbuds in his ears.

"Kieran."

Nothing.

I step closer. "Food's ready!" I call.

He startles violently. Then he drops his head, as if embarrassed. "Sorry," he says, yanking out the ear buds.

"I didn't know you painted." I try to see around him. "Is that…a tractor?"

He puts his hands on my shoulders for the first time ever—their weight is way too enticing—and steers me away from his work. "It's terrible. Let's eat."

His hands fall away as we jog down the stairs. "Did you always paint?"

"No, almost never," he says heavily as we enter the kitchen. "Can I have some of that wine?"

"Of course you can. I already poured your glass." I point it out on the counter. "But you have to pull the pork first. Here." I hand him two forks. "Easiest thing in the world. But you have to do all the steps yourself or it doesn't count."

"Count as what?"

"Something you made yourself. We're cheating already with the barbecue sauce." I open a bottle from the store. My cooking-school buddies would never let me live it down, but I didn't want to overwhelm Kieran with recipes just yet.

He gets to work tugging the meat apart, while my mouth waters.

"So why don't you paint more often?" I ask, because the wine has already obliterated my crappy impulse control.

He stops working for a second, as if trying to decide whether or not to answer me. Then he puts the forks down and looks me right in the eye. "When I was twelve years old, my mother was hanging one of my thousands of drawings on the refrigerator. And my father said, 'Don't encourage him. We don't want him to grow up to be a faggy artist.'"

"Oh," I say slowly. "And maybe that hit a little too close to the truth?"

"At twelve, I really didn't know..." He shakes his head instead of finishing that sentence. "I stopped drawing immediately. For, like, ten years."

My jaw hangs open. "Don't you draw at work, though?"

"I do now. A couple of years ago I said *fuck it* and picked up a set of colored pencils. It took me a long time to stop hearing his voice in my head." His eyes are deep pools of pain right now, and I just want to give him a hug.

"Shit. Don't I know it," I agree. "I still hear their voices in my head. It's fucking sad that you didn't draw anything for ten years. But maybe you're smarter than me. I took the opposite route, rubbing it in my parents' faces every chance I got. That's how I found myself living under a bridge when I was eighteen."

His eyes widen. "You did? For how long?"

"A few months. Then I found a program that helps homeless LGBT kids even after they're eighteen, and I went to cooking school on grant money. People tell you to be yourself. But not everybody can afford that luxury." I pluck his wine glass off the counter and hand it to him. "Drink some of this and paint some more. I won't tell anyone that you have a tractor kink."

His eyes crinkle in the corners. "I don't, really. But that's what I drew to piss off Dad. Seemed like a good place to start again."

"I would have painted him a purple rainbow tractor with unicorns in the meadow, because I never did know when to shut up." Like now. I don't ever want this conversation to end, because Kieran is finally confiding in me. He's so buttoned up with everyone that I feel like I won the fucking lottery.

"How did you, uh, know." He clears his throat, and his eyes are tentative.

"Know?" I feel so swimmy and bright that it takes a moment to understand what he's asking. "Oh, that I'm queer as fuck? I always knew. Sorry." I can hear myself babbling. "But everybody's different. I know some dudes who were thirty-five and married before they figured out how much they like cock."

I wait for it and—there it is! The telltale blush on his cheekbones. It happens whenever I mention sex. If I ever get this man into bed, I'm going to make him blush *everywhere*.

"You should experiment," the wine in my bloodstream says. "I'll help you make a Grindr profile. *Curious lumberjack with muscles seeks someone to sixty-nine.* They'll be like flies on honey."

Kieran looks horrified. He sets down his glass with a *thunk*. "No fucking way. I can't use an app. Shit. I can't even make barista conversation with strangers. People chat on that app, right? And if I actually saw someone interesting on there, they'd want to *talk*." He shudders.

I burst out laughing. "Oh the horrors! So you aren't afraid to suck a dick, but the small talk might kill you?"

"Maybe," he grumbles.

Giddy laughter bounces through my chest, and I feel drunk with unnamed possibilities.

Kieran braces a hand against the counter, studying his wine

glass like the secret to the universe might be written there. The man is seriously hard to read.

"Hey." A rush of affection makes me reach up to cup his face in my hand, so I can see his eyes. "If you ever decide to experiment with some lucky guy, just know that he's going to feel like he's winning at life."

Kieran goes absolutely still under my hand. And for a moment I think my compliment didn't land the right way. Maybe I've fucked everything up by touching him.

But then we lock eyes, and for the first time I realize that when Kieran gets quiet, it's not because he wants to chuck me across the room. He gets quiet when he's thinking. And right now he's thinking that we are standing *very* close together.

He does not move away.

And neither do I. Never one to back down, I stroke my thumb against his handsome, stubbled face. I'm rewarded by a sound of pleasure so low that it's almost inaudible.

His breath hitches as I move even closer. And then I bring us cheek to cheek, where I rub against him—stubble to stubble—like an affectionate cat. He smells like woodsmoke and outdoors.

Kieran makes a shocked little sound—half inhalation, half groan. But he doesn't pull away.

I take that as a green light. I turn my head and kiss his neck very slowly right under the jaw. One kiss becomes two. Three. I'm dropping shameless, open-mouthed kisses everywhere I can reach. And that's a lot of places, because Kieran lifts his chin to give me access.

Two hands sized for farm work close around my back with a clumsy slowness. His chest bumps mine as it rises with a gasping breath.

Standing on tiptoe so I can reach his ear, I whisper. "Kiss me. Do it." Because I've taken enough liberties with this gentle creature.

He makes another desperate noise and then turns his head, finding my neck with his eager mouth. My body flashes with goosebumps as he mimics me, measuring my neck with his lips, tracing an erotic path up to my jaw. He rubs my back slowly, as if in wonder.

And I can't wait any longer. I turn and catch his generous lips with mine. The first kiss tastes like red wine and the second one tastes like heat. He opens for me like he's starving. I slip my tongue inside his mouth and sigh into the kiss. I've wanted him for so long. And the vise-like grip he has on my back suggests he's been thinking about this, too.

I lose myself in his kisses. Each one is a little feistier than the next. Kieran is like a ball rolling downhill, picking up speed as we go. I push back on him until his ass hits the counter. And then I step between his legs and push my hips against his.

Yessss. My eager dick brushes his. Even through several layers of fabric I can feel him harden for me. My hand slips down, impulsively palming his ass through his jeans.

Kieran groans into my mouth. And the noise seems to wake him from this fever dream we're sharing. He jerks his head back suddenly, as if I've burned him. "Fuck," he curses.

I'm pretty sure it's not a request. In fact, his voice is charged with alarm. Somehow that pricks through the lust fog I'm in, and I take a step backward.

He buries his face in his hands. "Fuck," he says again. "I'm sorry."

"For what?" I gasp.

"I don't even know." He groans, and not in a fun way.

"Hey," I whisper. I plant a hand in the center of his chest. "Dude, it's me who's sorry. I took advantage."

"No." He shakes his head. "I've been thinking about that a long time."

I light up inside. "Yeah, I have too. But it's still not cool to jump your roommate. Not without discussing it first, anyway," I add, because hope springs eternal.

He lifts his face from his hands. "And I hate talkin'. So we're totally screwed."

I take a deep breath, because my brain cells need oxygen, and I'm so turned on we could power next month's electric bill with a single electrode to my aching nuts. "Look. Let's eat pulled pork. I'm drunk, and if we stand here any longer I'm just going to stare at you while I picture you naked."

His laughter sounds uncomfortable. "All right. Dinner."

KIERAN

I make a plate of food for myself and then carry it into the living room. But I'll be lucky if I can even taste it, because my mind is blown. I *kissed him*. And I liked it. A whole lot.

We sit on the new carpet, and eat at opposite ends of the coffee table that I brought home last night. It's another relic from my mother's attic. Absently, I pick up the giant sandwich and take a bite. And—Jesus. It's so good. The meat is tender and the bread is yeasty and perfect. To my embarrassment, I let out a little moan of happiness.

Roderick grins at me from several feet away. "Honestly, I'd be more upset if you didn't like this pulled pork than if you didn't want to fuck me."

I try not to choke on my next bite, because I don't know how to respond to that. I've never met anyone like him. I don't know any gay men at all. I mean—I've heard rumors. But I never met a guy like Roderick who calls himself "Gay AF" in a housing ad, or uses words like "cock" and "fuck me" in casual conversation. "You know, sometimes I can't tell when you're being serious and when you're joking."

He swallows a bite of our excellent dinner. "Here's a tip—I'm almost never being serious. Life is easier that way."

We chew in silence for a moment. It's becoming increasingly clear that Roderick has things he could teach me. Besides cooking. And those are things that I desperately want to learn. I'd like to be more like him—willing to name my desires. Unafraid to know what anyone will think.

But I don't have the first idea how you do that.

"Can I ask you a question?" Roderick says, breaking my reverie. "Have you ever dated men?"

I shake my head.

"So you date women?" he asks, looking perplexed.

"No, not really."

"Maybe I'm asking the wrong question. Do you have sex with men?"

Again I shake my head.

"Women?"

"Sometimes. Not for a while."

"How long is a while?"

I think it over. "A couple of years. Well, four or five."

His eyes bug out. "And you enjoyed it? Never mind. If you liked it you wouldn't have stopped."

"It was okay."

He seems to think this over. "Not everyone likes sex. I can't, uh, quite understand not liking it. But asexuality is a real thing."

"So I've heard," I say, and then take another achingly good bite of meat and fresh bread. It's occurred to me before that I could be asexual. It's true that I don't spend much time thinking about sex. I don't watch porn, and I don't hook up.

On the other hand, I spend a fair amount of time *avoiding* thinking about it. My life is complicated enough as it is. I watch my brother flirting and chasing women and making a fool of himself on a regular basis. And for what? A hookup after a night drinking at the bar.

Sex with strangers doesn't appeal to me. Women don't appeal to me half as much as they did when I was a horny teenager. And experimenting with random men off an app? That's just awkward.

I like the *idea* of sex. It's just that I've never worked out the details.

"You're thinking really hard over there," Roderick observes.

"Yeah. One of the reasons I wanted to move off my parents' farm is that…"

"Your dad is an asshole?" Roderick guesses.

"Sure, but that isn't what I was going to say." I have thought the word *asshole* many times while tangling with Dad. But my relationship with him is more complicated than that. I never asked to have a father who resents me, and he never asked to raise my mother's biggest mistake.

"What, then?" Roderick asks.

"I wanted the distance so I could figure it all out."

"Your sexuality," he guesses.

"That," I agree. "And my career, too. I need a better graphic-design job, and some more coursework. I don't want to hear Dad's opinions all the time. Not about that, and not about…"

"Steamy-hot man-loving?" Roderick offers, and I almost choke on my sandwich. "Sorry," he says with a grin. "I was born with no filter."

"It must be nice to say what you're thinking all the time. I can't really do that."

"And I can't stop," he says with a sigh.

"You never told me why you left Nashville in a hurry." One of the only tricks I know to get people to stop asking me questions is to ask one back. "Zara and Audrey are curious, too."

"Ah," he says, setting down the last bit of his sandwich. "It's not a very interesting story. I was in a relationship for three years with a country music singer."

"A famous one?" I ask, fascinated. I don't know of any gay country music stars.

He shrugs. "I won't tell you his name because I'd never out

somebody. I owe this man *nothing*, but it's the principle of the thing."

"Okay."

"We were a big fat secret, and I was okay with it for a long time."

"And then you weren't anymore?" I guess.

"Right." He looks glum. "The weird thing is I totally understood why he had to stay in the closet. Country music is a weird scene. Lots of conservative fans. But whenever I got frustrated, he always made me feel bad about it. Everything was always my fault and never his. If he had just commiserated a little, I might never have left."

"Oh," I say, hoping to sound supportive. But I've never been in a relationship, and I have no idea what that's like. "So you just had enough?"

Roderick laughs, but he's bitter. "I stayed, even as he got meaner about everything. He said I was too clingy. That hurt because I had completely arranged my life around his. I wasn't allowed to enter our house through the *front door*." He rolls his eyes toward the ceiling. "I know it sounds ridiculous. But I didn't give up until he cheated."

"Ouch."

"I know. Not only did he cheat, he set it up so that I'd catch him. It was the most cowardly thing in the world. I left Nashville right after I walked in on them. I got in my car and drove to this twenty-four-hour health clinic that performs STD tests. And then I drove home, walked through the backdoor like I always do, packed up my shit, and left."

"Holy crap." I cram the last bite of heaven into my mouth. "I'm sorry," I mumble.

"Me too!" He smiles brightly. "I should have bailed a year ago. I knew he was kind of a head case."

"He, uh…" I take a gulp of wine. "I guess you know a lot of those."

Roderick gives me a soft look. He has the most expressive eyes that I've ever seen on a human. "You're more honest about it, though. You said, 'I don't have my shit figured out,' but my ex was always trying to be two different people at once—the queer guy who wanted me to fuck him and the straight guy everybody else thought he was. And I was just supposed to be waiting at home when he got around to seeing me."

"That sucks," I say softly. Roderick deserves better than that. He's too accommodating already.

"I'm over it," he says, pushing his empty plate away. "I'll miss the sex, though. Brian wasn't conflicted at *all* when we were naked." He sighs and scrambles to his feet. "We have some cleaning up to do. But just think of all the leftovers we can eat this week."

He washes, and I dry.

I'm overly conscious of how close he is to me. And then we bump arms a couple of times, and I'm too conscious of that, too.

It's torture. I want him to kiss me again. It's all I can think about. But Roderick seems unaffected. He whistles as he scrubs out the Dutch oven, and then feeds his sourdough starter with a bag of flour he keeps in the cabinet. "There you go, William," he says to the blob in the jar. "Eat up!"

He washes his hands and dries them on our only dish towel. When he turns to me, I realize I'm staring at him like a creeper. His eyes light up with amusement. "Need something?"

"No," I say too quickly.

He gives me a comical frown. "Bummer. Because there are other things I could teach you besides cooking. Just saying." He takes one step forward and puts a hand on the center of my chest. "If you want to fool around with someone who thinks you look like a cross between Henry Cavill and Nick Pulos, you know where I live."

Then he plucks his phone off the counter and walks away. I

hear his bedroom door click shut a few seconds later, and I can still feel the heat from his hand on my chest.

Naturally, I go upstairs and google Henry Cavill and Nick Pulos. They are both hot as hell, but I sure don't see the resemblance.

And then I take a shower just because I needed to relieve a little sexual tension. As I stand there in the clawfoot tub, stroking my shaft, it isn't an actor or a burly stunt man I'm thinking about. It's a quirky baker with strong forearms and bright blue eyes. I picture him on his knees before me, opening his mouth and…

Eight years have passed since the first time I had lust-filled thoughts about Roderick. Now they're back and stronger than ever.

Maybe I should have followed him into his bedroom. But I didn't find the nerve.

I wonder if I ever will.

RODERICK

The following week is full of tension. The sexual kind.

After our kitchen make-out session, Kieran remains as difficult to read as always, but my crush on him expands to epic proportions. Subtlety was never my strong suit, but now I don't even try. At work I watch him like a puppy who's hoping the master will toss some table scraps in his direction.

Maybe we only shared a few kisses, but they were *hot*. Lava hot. I generally avoid assuming anyone's sexual orientation, but if Kieran isn't sexually attracted to me, then I'm the Queen of England.

Every time I think about his mouth on mine, I get all hot and horny. The grip he had on my body? *Rawr*. I want to feel it again. Next time, without clothes.

So now I'm watching for signs of further encouragement. As we stand shoulder to shoulder behind the coffee counter, I keep glancing in his direction. But Kieran is inscrutable as ever. He seems a little looser in my presence, though. Calmer. Quicker to smile.

If kissing me was the biggest mistake of his life, that wouldn't be true, right?

Unfortunately, there's no time for cooking lessons this week.

Kieran's new shift at the coffee shop is seven till noon, four days a week. Zara and Audrey cut his hours back at his request, so that he could do more farm work.

I've never lived on a farm, and I don't really know what it's like. When he talks about farming, I mostly watch his lips move and wish I could kiss them, but a few things have sunk in. Like, I'm pretty sure this week he's been busy using macho tools to fix a broken water pipe. Or something that lets the cattle have a drink of water after they've snacked on oat stalks. I think.

He might have also mentioned something about breeding the cattle. I only remember that bit because I have a filthy mind.

Let's face it, I just want to do him. Or vice versa. And if he decides to explore his sexuality with someone who isn't me, I'm going to be crushed.

"Roddy," Zara says, snapping me out of my reverie by literally snapping her fingers in front of my face. "You're in a kneading trance there, buddy."

I look down at the dough I've been working and see that it's supple and smooth already. "Right. What do you need?"

"Two things. First one—can you set up a batch of biscotti for the morning? I'm opening with you, and I'll be hung-over."

"Sure." I chuckle. "How come?"

"That's the second thing I need from you. My place, seven thirty. Hockey-viewing party—Brooklyn versus the Bruins. My honey is playing, and I just ordered up satellite TV so I could see every game. There will be food and tequila."

"You need me to cook for that?"

"No way." She gives me a face, like I've said something dumb. "I need you to *come*. We'll have a good time."

"Oh." I feel a rush of gratitude. "What can I bring?"

"Nothing. Except your roommate. That boy works too hard. Do you like hockey?"

"Well, I never watched before. There's too much padding concealing all that male hotness."

Zara gives a belly laugh. "You have to use your imagination. I know I will. See you tonight."

After work I'm on the prowl for ripe avocados. I strike out at two different grocery stores, but I'll be damned if I show up to Zara's party empty-handed. Luckily I find them at a store in Montpelier.

When I pull up to the house, Kieran's truck is already in the driveway. *Yes.* I can teach him to make guacamole. Every man should be able to make a fresh guacamole.

"Hey, Kieran," I say as I come through the backdoor. "Want to learn how to make the food of the gods?"

"Maybe," he calls from the living room. "Need a minute." His voice drops down to a softer register, and he says something I can't quite catch. I decide he's on the phone. But then I hear a distinctly non-Kieran squeal.

Curious, I deposit my grocery bag on the counter and then tip-toe into the living room. I find Kieran on the couch, and he's not alone. There's a very beautiful redhead on his lap. But I'm only a little jealous, because the girl in question is only one or maybe two years old.

They are reading *Frog and Toad are Friends.* It's so freaking cute that my heart melts like a lump of butter in a hot pan.

Kieran looks up at me with an embarrassed grin. "Zara ran out to the store. Have you met Nicole?"

"Hi, baby," I say, giving her a wave. I don't really have any experience with kids.

"That's Roderick," Kieran says in a gentle voice. "He's coming to your party, too."

"Watch. Daddy," the little creature says.

"Right," Kieran agrees.

"More," Nicole says, pointing at the book.

"Yes, ma'am." He smiles, and I turn to mush inside. Could Kieran be any cuter?

I leave the two of them to their book. In the kitchen, I cut the avocados and scoop the flesh into a mixing bowl. I mince garlic and squeeze limes. And I listen to the low sound of Kieran's voice reading about Frog and Toad, until finally it stops.

A moment later he appears in the kitchen. He's still holding the toddler, but she's passed out on his shoulder.

"Wow," I say.

"Actually, this happens a lot when I talk to women."

I let out a bark of laughter. It's awfully loud, so I clap a hand over my mouth. Kieran doesn't make jokes that often, but they're usually dry and terribly funny. I've got it so bad.

"You couldn't be any hotter than you are right now," I point out. "Just saying."

His eyes widen a trace. "Hold that thought for a few hours," he says. "I'm going next door, because Zara's car just pulled in. I'll see you over there a little later, unless you need help here?"

"I got it," I assure him. "Text me if Zara needs anything else."

He leaves, and I turn on some music while I finish the guac. Not country and western. I think I could go a lifetime now without listening to anything twangy. Been there, done that. Got the broken heart to prove it.

In fact, I put on some old eighties New Wave stuff. Depeche Mode, Erasure, and A-ha. Brian would *hate* it. That's why it's perfect. I haven't listened to this stuff in ages. I like a lot of different music, so I always let him pick.

Of course I did.

When the guacamole is perfectly seasoned and nicely blended, I cover it with plastic wrap and take a shower and shave. I'm not in a rush, because it's dawning on me that I won't know very many people at this party. Except for Kieran, Zara, and Audrey.

I mosey over there around eight, letting myself in the kitchen door. Audrey is the first person I see. "Roddy!" she says. "Help me carry these trays into the living room?"

"Sure thing, sugar pop." I grab a tray and follow her.

"Look who I found!" Audrey announces to the living room. "Roddy brought guacamole. And he said it's all for me."

"Sure he did," Zara says from the sofa. "Pour yourself a margarita?" she adds without taking her eyes off the screen. "Dave's shift is on."

I guess that means he's playing. All I see is a bunch of dudes skating around bumping into each other.

"Everybody, this is Roderick," Audrey says. "Our newest Busy Bean."

I receive friendly greetings as several heads turn, including Kieran's. He and two other guys are sprawling on beanbag chairs. He gives me a quick smile that does nice things to my insides.

"That's Kyle Shipley," Zara says, "Kieran's brother. But you probably know that already." Kyle must be the one that Kieran argues with on the phone. "And you've met Griffin," she says, pointing at the biggest lumberjack in the room, "whom Audrey was kind enough to marry." Everyone laughs. "And Dylan, the sweetest Shipley."

They all say hello, and I'm struck by how much alike Griffin, Kyle, and Dylan look. Kieran has the same build, but his eyes are different. Moodier.

Finally, I'm introduced to Zara's brother Benito—a cop with flashing dark eyes—and a couple named Sophie and Jude who live nearby. It's quite a crowd.

The Shipley boys have already turned the hockey match into some kind of drinking game. "There it is!" Griffin laughs.

"Drink!" someone yells. Kieran picks up his margarita and takes a sip, as do the others.

I resolve not to stare at my roommate all evening, because people will notice the raging crush I have on him. And I also resolve to drink slowly, because the first margarita always goes right to my social skills.

The men on the floor look like a happy pack of puppies. Kieran grins and nudges Kyle. "Go on, you lightweight. No stalling."

"I'll show you stalling..."

I make myself busy pouring a margarita while I eavesdrop on their patter. It's fun watching Kieran in his natural environment.

"Butt shot!" Audrey yells. "Drink!"

I glance at the screen and note that the camera is, indeed, focused right on the goalie's ass. It fills the screen. Zara, Audrey, and Sophie all take a drink. Audrey's is ginger ale, though. Much of the furniture is taken, and I can't figure out where to perch.

Zara notices my plight and scoots over. "Come here. We have the good cheese and charcuterie."

I take a seat among the women just as the hockey game goes to a commercial. "Your baby is so cute," I tell Zara.

"She is delightful, a perfect child," Zara says with a cheeky grin. "And by the way, do you babysit?"

"No." I laugh. "I mean, I have no experience. But if you're ever in a bind, I'm always ready to help."

"Our Roderick is a pleaser," Audrey says, patting my arm. "So many chefs are."

"What do you mean, a pleaser?" I help myself to a slice of brie on a cracker.

"You give a lot, and you hope others will do the same. And since you're above average, they let you down a lot of the time."

"What, are you my shrink now?" Although that sounds an awful lot like me.

"You can ignore her advice," Zara says. "I always do."

The thing is, Audrey is right. A lot of chefs are trying to buy the world's affection with their cooking. Audrey gives me a knowing little wink and reaches for a piece of salami.

"Where's mine?" says her husband from the floor.

"Don't ask me to find your salami in front of all these people, honey."

There's a roar of laughter. And then Zara announces that the chili is ready in the kitchen, and all the guys get up fast and hustle into the other room.

"How to get the Shipley men moving in one easy step,"

Audrey says. "Roddy, you'll have to muscle in there and get yourself a bowl. But first, can I have a sip of your margarita? I really miss alcohol."

"Sure." I pass her the glass and she takes the world's tiniest sip.

"That'll have to hold me another three months."

My phone makes a noise from my pocket. It's not a Grindr notification. It's something far more surprising. A text from Brian.

Where are you, baby? I've looked everywhere.

And even though I know better, my heart gives a startled little kick. All I ever wanted was for Brian to love me back. The fact that he's looking for me might have sent me running back to him, if I didn't know better. And I *do* know better, right?

Stop it! I give myself a mental slap. *This man canceled your credit cards and froze you out of our bank account.*

That's not how you treat someone you actually love. Not to mention all the shitty things he said when I caught him fucking a groupie in his dressing room. Even then, I was mindful of his status in the closet. I didn't call him out until he caught me backing out of the driveway just as he finally arrived home.

Don't be a whiny little bitch about this, he'd said. *You don't own me.*

Those aren't exactly words of love.

Even so, I stare at that text for a long time. I don't respond.

"Everything okay?" Audrey asks beside me.

"Yeah," I say, flipping the phone over. "My ex-boyfriend is texting me, though. Nobody let me drunk-text him later, okay?"

"I'll hold that for you," Zara says, taking my phone away. "Even better—we'll give this to your roommate. Catch, Kieran."

Oh shit. I watch, panicked, while my phone arcs through the air toward the men returning from the kitchen. I can't afford to replace that if it breaks. But Kieran lifts his hand immediately and the phone lands neatly in his palm.

"Friends don't let Roddy text his ex-boyfriend," Zara says. "Keep that till morning."

All the boys are studying me now, curiosity in their eyes.

Luckily, the hockey game comes back on. Zara sits up straighter and yells, "Power play!" Whatever that means. Kieran tucks my phone into his shirt pocket and looks toward the TV.

All eyes are glued to the hockey, so I get up to make myself a bowl of chili with all the fixings.

Vermont doesn't quite feel like home yet. But I suppose it could get there one day. The men are hot and the food is good.

It will have to do.

KIERAN

I almost never get drunk.

In the first place, it's expensive. Also, I'm the guy who usually has the forty-minute commute home. But not tonight. Griff's in the mood to drink, because his pregnant wife can drive him home, and so we're playing some kind of stupid drinking game that involves getting me a little drunker every time the guys calling the game use the word "stick."

"Kieran has to do my shot," Kyle says. "I'm done drinking for the night."

"You could crash at your brother's place," Griff says. "Is there a spare bed?"

"Nope!" I say sloppily. "There's barely any furniture at all."

"Are you going to show us your pad?" Griffin presses.

"Sure," I say. "After the game."

When the time comes, I rise unsteadily to my feet. The alcohol is swimming through my bloodstream, leaving me feeling pleasantly loose and carefree. It had been too long since I'd hung out with this crew, and it was nice to just watch TV and talk smack with my brother and cousin.

I thank Zara for having me over. "Is there anything I can help you with?" I ask, giving her what is probably a sloppy grin.

"No." She laughs. "Go home. Your more sober roommate already scrubbed the chili pot for me. Besides—you helped me out with a little childcare earlier."

"That was nothing."

"Don't say that or I'll ask you again."

"You can," I insist.

She grabs my shoulders and points me toward home. "Drink some water before you go to sleep."

"Good plan."

When I step outside, Kyle is puffing on a cigarette. "Two seconds, okay? I need it to wake up."

"Filthy habit," I say. Although I've been known to smoke after a party. I consider asking my brother for one, but then change my mind. The truth is that I don't want to sober up right away. It's nice to feel loose and carefree, for once. Although the cold November air is bracing in a good way, and I feel my head start to clear, regardless.

"Let's see this place," Griffin says, exiting Zara's kitchen door a couple minutes later.

Kyle crushes the cigarette under his boot. "Cool. Let's do it."

"Pick that up," I insist. "Don't litter in my hood."

With an eye roll, Kyle bends over to retrieve his butt, and then follows me across the yard and up the front path.

"Nice house," Griff says.

"I couldn't afford it if I were paying the market rate," I admit, unlocking the front door.

"You need chairs on this porch," my brother says.

"It can wait. I need a hell of a lot more than that."

When we step into the living room, they chuckle at its barrenness. "You've got the couch," Griff says. "But no TV?"

"Later," I grunt. It's not like I ever have time to sit down.

I show them the kitchen, where I spend a lot of my time, anyway. I toss my keys and phone onto the counter. Then I realize I still have Roderick's in my other pocket, so I set it down where he'll find it later.

"Hey," Kyle says. "You didn't tell me your roommate was a queer dude. Isn't that kind of weird for you?"

Everything inside me sort of freezes up.

"Jesus." Griffin gives Kyle a non-serious slap to the side of the head. "Don't be that guy. What does Kieran care?"

"I only meant that maybe if he brings guys home with him, Kieran would have to listen to 'em…"

"Oh, shut it!" I sputter, finally finding my voice. "Jesus."

That's when I hear Roderick's door close softly, as if someone has just attempted to shut it noiselessly.

"Oops," Kyle says, and I want to punch him.

"He's probably heard worse," Griffin whispers. "But you could apologize, maybe."

Kyle's gaze flicks toward the back of the house. I can't imagine what my boneheaded brother might say for an apology. He might actually make it worse.

"No," I grunt. "I'll talk to him."

"Show us your room," Griff suggests.

"Nah," I say, suddenly eager for them to get gone. "Nothing there but a bed and a desk. I don't even have a dresser, yet."

"I think Mom has an extra one," Griff says. "Want me to ask?"

"Sure," I say, just hoping they'll leave. "Thanks."

Griff squeezes my shoulder. "Good to see you, dude. You're pressing cider with me tomorrow night, right?"

"Yeah, but I'll be late," I point out. "Somebody has to water the cows."

"Ah," he says. "Is your dad doing better?"

"Still kinda rough," Kyle says. "Progress is slow."

They make their way out, and I say my goodbyes while trying not to sound hasty.

When they're finally gone, I head toward the one place in the house where I never go—Roderick's room. The door is shut, but there's a strip of light showing beneath it. I knock. "Hey man, can I come in?"

"Sure."

I open the door and find him lying on his back on top of his sleeping bag, hands folded behind his head. "What's up?"

"I'm really sorry about that."

"About…?" He looks confused.

"My brother talking like a doofus. Maybe you didn't hear him. But he was wondering whether…"

He holds up a hand to stop me. "I heard him fine. But—like your cousin said—I've heard worse. Kyle was just thinking out loud, displaying his discomfort with listening to two guys get it on. I hated it for you much more than for me."

"Why?"

Roderick sits up and looks me right in the eye.

"Oh," I say slowly. "Yeah." Because I'm not as straight as Kyle thinks I am. And won't that be a fun little chat someday? I can't even imagine.

"Your cousin seems nice," Roderick says. "Griffin. Another lumberjack."

I grin, because he really does look like one. "Totally. That side of the family is great." I sort of look around for a place to sit, but there's only the floor. I lower myself down, still feeling tipsy.

Even though there isn't any furniture in here, Roderick's room is nicer than mine. He's begun to hang things on the walls, I've noticed. There's a poster of a baker kneading a loaf, announcing a contest that took place a couple of years ago. And postcards from here and there dot the walls.

"You're more moved in than I am," I observe.

"I work fewer hours than you do," he points out. "Although—look at you! Drunk on a Thursday night."

"That was intentional," I admit. The last drink especially. I did a final shot of tequila to amuse Griffin, but also to loosen me up. "Liquid courage."

"For?"

"Well…" I clear my throat. "I need to ask you if you were serious. About what you said."

Roderick sits up a little straighter. "About...you being as hot as Henry Cavill?"

I laugh, which is proof that I am still drunk. "I'll take the compliment. But I meant about you being willing to, uh..."

"Tutor you," he guesses.

"Yeah."

"Any day of the week, hottie. Except for right now. Because you're wasted."

"Not *wasted*," I argue. But it doesn't help that I slur the word a little. "I'm a little drunk, but I did that on purpose."

Roderick chews on his lip, and it only makes me want to push him down and own his mouth. But then he shakes his head. "Nope. If you have to get drunk to let me suck your cock, then it definitely isn't a good idea. That's a big problem for me."

I let out a groan that's half frustration and half lust. "You have it wrong. I don't have to be drunk to do it. I have to be drunk to *ask* for it. I hate talking." And just to demonstrate my willingness, I lean forward until I can cup the side of his face. With my thumb, I trace the shape of his top lip. I've been picturing this mouth on my body for quite a while now. Years, if I'm honest.

Roderick's eyes gleam. Then he stuns me by opening his mouth and sucking the pad of my thumb inside. Those eyes are full of challenge as he gives a good, hard suck, his tongue sliding hotly against my flesh.

I make an unrecognizable noise as my body flashes with heat. Everywhere. "Jesus." And it's only my thumb. If he puts that talented mouth of his on my cock, I'll probably die.

Roderick pops off me and sits back, grinning. "You're drunk, and I have poor impulse control. What a pair we make."

I'm breathing too fast, and my dick is already hard inside my jeans. "Look. If you won't come upstairs with me, you know I'm just going to go up there and jerk off. And the whole time I'll be thinking about your mouth on me." *This wordy bit of honesty brought to you by Jose Cuervo.*

He lets out a dramatic sigh and then falls back down on his

pillow. "Nobody is fucking anybody while drunk. But I want to watch."

"What?"

His eyes find mine. "Show me how much you want it. And then some other time we'll fool around."

"Seriously?"

"Sure." He shrugs, as if he's made a totally normal request. "I used to put on a show for you. Seems like you're overdue to return the favor."

I blink. Is he even serious? Right now I'm not thinking very clearly—he was right about that. But I'm overheated and horny and about to pop out of my skin. "Okay. I'll be upstairs. Show starts now."

I stand up and walk out of his room. I take the stairs two at a time. In my room, I don't bother turning on the light. In the street lamps' glow, I begin to shuck my clothing.

First my shirt hits the floor, and then my shoes. Socks. My jeans land with a jingle. I've lived in a small house with my family my whole life, so I'm almost never naked unless I'm in the shower.

That seems like a mistake now.

I pull my comforter down and expose the white sheets. They're the brightest thing in the room. I lie down diagonally across my new bed. It's no accident that a bed is the first thing I purchased. I've waited too long to unpack certain truths about myself—things I never felt comfortable exploring before. One second after my back hits those sheets, my hand is on my cock.

The house is quiet, though. I guess he wasn't serious after all. But, fuck it. I need to come.

Touching myself isn't something I ordinarily do. I could blame the thin walls of my parents' house, but my reasons were bigger than the limitations of four walls. I'd felt claustrophobic because of the constant sense of being judged, being found wanting.

That place is behind me now. So I make myself comfortable, curving my hand around my aching dick. I'm desperate for relief, but I make myself go slow. First I just touch the shaft. I let my fingertips drift low, measuring the weight of my balls in one hand. I spread my legs wider, because this is my house and the only other person home is the one I'm fantasizing about.

I picture Roderick crouching between my legs, his eyes on me as his cheeks hollow…

Then I hear a beautiful sound—the creak of a stair tread. And then another. He's walking slowly up the stairs. Or at least considering it.

"Get your ass up here," I growl. I don't sound like myself at all. But I don't feel like the same old me, either. That's the point.

Roderick appears in the doorway a moment later, his big eyes taking in the scene. "Hello, fantasy. Wowzers."

I close my eyes and stroke myself. Faster now. I love that he's watching, even if I'm way past my comfort zone.

Again, that's totally the point.

With my thumb, I catch a bead of pre-come on the tip of my cockhead and smear it around. I'm rewarded with a breathy little sound of appreciation.

He's watching. And he likes what he sees.

I've got goosebumps up and down my body now. I feel his eyes on me, and it's invigorating.

"Touch your nipples," he whispers.

With my free hand, I do it. Circling one and then pinching the other. A new bolt of lust runs through me.

The bed depresses slightly, and my eyes fly open. He's *right* there, eyes wide, pupils enormous. "Close your eyes," he orders.

So I do.

"Rub your taint."

"My what?"

"Your…" Roderick swallows a laugh. "Below your balls."

I drop my hand to that stretch of skin, and everything tingles when I probe there.

"Unngh," Roderick says with a sigh.

"Touch me," I beg, opening my eyes again.

"I'm here to watch," he says. "Not that it isn't tempting." Roderick lifts his shirt over his head and tosses it off the bed, and I feel like cheering. Now I can see his lean, seriously fit chest, and those strong arms I dream about. He's a smaller man than I am, but the proportions are *nice*.

"Close your eyes," he repeats quietly.

"Why?"

"Because I'm a bossy little fuck," is his response. "Close them."

I do it, because arguing would just take longer. I feel his hand land on my thigh. He lets out a sigh, runs his hand up to my hip, and gives me a squeeze. "So fucking hot. I thought so when you were seventeen, too. But the view is even better now."

The words of praise make me swell with pride. Fine—they make me swell, period. My cock has never been so hard. With my eyes shut, I can't anticipate Roderick's next move. All I can do is take a deep breath and experience the drag of his fingertips across my stomach. My abs clench under his touch.

"Nice," he whispers. "Turn your head away from me."

I do, not knowing why. But a moment later, his lips drag along the sensitive skin on the underside of my jaw, and I groan from the contact. "Yes, fuck. Kiss me," I beg.

Those firm lips find my neck, then my clavicle. Slowly he kisses his way to my chest. I'm dying as he licks and sucks and nibbles across my ribcage. I weave my fingers into his hair and rub my hands all over his bare shoulders and back. I want everything at once. I want kisses and a blowjob, and I want his hands to roam the way they are right now—over my knee and up my thighs.

Being tortured by Roderick is the hottest experience of my life. Not that there's a great deal of competition for that title. I spent my teenage years trying to pretend that I was attracted to girls. Although when Susie Nordstrom put her hand down my pants on prom night, it felt pretty great. Teenage hormones powered me through a few hasty sexual encounters. I lost my virginity on the backseat of a pickup truck, like every other kid around here.

But nothing I ever did before felt as right as this. Every inch of me wants Roderick. I'm made up of yearning. And it's not because of the tequila.

He lifts my hand to his mouth and repeats the torture he began when we were downstairs—he sucks on my thumb. On my forefinger. Then he places my wet fingers on my dick. "Jerk for me," he says. "I want to watch you shoot."

Making another desperate noise, I start stroking. That's when he leans down and kisses me hotly on the mouth.

I lose my rhythm, because I'm busy adjusting the angle of my head and pushing my tongue into his mouth. *Fuck*, the heat and taste of him are just what I need. Stubble scrapes my lips and I just want more. I grab him with both arms and pull him down onto my chest.

"Unnngh," he says into my mouth. He pushes his body closer to mine, scrambling to get his legs onto the bed.

His weight on my body makes me feel crazy. I wrap my arms around him and squeeze. His chest is hard and warm against mine. Our mouths are fused together, and I never want it to end.

Roderick is kissing me like there's a meteor heading for the earth, and we have five minutes to live. Each time his mouth leaves me, it returns instantly, as if he can't get enough.

I know I can't. I have one hand on his ass now, for leverage. I grind against him, finding a slow rhythm, but I still want more. I snake one shaking hand to the front of his jeans and pop the button.

Maybe he'll argue. But no—he reaches down to help me, instead. We both tug down his clothes. I'm sure his jeans and underwear are still stuck around his ankles when I roll on top of him and fuck his mouth with my tongue once more. His fingernails are scratching my back, and I let out a bellow as our dicks line up and slide together.

Roderick yanks his head to the side, licks his palm, and

reaches down between us, taking both of us in hand. "Go," he says hoarsely.

I kiss him in fevered pulls as he jacks us together. "Gonna come," I pant less than a minute later.

"Shoot all over me," he gasps.

As if I have a choice. I blow like a canon with a moan of pure relief. I spurt twice more, seeing spots before my eyes. There's a rush of excess heat as Roddy shudders and comes against my belly.

I collapse in the mess of us and groan, my limbs quivering, my heart racing.

"Jesus Lord," he says in a whisper. "You don't disappoint."

I'm silent because my brain is *gone*. I manage to slide a bit sideways, so I don't crush him. But then I bury my face in his hair and just try to breathe. Stillness settles over us while my heart rate tries to slow down.

"Are you okay?" he whispers eventually.

"I have honestly never been better," I mumble.

His laugh is a sharp, surprised bark. "You went quiet on me."

"Don't like talking. Can't top what we just did, so what's the point?"

I can feel his smile against the side of my face. "If you regret this, I'm not going to feel okay about it."

"I won't. Promise."

"A man of few words." He reaches up and rubs one of my shoulders.

"Feel free to keep doing that." I am spent, but my senses are still dialed up to eleven. The brush of his skin against mine is heaven. His fingers are divine.

He rolls onto his side, forcing me to do the same. "Can I kiss you again?"

Since I've already stated my position on excess chatter, I just lean in and offer my mouth.

He kisses me slowly, and then sighs. "I need to clean up a little."

"I'll bet," I mumble. That sounds like a fine idea but I'm not up to moving. Not yet.

Roderick slips out of the bed and goes downstairs, where I hear the squeak of water pipes as he turns on the shower. A few minutes later, he reappears with a wet paper towel in his hands. "Here. You'll regret it if you fall asleep like that."

"Thanks." I take the paper towel and wipe myself up the best I can.

Roderick takes it from me and throws it away somewhere. Then he reappears, tugging the comforter into place over me. "I'm staying," he says. "Your bed is nicer than my floor. And you're catatonic anyway. You won't even know I'm here." I feel the other side of the bed depress as he climbs in.

I'm too sleepy now to turn my head. But I reach a hand out, finding his chest. I stroke it once, lightly. "Thank you."

He doesn't ask what for. "You're welcome," he whispers. "Sleep tight."

I do.

RODERICK

I'm not getting up.

Maybe ever.

My limbs are heavy against silky sheets. I'm stretched out on a thick mattress. My body hasn't known such luxury in weeks. And when I open my eyes, I see the honeyed skin of a naked man spread out on the bed beside me.

It's basically my version of heaven.

But as my consciousness comes fully online, paradise crumbles like a poorly made pie crust. In the first place, that's my room-mate, coworker, and landlord who's naked beside me. And I distinctly remember telling him that I wouldn't corrupt a drunk man.

And then I did exactly that.

Secondly—and I'm just realizing that this is far worse—it's not nearly dark enough in this room. The gray sky outside Kieran's window means morning is arriving.

Morning. On a day when I'm supposed to open the kitchen. *Oh my God.* What have I done?

I bolt upright and slide out of bed, almost stepping on my phone where it rests on the floor beside my underwear. I never plugged it in last night. And now it's obviously dead, because the alarm failed to go off at five thirty like it was supposed to.

Grabbing my dead phone as well as the underwear, I sprint for the door, nearly turning an ankle as I go tipping down Kieran's staircase, like some loser Cinderella whose job is about to turn into a pumpkin because he had some tequila and forgot to keep his dick in his pants.

I'm so dead.

Three minutes later, I've dressed and brushed my teeth. I don't glimpse a clock until I crank the engine of my car, and the dashboard comes to life. And there it is—proof of my complete failure to behave like an adult. It's 6:53 a.m.

I'll be arriving at work an hour and a half late. When the coffee shop opens in seven minutes, there won't be any bagels. Or pretzels. Or muffins. The coffee won't even be ready.

I zoom down the hill and barely come to a stop in the gravel parking lot before flinging myself out of the car. When I reach the door, I'm face to face with Benito—one of Zara's brothers.

"Driving a little fast, there," he says mildly.

"Sorry," I sputter, remembering that he's a cop. I shove the key into the lock and wave him in after me. "I got bad news. I'm very, very late for work, and there aren't any pastries."

"Oh shit," he says, which pretty much sums it up.

"Benito?" calls Zara from the kitchen. "There will be muffins in a half hour. It's the best I can do."

My stomach quivers with fear.

"Anything day-old?" Benito asks hopefully, walking over to the basket where we offer day-old pastries, individually wrapped, for half price.

"Just take whatever you want!" Zara yells. I hear the oven door slam. "Roderick, get the coffee on. Hurry."

"I'll do it," Benito says. He slips behind the counter and turns on the grinder. "Go bake something. Your public needs you."

I duck into the kitchen and grab an apron. "Zara, I'm so damn sorry. My phone died."

"It happens," she says tightly. "What can you bake the fastest?"

I close my eyes and fight off a wave of pure panic. I *cannot* lose this job. I've got to stop being the guy who screws up every break people give him with some stupid decision or another. "Biscuits," I decide. "Soda-leavened biscuits. And then scones."

"Okay, get to it," she says. "I have to open up out front."

For the next twenty minutes, I'm the Tasmanian Devil cartoon character—spinning around the kitchen like a maniac. Cubed butter, flour, salt, and soda all land in a bowl. The mixer paddles are a blur. I fold in some shredded cheese and chives, and plop the dough onto baking trays at top speed. They go into the oven the minute Zara's muffins are out. I burn my fingers when I dump the muffins from the pan before they're ready and line them up on a tray.

I rush the tray to the counter, where Zara avoids looking me in the eye. The customers are five deep because she's working alone. Usually I work the morning coffee rush behind the counter to avoid exactly this situation. "You want me to help with…?"

"Make the scones, please," she says, her voice cool. "And we'll need rolls for the lunch crowd."

I'm so screwed. But I head back into the kitchen and start a batch of scones anyway. The dishes are piling up in the sink, and a headache has moved in behind my eye sockets. I haven't had any coffee or food, and after a few hours of frantic baking, my hands start to shake.

"Roddy?" Zara calls. "Can you come out here for a minute?"

"One second," I croak and quickly wash the butter off my hands.

When I arrive out front, Zara unties her apron. "I just need a five minute break, okay? Can you make a double cappuccino for this gentleman? Then start on the next in line."

"Sure. Of course." I start the espresso drink as Zara disappears toward the women's room. Or maybe she's heading to the tiny office that's also back there, perhaps to write me a half-week's check and fire me.

The next order is complicated, of course. The line grows longer while I make four fussy takeout drinks for a woman who's treating her coworkers back at the office. When Zara comes back, she can tell I'm in the weeds.

"Shall I help you work this line down?" I ask. "Or bake the rolls for lunch?"

"The rolls," she says, then immediately shakes her head. "No, the line." It's hard to make up your mind when you're in an impossible situation.

"Hey, are there any of those bagels left?" the next customer asks. "I promised my wife one of those new bagels you got."

"Not today, sorry," Zara says.

"They'll be back, though," I stammer, realizing how pointless it is to prove how indispensable you are if you then dispense with yourself for a crucial, two-hour period.

I work down the coffee rush for a little while until I find myself elbow to elbow with Zara at the espresso machine. "I'm so sorry about this morning. It won't happen again."

"It had better not," she says tersely. "If you could have just called me to say you'd be late, I could have called someone else in to help. We look like idiots today."

"I know. And I feel terrible about the lost revenue." Because that's what a guy who's hanging by a thread should do—point out how bad it really is.

"Just…" Zara sighs. "Just don't do it again, okay? I really need you to be *reliable*. Now go bake some bread so we don't starve everyone to death at lunchtime. Can I help you?" she asks the next customer, essentially dismissing me.

I step out from behind the hulking espresso machine to maneuver past Zara. But then I hear the next customer in line gasp.

It's my mother. "Roderick," she whispers. "Never thought I'd see you here."

"Now you know," I say icily. "Better buy your coffee elsewhere."

Zara's jaw drops. I stalk into the kitchen and turn the water on at full force, spraying those dirty mixing bowls down as if they were on fire.

I'm well aware that snapping at customers is just digging my hole a little deeper. But Zara is already mad at me. What difference could it make?

This is how it works with me. One step forward, two steps back. I'm twenty-six years old now. At some point you run out of people to blame. It's all on me. I never rein myself in when it really matters. And if I don't overhaul my behavior, it's always going to be this way.

Ten minutes later, I've cleaned almost every pan and bowl in the kitchen when Zara leans over me and shuts the water off. "I'm just about to bake the rolls," I tell her.

"Screw the rolls," she says. "Who was that lady? Your mother? You have her eyes."

"So I've been told." I grab a dish towel and furiously swipe at a mixing bowl. "We're not very close."

"Weren't you staying with your parents?"

I shake my head. "Not, uh, really. Renting from Kieran is better for everyone."

She frowns at me like I'm a puzzle she's trying to solve.

"It's embarrassing, Zara," I mutter. "My parents don't approve of my so-called lifestyle."

She blinks. "Oh, screw her, then. She can keep her five bucks."

I shrug like it doesn't matter to me. But it absolutely does.

"Can't believe I bitched at you in front of your mom." Zara grabs a towel and dries off a cookie sheet. "I'm sorry. I was stressed out."

"I'm pretty sure I had it coming." I still just want to crawl under a rock and hide. Sleeping in when it's my job to open the kitchen? What a dick move.

And I don't think Zara would be half so understanding if she knew the whole story of where I woke up this morning. Kieran is like family to her, and I took advantage of him.

"You need a break," Zara says. "That's the other thing I came back here to tell you."

"No, I'm fine," I insist, even as my stomach gurgles. "You'd better get back out there. I'm baking the rolls next. They'll be out of the oven in thirty minutes."

"Okay," she says with a sigh. "Back to the trenches. It's strangely busy today, with everyone asking for your wares. Those biscuits were dynamite, by the way. If that's your go-to emergency recipe, we'll all be okay."

I gave her a weak smile and get back to work.

Lunch is a single misshapen roll with butter. Today's only blessing is that Kieran isn't on the schedule. We could have used the help, but I'm not ready to look him in the eye yet. Not after last night.

When the day is finally done, I get my things together and prepare to leave. My heart almost fails when I see that I have a text from Audrey. I'm expecting it to say: *What did you do last night?*

But it doesn't. There's an address, followed by: *See you whenever you can get here.*

Oh boy. I'd forgotten about Audrey's invitation to the Shipley farm. Tonight, the family is doing some kind of late-season push to press apples into cider.

"There will be food and a bonfire! And you can taste the cider," Audrey had said.

Last night, with some tequila in my bloodstream, going to the Shipleys' place had seemed like a fine idea.

It no longer does. And yet I know I have to go anyway. Besides, free food.

I am so easily bought.

KIERAN

My father grew up at Shipley Farms, pruning the apple trees and milking the cows. There's a picturesque apple orchard, with the trees lined up in rows like soldiers, and Jersey cows in the distant meadow. On fall weekends, crowds of people pick apples and take selfies beside the scarecrows.

Now the apple trees are stripped bare, but there's still plenty of work to do. Once in a while—when my cousin Griff needs some extra pairs of hands—he'll throw a bonfire party and invite all of us to eat dinner and make cider.

I've hefted bushel after bushel of apples into the water bath. First the apples are washed and then they climb a mechanical ladder into a machine that grinds them up into mush, cores and all.

This apple slurry is squirted through a hose into the baffles of the apple press. Then a hydraulic machine squishes the press, forcing cider to run out into a tank. When the pressing is done, all that's left are caked sheets of apple cellulose, which are surprisingly dry. The cellulose is fed to animals or composted.

When my grandparents ran the place, they only dabbled in cider. They had two sons—my dad and Griffin's father, my uncle

August. It was August who learned to make hard cider, and it was Griffin who figured out how to make it profitable.

So here we are, squeezing apples into gold on a chilly night in November. My belly is full of Aunt Ruth's pulled pork, and I've got another hour of work in me at least. The cider house smells like a cross between the inside of an apple pie and a wine cellar. This is the nicest place in the world.

My cousin May arrives with another bushel in the wheelbarrow. "Griff? Is this the kind you wanted next?"

Griffin stops what he's doing and eyes the apples she's brought in. They have ugly skin the color of a paper bag. Cider apples can be really funny-looking. "Yep. Thanks. Keep 'em coming."

I take the bushel from May and pour it into the water bath.

"How's your father?" May asks me, putting a hand on my arm.

"The same," I say, handing the empty container back to her. "Back surgery looks like hell."

"Oh, man," she says. "I hope it's over soon."

"You and me both." I stir the apples in the water with a big wooden paddle, while the machine clanks away.

Before I was born, my father decided to leave the Shipley orchard and raise beef. He was already having back trouble, and he had the idea that a beef operation would require less of his body than apples and dairy cows. So he found our land in Hardwick and his father helped him finance it.

And it worked, I guess. He does all right. But I've always loved the orchard and my grandparents' farm. August and Ruth always made me feel welcome here, even if I feel like an extraneous Shipley. An outsider. Whenever someone local hears my name, they say, "Oh, I've heard of that fancy cider. That's your family?"

I can never decide whether to say yes or no. Because it is and it isn't. And the people who ask about it have no idea what they're really asking.

"Hey, I got a jam in the hose," Griffin says. "Shut 'er down a minute?"

I skirt the edge of the cider press and pull a lever that stops the machine from pulling new apples into the hopper.

Griffin pokes at his ancient equipment, humming to himself. I glance out the doorway of the cider house. In the distance, the bonfire burns, and, in a nearby chair, my grandpa gestures wildly with his fork, telling one of his tales. My cousin Daphne is setting desserts out on a table.

The fire's orange flames are reflected in Audrey's shiny hair as she walks toward the cider house, talking a mile a minute to someone beside her. "This is where the magic happens. We press apples from September through the springtime, but most of the heavy lifting happens between October and Christmas..."

When they're close enough that I can see who she's talking to, my stomach does an unfamiliar swoop and dive. And then my skin flashes hot everywhere. *Roderick*. He's here.

The two of them pass by the door, as Audrey shows off the oak barrels that are used to age the cider. It isn't until a moment later that I finally remember to breathe.

This is new for me. And I don't mean getting naked with a guy and coming in his hand, although that's new, too. The really new thing is feeling so stirred up and wild inside.

Today I had the day off from the bakery, but I spent all my free time thinking about Roderick's mouth on mine and the heat we made between our bodies.

It wasn't just that I liked it—which I totally did. It's that I didn't realize I was capable of letting go like that. He thrilled me with his bold hands and wicked mouth. He surprised me with his tight, fit body and his flashing, desperate eyes.

But I surprised myself even more. First I told him what I wanted. That never happens. And when he showed up to give it to me, I made the most of every second. I kissed him like the world was burning down, and I held nothing back.

Before—during every other one of my admittedly scant sexual

experiences—I'd felt like an outsider looking in, an observer in my own life. *Should I put my hand here? Does she want me to unzip this? Does that moan mean I should stop or keep going?*

Last night was on another level entirely. Never mind that I'd never gotten off with a guy before. Lust made me confident. Heat made it easy. I've never kissed anyone so deeply that the taste of him became part of me. I wanted it to last forever.

I want it again right now.

"All set," Griff says, snapping me out of my dirty reverie.

We go back to work, but the next few minutes are torture, because Roderick's nearby, and I'm stuck feeding apples into this machine. Lord knows what I'd do right now if my hands weren't busy. Run outside and hump his leg, probably.

"These are the fermentation tanks," Audrey says, continuing her tour. "And this big thing is the cider press. One person can run it, but it's better with two or three…"

I can't stand it anymore. I have to turn around and see him in the flesh. And there he is, flashing a smile at Audrey, holding an apple slice that she probably cut for him so he could experience the tannins in a cider apple. His cheeks are ruddy from the cold, and he's wearing black jeans that skim over his trim hips and a wool sweater in a cranberry color. I could lift it right over his head…

We lock eyes. Immediately his smile drops, and the look on his face is guilty.

Uh-oh.

"Hey guys," Audrey says. "I'm here to announce that dessert is served. Shut 'er down after this batch, yeah?"

"Sure, baby," Griff says. "Save me a piece of pie. Roderick—want to press this batch?"

His eyes flick toward me for a split second before he looks at Griff. "Sounds like fun, but I told your sister that I'd help out in the kitchen."

"If you say so." Griffin shrugs. "Pour the man a cider, Audrey."

"Don't you worry, I will." She gives us a wave, and the two of them disappear, with Roderick in the lead. He couldn't get out of here fast enough.

I paddle more of the floating apples toward the ladder and try to absorb this disappointment. Roderick is avoiding me. Although maybe he's just being discreet. There are a lot of people around. And I really don't need my family asking questions.

Those guilty eyes, though. I don't like it. What happened last night was a revelation to me. But maybe it wasn't for him.

I need to find out.

Outside, Griffin throws another log on the bonfire, and my cousin Dylan picks up his fiddle and begins to play. I glance around for Roderick, but he isn't anywhere in sight.

Someone hands me a plate with a slice of Aunt Ruth's apple-cranberry pie. I use the fork to slide a big bite into my mouth, and the tart apples burst against my tongue. This is why people come to Vermont—the romantic fools, anyway. They come for the food and the hot cider and the smell of pine in the wind.

Even on my worst days—when I want to scream from the rut that my life is in—I never really consider going somewhere else. I may have problems. I may not belong to this place. But I'd like to, and I don't think that feeling will ever go away.

The screen door bangs, and I look up to see Roddy standing there, hands in his pockets. His shoulders are square, and his head is held high. He's a confident man by all outward appearances. Even so, when I look at him, I see someone who's a little lost like me.

Maybe I'm just projecting. Maybe I only see what I want to see. *Look over here*, I silently ask of him. *Look at me.*

But he hops off the stoop and walks over to talk to May and Audrey.

RODERICK

"Taste this, Roddy," Audrey says, passing me a tiny cup. "You're driving, right? That's why I gave you such a small pour."

"I am driving," I admit. "And not looking to get drunk anyway." Not after last night's fiasco. "But look at me, getting out two nights in one week," I say, sipping my excellent cider. The flavor is deep and a little bitter. It's like nothing I've tasted before.

"Party animal," she says with a wink. "And you definitely need a slice of this pie."

She shoves a plate in my free hand, and I have to finish the cider in order to take the first bite. "God, that's good."

Audrey winks. "Ruth! Come and meet Roddy Waites, our new baker."

"Nice to meet you, honey," says the middle-aged woman who hurries over. "I'm Ruth Shipley."

"Mother to Griffin, Dylan, May, and Daphne Shipley," Audrey clarifies. "Aunt to Kyle and Kieran."

"That's a lot of kids," I say without thinking. Then I offer her my hand.

"There were days when it felt like too many," Ruth agrees with a smile as we shake. "Would you like another piece of apple pie? Just don't tell me if it's not up to snuff."

"Oh, please," Audrey says with a grin. "Her pie is exquisite. I've seen wrestling matches over the last piece. Ruth—I think I told you that Roderick is teaching me about sourdough."

"Yes! I've already sampled your wares," Ruth says. "I ate a pretzel that Audrey brought me, and it was divine."

"Thank you!" I feel a rush of satisfaction. "I'll make another batch tomorrow." There's nothing better than hearing praise over your work. "I might experiment with pretzel bagels. And pretzel sticks with dipping sauces."

"That sounds decadent. Did you say your last name is Waites? There's a couple by that name at our church in Colebury."

"Ah." Just like that, my appetite dies. "Those would be my parents."

"I see the resemblance. I don't know your parents, though, except by name. They must not stick around for the coffee hour very often."

"Well," I say slowly. "I wouldn't know. We're not in touch."

"Oh," she says, looking startled. "I'm sorry. I didn't realize."

"It's their choice," I add, because I don't want Kieran's aunt to think I'm a monster. Also, I kind of need to know the Shipley stance on queer dudes. I'm curious what Kieran is up against if he decides to pursue men. The way he kissed me makes me think that he will. "My parents kicked me out because I wouldn't consider conversion therapy."

Ruth Shipley recoils. "What? Why?"

"They don't want me to be gay," I add, just in to clear up any ambiguities.

"I don't see how that's up to them," she says, her face full of understanding. "I'm so sorry, honey."

Now I feel like a drama queen. "No, it's fine. Just putting that out there so you won't greet them on Sunday and expect a friendly response about me."

She flinches. "Not everyone at church feels that way. God doesn't make mistakes."

"Good to know," I say quickly, because I need to parachute out of this conversation. For Kieran's sake, I hope the whole Shipley clan shares Ruth's viewpoint. Kieran deserves better than what I get at home.

Everyone does.

I listen to some fiddle songs and consider my departure. Kieran is on the other side of the bonfire casting *fuck me* eyes in my direction. Maybe it's cowardly of me to avoid him, but what's the alternative? He and I need to have a conversation, and this is neither the time or place.

As soon as Kieran walks off toward the cider house, I carry my plate into the house and say my goodbyes. "Wonderful party, Ruth," I say, tucking my plate into the dishwasher. "Thank you for having me."

"Come back anytime!" she says. "We have a big dinner most Thursdays. Come with Audrey sometime."

"Sounds like fun." I make my excuses and slip out into the dark. I head down the gravel drive, away from the music and the party. Seeing as I was the last to arrive, my car is at the end of a long line of pickup trucks.

It's a long driveway, and I start wondering whether I could be snatched up by a bear or a coyote before I reach my Volkswagen. Bears hibernate, right? So I'm probably safe. Coyotes, though. And are there wolves in Vermont?

Just as I'm thinking these thoughts, a loud hoot erupts from somewhere nearby in the darkness, and I startle violently. "Holy shit," I curse, hurrying my pace toward the car.

That's when I see the orange glow of a cigarette. There's someone leaning against my car. And from the sound of the warm chuckle he lets out, I can tell it's Kieran.

"Don't laugh," I mutter. "I forgot how to be a country boy."

"Sorry." His voice is a soft caress, and I hate myself for wanting to roll around in it a little longer.

Telling him to fuck off is going to hurt both of us. "Did you need a ride or something?"

The cigarette moves as he shakes his head.

"Just enjoying a cancer stick against my car?"

"Something like that."

"You got another one?"

"Think so." I make out the flash of the wrapper as he pulls a pack out of his pocket. "I took these off my brother."

"I've never seen you smoke before." He holds a cigarette out, and since my eyes are finally getting used to the dark, I can see well enough to take it.

"Smoking is spendy." His rugged face is illuminated as he lights my cigarette. "I'm too cheap to get cancer."

"Same." My only use for cigarettes these last few years was to give my hands something to do while I waited for Brian to chat up the important people at parties.

I'm not doing *that* anymore.

"So what's the story?" Kieran frowns around his cigarette and looks hot doing it. But I will be *strong*. Celibacy is my new middle name. *Roderick Celibacy Waites*. It has a nice ring to it. "You're avoiding me tonight."

"Maybe a little," I admit, exhaling into the crisp air. "I mean—I'm flattered that you're giving me the fuck-me eyes. And I'm glad you're not freaking out about our little drunken thing last night."

"Our *little drunken thing*," he repeats slowly.

"Yeah, we shouldn't have done that."

"Huh. Well, I really enjoyed it. But I guess you didn't," Kieran says flatly.

"Hey—that was *not* the issue."

He snorts. "Then what is? Did I do something wrong?"

"No *way*. It's me who's the fuckup." Isn't that obvious? "It's not okay to jump your drunk, horny roommate."

"Really? Even if he wants a repeat?"

"Even then." I take a puff and try to explain. "See, I have a bad track record. I threw myself at you, with no thought of the consequences. I've done this before, too, and then I can't figure out why I keep blowing up my own life. For once I have to stop being impulsive, and act like a damn adult. There aren't enough bakeries in America to hire me every time I fuck up."

Kieran narrows his eyes. "So *you're* the one who's freaking out after last night? That makes no sense."

"Yeah, I know. But that only proves that I'm the asshole here. And I'm sorry, okay? But when I said we shouldn't fool around, I was right."

"First you said you could. And last night you said you couldn't. And then you did it anyway," he points out.

"Yup." I nod vigorously. "See? That's how it goes with me. Bad decisions, followed by regret. Trust me—you won't be missing anything if we don't get together again. I only seem like a good idea when you're wasted and horny. In the cool light of day, it'll be easier for you to forget it ever happened."

"Really?" Kieran tilts his big, handsome face toward the sky. "Because I spent every daylight hour today thinking about you."

I'm a praise junkie, so naturally my stomach flutters. *Kieran can't stop thinking about me.* Then I give myself a mental slap. "Thinking is different than doing. Are you sure you even want to have this conversation with your family all around us? You seem like a very private person."

"I am," he admits. "I don't share. But the thing about my family is that they don't pay attention, especially when it comes to me. We could be making out like movie stars right now and nobody would notice."

When he says "making out," I just want to jump into his lumberjack arms and ask him to haul me off to a hay loft for naughty fun. There has to be a hay loft here somewhere, right? That's my fantasy.

But that's all it can be—a fantasy. I have to get my act together. "Sorry," I say, crossing my arms. "Last night was super fun, but it can't happen again. I'm probably not even going to stick around Vermont, you know? I'm a bad bet."

He's silent for a beat. "So that's just it?"

"Yes," I insist, even as my heart wavers. The truth is that I *like* Kieran. A lot. Which only means that turning him down is the right thing to do. He doesn't need an impoverished, slightly desperate man hanging on his arm. And I need to stop being that broke, needy person who left most of his self-esteem back in Nashville.

"I've got one question."

Aw. He has questions about gay sex? "Go ahead and ask. I'll tell you anything."

"Will you still teach me to cook?"

I chuckle. "Yes. Absolutely. Cooking is the one thing I do reliably and that people appreciate me for. Definitely take advantage of the single perk there is to having me as a friend."

"Not the only thing," he says drily.

Sure, but my track record speaks for itself. And there's no point in arguing. "What do you want to learn next?"

His grumpy frown becomes a little less grumpy. "I don't care. You pick. Something meaty?"

Oh, the dirty jokes I could make right now. But I don't want to send mixed signals. "You got it. I'll come up with something."

"Thank you," he says. Then he turns and walks away so quickly that there isn't even enough time to ogle his ass before he disappears in the darkness.

Which is really just as well.

RODERICK

Remember when I thought living with Kieran would be awkward, because he didn't like me?

Yeah, the joke's on me. Living with Kieran isn't awkward, but it sure is horny. Neither of us has been able to forget our time together in his bed. Lately, we've shared a lot of lingering glances, and some of them have been all my fault.

Last night he arrived home just as I was stepping out of the bathroom wearing only my towel. We ended up doing an awkward dance in the narrow hallway, each of us stepping aside to let the other pass at the same moment, thereby prolonging the impasse.

Meanwhile, his eyes roved my bare chest. All my blood rushed south as I remembered the rush of his skin against mine, and the vibration of his moans against my tongue. Back in the safety of my room, I had to read the political headlines for ten minutes to get my dick under control.

But I don't regret my newfound self-discipline, because my life is on the upswing. My reputation at the bakery is on the mend. Zara is finally starting to trust me again. Those cheddar biscuits are a permanent fixture on the menu, too.

What's more, I've used my screw-up—when I was late on that

fateful day—as an opportunity to rethink the way we prepare each morning's offerings.

"Hey guys, can I show you a couple of ideas?" I ask after work one day, when Audrey and Zara are both present. "I think we should create a three-day plan for yeasted breads. On Monday afternoon, we'll stir together Thursday's dough and put it into cold fermentation. And Tuesday we make Friday's, and so on. If I'm careful, there'll be enough refrigerator space."

"What's the benefit?" Zara asks.

"Two things—better flavor development and a shorter turn-around time in the morning."

"You think we should come in later?" Audrey asks, tilting her pretty face toward mine. "I could get behind that."

"Not really," I say hastily. This isn't a plan to let me sleep in. "I just think we'll have an easier time of it in the morning. We'd be shifting some of the work to later in the day, when we're often standing around. Like we are right now. We can also freeze a couple of batches of biscuit dough for unexpected traffic during the morning."

"I like it," Zara says, cracking her gum. "This is good work, Roddy. This is the kind of thoughtfulness I'd hoped we'd get by hiring a full-timer."

"Thank you," I stammer. Honestly, it's not rocket science, and I didn't invent cold fermentation. But I sure don't mind hearing praise. It makes my situation feel less precarious.

The next Thursday afternoon I wake up from a nap to discover that the house smells amazing. I can hear Kieran whistling in the kitchen. I wander in, yawning, to find that he's roasted a chicken all on his own, with the compound butter that I taught him to make. And he's made a pot of rice in the rice cooker I found at a yard sale for eight dollars.

"Damn, look at you go!" I enthuse, rubbing my hands together.

"There's enough for two, so long as you tell me when our next cooking lesson might be." He hands me a plate of food.

"Soon," I stall. "I need to find you another go-to main dish. A pork roast maybe."

"Sounds good." He licks the chicken fat off his fingertips and gives me another hot look.

I should probably start looking around for another rooming situation. Kieran doesn't press me for sex. He doesn't bring it up or pressure me. But his hunger feeds mine, and I trust myself far less than I trust him.

"Beer or water?" He asks, turning to open the fridge. "That's all we've got."

"Water," I say huskily. My tolerance for alcohol isn't great, and it probably gets even worse when he's around.

"Suit yourself." He grabs a glass and fills it for me out of the refrigerator's dispenser. He hands it over, and I leave the room to put some space between us.

The respite is short-lived. I hear the fridge open and then shut again. Kieran arrives a moment later with his plate, a beer dangled between two fingers, and my phone in his other hand. "Roddy, I know that cold fermentation is one of your favorite tricks. But I'm not sure your phone could benefit from any time in the refrigerator." He sits down on the sofa at a respectful distance away from me and hands over the phone with a smile.

"Oh, my phone and I just needed some time apart," I explain.

His beer pauses on its way to his mouth. "You put it in there on purpose?"

"I once had this friend who did this thing where he'd freeze someone out of his life. Literally. He'd write their name on a piece of paper, put it in a baggie with some water, and put the whole thing in the freezer. But baggies are bad for the planet, and I'm lazy."

Kieran's sideways glance doesn't know whether to be amused or skeptical. "So you decided to refrigerate your contacts list?"

"Something like that." Plus, there was a danger that I'd throw my phone across the room. "My ex has been texting me again."

Kieran goes very still beside me. "Are you getting back together?"

"Oh *hell* no." I startle both of us with the volume of that statement.

Kieran relaxes and takes a bite of his chicken. And, whoa, was Kieran *jealous*? "What does your ex want?" he asks.

"Well, I didn't tell him where I was going when I left. And he says he's been looking for me." That doesn't mean it's true, though. He wouldn't actually exert effort. "I was ignoring his texts. But this morning I finally responded and told him that I wasn't coming back. That's when he got ugly."

I tap the screen and see that he hasn't stopped, either. *You stupid little fuck. You'll come crawling back. This is so manipulative. You wanted me to come chasing after you, don't you? Just gonna string me along now?*

That's not even a little bit fair. I've always been honest with him. More honest than I was with myself. *The point of leaving was leaving*, I type. Then I erase it and sigh. I know better than to prolong the conversation. You can't negotiate with terrorists.

I hand the phone to Kieran. "Look. It's embarrassing to me that I put up with this man for so long."

Kieran wipes his hand on a napkin and then scrolls up, reading Brian's vitriol. "What a turd," he says gruffly, and his choice of words makes me laugh. He doesn't think it's funny at all, and says, "This is abusive. Was he always like this?"

"No." I shake my head quickly, so that Kieran doesn't think I've always been a doormat. "He can be the most charming man in the world. People love him. Sometimes when we fought, he would get this way. But the next day he would always go crazy trying to make it up to me. And I know that's how abusers operate. But I swear we had a whole year before he started acting this way. I just kept hoping it would get better."

When his last album didn't do very well, his mood tanked for good, and I finally realized that things weren't ever going to get better. And I *still* hung around too long, because it seemed so mean to desert a guy whose career was in a downward spiral.

"Do you think he might do something crazy?" Kieran asks suddenly.

"What do you mean? Like what?"

He gazes at me with those big brown eyes that I like so much. "Would he try to hurt you physically?"

"No," I say quickly. "In the first place, he doesn't know where I am, and he's not likely to come to Vermont. Also, violence really isn't his style. He'd rather bruise my self-esteem than my face."

Kieran winces. "Why don't you block him? Serious question."

"I guess…" The truth is embarrassing. "I was hoping to get my guitar back after he calmed down. But if I'm honest, what I really wanted was an apology. It's never coming, though. I guess that's what adulting really is—living your best life in spite of all the apologies we never hear."

Kieran's warm eyes take me in for a long moment. Then he puts down a chicken bone and gives me a shy smile. "Not bad, Roddy. I think that idea is ready for the big time."

"Oh." For a second, I don't understand. But then I do. "You mean I should chalk it up on a beam at the Busy Bean?"

"Yup." He digs into more chicken and smiles at me.

I take a bite of crispy-skinned chicken and let out a noise of pleasure. The seasoning is terrific, and he roasted it to a deep brown. "This is so good. My compliments to the chef."

"Thanks." When I glance at him, his face is slightly flushed. "Maybe you shouldn't moan while you're eating it, though. Just as a favor to me."

"Sorry." I glance at him, and he actually winks. Winks! Kieran Shipley is *flirting* with me. What are the odds?

But of course I can't flirt back, because that would send mixed signals. So I'm silent while we devour crispy chicken and rice.

"Hey," he says eventually. "I've been watching *Silicon Valley* on Hulu. You want to—"

"Great show," I say quickly. A comedy is exactly what we need to dissolve the sexual tension in here. "Turn it on."

"Cool." Kieran wipes his hands and reaches for his laptop on the coffee table. He flips it open and pecks at the keyboard until we're watching Richard Hendricks stumble around trying to extract himself from another fiasco.

Maybe that's why I like this show. Richard and I have a few things in common.

Kieran chuckles quietly on the sofa beside me, and I lean back and relax. It's nice in this room, where the lamplight burnishes the floorboards, and there's a hot farm boy who makes me feel appreciated.

It's cozy. Almost domestic. If I weren't so good at torpedoing my own life, I could almost imagine a future that looked like this.

Almost.

KIERAN

"Whoops, no. The lunch special is a spinach and feta turnover," Roderick says from several feet below me.

"Wait, really?" I'm standing on a stool, chalk in hand, trying to write the daily specials on the board. "I thought you were doing ham and cheese croissants?"

"Last-minute change," he says. "Audrey brought in a whole lot of spinach, and I wanted to use that first."

"Okay. Sure." I use my fist to wipe off the word ham, but it smears. "I can't work under these conditions. Would you mind tossing me a damp rag?"

Chuckling, Roderick grabs the bar towel and tosses it up to me. "Just pivot, like Jared. Okay?"

Despite my unsteady position on the stool, I laugh at his reference to a funny scene from *Silicon Valley*. "So I'm Jared, now?" I guess it fits. Jared's an outsider always trying to fit in.

"We're all Jared," Roderick says. "I guess I'm Erlich Bachman —not very self-aware. Always trying to get people to like him."

They do, though, I think to myself. Everyone likes Roddy, even me. *Especially me*. But I don't say this out loud. "Anything more to add before I get down from here?"

"Um." Roderick strokes his perfect chin, and it makes me want to jump off this stool and stroke it for him. Time hasn't dulled my attraction for him, and I don't know what to do about that. There doesn't seem to be anything *to* do, except look around for some other guy who cranks my engine the way he does.

Except I don't want another guy. I want this one right here.

"Okay, can you add this? 'Now taking orders for holiday cookies and pies.'"

"Sure. Not cakes?" I start on the letters in a new shade of chalk.

"I don't know how to decorate cakes," Roderick says.

"That wouldn't stop the guys on *Silicon Valley*." Our TV habit is totally a thing now. On the nights when I come home early enough, we always watch a couple of episodes together.

"Which character am I?" Zara asks, emerging from the kitchen.

"You're Monica," I say without hesitation. "She's sharp and doesn't take any bullshit from anyone."

"Is she hot?" Zara asks, sliding a tray of muffins into the case.

"Very," Roderick assures her. "I should get the bagels into the water bath." He ducks into the kitchen.

"Very nice," Zara says, inspecting my work on the board.

"Thanks. It's just a couple of additions."

"No, I mean..." She drops her voice. "You seem happy enough with Roderick around. I'm glad that worked out."

My neck gets instantly hot. "Yeah, it's fine. He's all right."

"Good."

Luckily, I'm saved from this conversation by two new customers walking into the cafe. The morning rush is about to kick in. I can feel it.

I make someone a skim-milk mocha, and then the door opens again and four more people enter. Zara and I handle the rush together, filling orders on autopilot. Roderick steps out of the kitchen with a new batch of bagels, and I actually sense him before I see him. All he does is slide the platter onto the counter and walk away. Even so, my eyes follow him, and my heart hitches.

This is how I am all the time now. He walks into the room, and all my attention goes straight to him. I've never felt like that about anyone, and I don't know how to shut it off.

I'm not even sure I want to. Zara's right. The more I know of Roderick, the more I like him. He's funny, for starters. Who knew you could have a hard-on for a biting wit and a snarky tongue?

His snark is just a front, though. Nobody tries harder than Roderick. Nobody is quicker to lend a hand, or more eager to satisfy the customers.

Audrey and Zara are smitten with him, too, in their own ways. No matter that Roderick was late to work that one time. Our bosses have completely forgiven him. Last week Zara offered him an extra shift in the early morning, and this week Audrey did. They're both a little drunk on the idea that there's someone else available to work the brutal five thirty prep shift.

The result is that Roderick is *tired*. He has circles under his eyes. They're not as deep as those early days when he was sleeping in the car. But he never says no when they ask him a favor, and he likes the extra hours in his paycheck.

The fact that he goes to bed so early all the time is making a serious dent in our hang-out time in front of Hulu. And forget about learning to cook. I haven't gotten another lesson yet.

Then again, I haven't asked. So when Zara takes her break, and Roderick and I are working together, I bring it up. "Look, I know you're burning the candle at both ends, but let's not neglect my education. You promised."

"Your, uh, education?"

He turns to me with a surprisingly heated gaze, and it catches me off-guard. Roderick is thinking about sex right now. *Sex with me. Hallelujah.* There's hope for me yet.

"Look," I say. "I'm down for anything. But you should know that I meant cooking lessons." And I can't help smiling, even if my face is turning red.

"Oh!" He throws his head back and laughs. "Of course. I'm sorry. You should have spoken up sooner. I've just been—"

"Super busy working extra shifts. I know."

"Yeah, but I made a promise. Tomorrow night? Unless you've got chores?"

"I'll get out of it," I promise. Now that the cold weather is upon us, I don't have to work as hard. My dad's back is still a mess, but there isn't as much farm work. "What do we need from the grocery store?"

He rubs his hands together. "I'm not sure yet. It will be a game-time decision. Let me handle the shopping."

"Sure." I pull twenty bucks out of my wallet and hand it to him. "For my half. I'll be home by six."

"Great." He puts the money away. "See you then."

RODERICK

I spend parts of the following morning daydreaming about cooking with Kieran.

Unfortunately, daydreaming is bad for business. Happy thoughts about a certain hot farmer distract me as I'm tallying up a catering order. And I end up undercharging the buyer.

So I do the only reasonable thing and put fifteen bucks of my own money in the till.

Ouch. That's what I get for letting my mind wander to a man that I've already sworn off of once. You'd think I'd learn.

We're going to be *cooking* tonight, damn it. Just cooking.

When the work day finally ends, I head to the grocery store. I buy all the ingredients to make a roast pork loin with ginger and lime, plus a mushroom risotto and green beans on the side.

I don't buy the bottle of wine I was planning to pick up, because I spent that fifteen bucks already. Otherwise, my dinner plans are still on track. But after I load everything into the back of the Bug, things go wrong again. My engine starts up fine, but then abruptly cuts out when I shift into reverse. It just dies.

I should mention that I'm completely useless when it comes to cars. All I know how to do is put the key in and drive. Or call AAA. Which I do.

"Are you a member?" is the first question they ask.

"No, but maybe I should be."

"I'll need a credit card number."

Yeah, I really should have seen that coming. "I don't have a credit card, but I have a debit card. Or I can pay cash." There's a bank machine in view inside of the store. It's the kind that charges an extra fee, but that's the kind of day I'm having so I shouldn't really be surprised.

"I can't send out a tow truck without a credit card number."

Of course you can't. I hang up, because it's either that or say something rude. I end the call and find the number for a local garage. But it's now after five thirty, and they're closed.

I'm ten miles from home, the temperature is dropping, and my pork loin and risotto need at least an hour's worth of attention. What to do?

Out of ideas, I call Kieran to ask if he knows a mechanic.

"Sure," he says, his rumbly voice soft in my ear. "What's the problem?"

"I dunno," I mumble. "Maybe I need a jump or something. What's his number? Still hoping to cook this dinner."

"Where are you?"

"In Montpelier, unfortunately."

"*Where* in Montpelier?"

"Outside the Shaw's."

"Leaving now. It'll take me twenty minutes to get there."

"You don't have to…"

Click.

Hmm.

I go back inside the store and make a small ATM withdrawal. Then I buy the bottle of wine I skipped the first time, as a thank you for Kieran.

He rolls up in his truck and stops beside my car. He hops out and smiles at me. "Want a jump? I have cables."

"Sure. I hope that's it, though."

"Tell me what happened."

Kieran frowns after I explain the sequence of events. "It just cut out? How long was the engine running before you shifted into reverse?"

"Uh, sixty seconds? Maybe longer. I was checking my phone for emails."

"Doesn't sound like the battery," he says. "Sounds like a belt."

"Oh." I think about that for a minute. "A belt is just a piece of rubber, right? I hope it's cheaper than a dead battery."

He winces. "Depends. Let's try a jump just in case."

I'm not exactly stunned when it doesn't work.

Kieran ends up calling his friend Jude, who sends a tow truck. By the time we're rolling toward Colebury in Kieran's truck, it's after seven.

"Dinner is going to be late," I grumble. "I'm sorry."

"Hey, it's no big thing," he says, switching on the radio.

"Except I'm starving. Aren't you?" I hate my life right now.

"Yeah," he agrees. "Will the ingredients keep until tomorrow? We could just grab a pizza instead."

"I guess?" They'll totally keep, but I just spent all my cash. "I'd need to hit the bank again."

"I got money," Kieran says. "Here." He unlocks his phone and hands it over. "The place is listed in my contacts under *Pizza*. Because I'm subtle like that. Order a large. Half with sausage and olives, half with whatever you like."

I hesitate a second.

"Don't tell me you don't like pizza?" Kieran says.

"I do," I say quickly. "I just don't want to be like your brother —always taking advantage of you."

"It's a pizza. Jesus. And it was my idea. Order, okay?"

So I do. I get the whole thing with the toppings he suggested, in case there are leftovers. After I hang up, he turns up the dashboard radio. And wouldn't you know? Kieran listens to country music. The sounds of Nashville hum through the truck, and for the first few minutes it doesn't bother me that much. We hear a Darius Rucker tune, and then a crossover song by Delilah Spark. Inevitably, a Brian Aimsley song comes on. It's his new one, "So Happy I'm Yours."

I grit my teeth through the first verse, and I'm suddenly aware of an uncomfortable truth—I've never wondered if a Brian Aimsley love song was secretly about me. Songwriters collaborate like crazy, and Brian rarely wrote a song by himself.

But as I listen to him singing about the way his heart lifts when he sees that special someone's smile, it occurs to me to realize I should have expected for more. I mean—I would never demand he sing about me in an obvious way. But why shouldn't he have *wanted* to?

He never did, though, and I never asked why. And although I'd sometimes demanded more of Brian's time, I'd never demanded more of his heart.

I'd sold myself short from the start. Brian was a first-class dick, yeah, but putting up with it was on me.

"Can we shut this off?" I blurt out.

"Sure." Kieran smacks the power button and the radio falls silent. "Sorry."

"Don't be sorry. It's your truck."

"Not a fan of country?"

"Hate it," I confess. "Spent too many years in Nashville." That's for damn sure.

He gives me an appraising glance before pulling into the pizza joint parking place. "Be right back."

The truck smells like pizza on the way home.

And that's when I realize that I never transferred the groceries from my car to Kieran's truck. I let out a groan of pure unhappiness at the thought of my pork loin being towed to a garage right now.

"What's the matter?"

Embarrassed, I explain the problem to Kieran. It's not like he won't notice when I have no ingredients to unload into our fridge. Today is like a bad dream I can't wake up from. "I can't believe I did that. I'm sorry about dinner."

"It's only thirty degrees out right now. Your groceries will be fine sitting in the car all night. We can get them tomorrow."

The idea of Kieran having to drive out to get them makes me want to howl. I'm so tired of being a hot mess. But I don't know how to stop being one. "I'm so sorry."

"For what? Cars break." He makes the turn onto the town green. We're almost home.

"For being your crazy, unreliable roommate. *Again*."

"You had a shit day Roddy, they happen. They happen a lot, honestly. We're going to eat pizza and drink a beer. Wait. Do you not like beer?" By the sound of his voice I can tell the question alarms him a little.

"I like it fine. But broke guys don't drink beer." I *am* a broke guy again. Thinking about my car repair bill makes me want to howl, too.

"Look," he asks as the house comes into view. "Are roommates supposed to tally everything to the penny? Am I doing it all wrong? I'm new with this."

"You haven't done anything wrong. Not one thing." I swallow hard. "I'm the dysfunctional one in this vehicle. The roommate rules *clearly* state that you don't jump your hot, drunk roommate, and then act like a drama queen afterwards. You probably think I'm insane."

"Nah." He makes a dismissive sound. "You told me your issues. I get it." He pulls into the driveway and cuts the engine and the lights.

"Why do you have to be so fucking decent?" I ask into the sudden silence. "It makes the rest of us look bad."

Kieran sits still in the darkness, as if this was a serious question. "I'm just like you, though. Just trying to figure my shit out. You've already helped me with that, by the way."

"Because I made your dick stand up and cheer?"

He snorts loudly. "The things you say. You're fearless."

"Yeah, but not wise." I unclip my seatbelt and reach for the door handle.

"Maybe just ease up on yourself for one night?" Kieran says, pocketing his keys. "We're going to watch a little TV and have some pizza and a beer. Or not the beer. Whatever. I offer it to you with no expectations. It doesn't have to be a big deal. You just seem like a guy who could use a piece of pizza and a hug."

"Ha. You of all people are *not* a hugger."

He shrugs those big shoulders. "That's just it, though. You make me feel like I could be someone who does things instead of just thinking about them. You probably don't understand, but I get a lot out of having you around."

Oh, man. Now he's done it. I'm full of warm fuzzies. "I'll take that hug now," I say before I can think better of it.

He turns slowly in my direction. "You sure about that?" It sounds like a challenge.

"Yup." I hitch myself closer to him on the seat, and open my arms wide. Kieran's response is to grasp the halves of my jacket and haul me closer.

And I like it so much that I skip the hug entirely, and dive straight into a steamy kiss. I lay it right on him.

Kieran lets out a grunt of surprise, but slides right into the kiss like a champ. Thick arms wrap around me and soft, hungry lips slide over mine. He kisses me like he's been thinking about it for weeks. And I kiss him back like I'm starved for it.

It's all very magical until my elbow beeps the truck's horn, and we startle apart.

"Inside," Kieran growls. "You know you want to."

I open my mouth to argue, but then I realize resistance is futile. "Yessir," I say instead.

Pizza forgotten, we slam the truck's doors and hustle into the house. Once the door clicks shut, Kieran lets me push him up against it. And then we're making out like teenagers again—fast and messy. Every lingering glance we've shared, every frustrated night sleeping in separate rooms. Is there any real surprise that we'd end up here—trying to fuse our mouths together in the darkened hallway?

No surprise at all, really.

Kieran's woodsy scent overpowers me, and his kisses are scorching. I'm done trying to fight all the things I feel for this man. I may end up ruining our friendship. I may even get my heart broken.

But some people are worth the risk, aren't they? I have a feeling in my bones that Kieran Shipley is one of them.

KIERAN

One kiss. That's all it took to untie my control.

I've tried to be so fucking patient. But the moment he looked at me with those liquid eyes in the truck, I just snapped.

And so did he. There are two strong hands on my shoulders, telling me what he needs. Every kiss draws us closer. I didn't know kisses could run so deep and dark. I taste more of Roderick than of myself.

I am amazed by so many things. The scent of his skin. The force of his tongue against mine. And my own boldness as I latch my hand to the back of his neck and whisper against his lips, "I want you." It's the truest thing I've ever said in my life. I am made of wanting.

In answer, Roderick's hand slides down my chest. And when it keeps going—his fingertips parting my jacket, grazing my abs, searing me through the thick cotton of my shirt—I break out in a sweat. Then he reaches for my belt buckle.

And tugs.

I make a noise of shocked elation when he unbuckles my belt and pops the button on my jeans. My old fantasies keep unspooling as he lowers my jeans by a couple crucial inches and drops to his knees.

I hear myself gasp as Roderick curls a hand around my hard cock. I stare in wonder as he draws it out of my briefs. And I can't stop a low groan from escaping as he lifts his chin, looks me *right* in the eye, and takes the head into his mouth.

Liquid heat. Pressure and bliss. This is how my obsession with him began, isn't it? A hasty blowjob in the dark. His eyes glittering with lust.

I wasn't ready for him back then, though. I could only watch, never speaking my desires aloud. But I'm not that frightened boy anymore. My head thunks against the door as he weighs me against his tongue. His expressive eyes lift to show me how invested he is in pleasing me.

Waiting eight years almost seems worth it right now. For me, this is so much more than reliving a teenage fantasy. I run a hand through Rodrick's hair the way his partner feared to do all those years ago. It's incredibly soft against my palm. Maybe I'm a late bloomer, but I'm all in now.

And not for just any guy. I'm all in for *him*.

Roderick slows his movements, teasing me, watching me with wide, curious eyes as I respond to each new thing that he does. He's not hesitant. I can tell he's just enjoying putting on a show.

I drop my hand beneath his chin, cupping his face. Slowly, I trace my thumb over his top lip, where it stretches around my cock. He closes his eyes and lets out a little moan that I can feel all the way through my groin. Then he takes a deep breath and gives a firm, measured suck, and another and another.

Before long, he's found a rhythm that I can't resist. My breath comes in shocked gasps. I am not used to getting what I want even when I manage to ask for it, so it's pretty overwhelming when it finally happens.

I can't hold still. I have to thrust my hips, pushing myself into Roderick's willing mouth. And I may or may not be making loud, desperate sounds as he takes me deeply again and again. It's too much, and it's going to be over too fast. I'll lose him again. I'm sure of it.

Somehow I find the will to catch his perfect face in my hand. "Wait," I rasp. "I need to touch you." If tonight is all I get, I need to make it last.

He pops off me, his lips red and swollen, his eyes flashing. I tug him to his feet and then kiss him again, because I can't help myself.

Clumsy with lust, and unwilling to break our kiss, I begin to guide him toward the living room. The fire I'd made in the fireplace is down to orange coals. It provides just enough light to steer Roderick around the sofa and onto the rug.

I give him a little shove, hoping he takes my hint.

By some miracle, he lowers his body down to the rug, then looks up at me with big eyes. For a moment, I could swear that he's about to come to his senses and bolt. But that's not what happens. He lifts his shirt over his head, showing me that tight chest that makes me so thirsty, with its trail of dark hair leading south into his jeans. "I like the way you think," he says.

I kneel down and practically pounce, popping the button on his jeans, then unzipping him.

He seems completely in control as he lifts his hips to let me tug the jeans down. Like getting naked in the living room is no big deal. Maybe it isn't for him.

It sure is for me. I can't stop staring at his golden body in the firelight, where shadows play over his lean, muscular thighs. I reach out and run a hand down his quadriceps, admiring the scrape of hair against my palm. This time I'm sober. This time I plan to remember every little thing about touching him.

He doesn't make me wait, either. He kicks off his shoes and socks until there's nothing left but miles of skin and a jutting erection. It's the only part of him that isn't smaller than me.

"Damn," I whisper at the florid sight of him. I want to reach out and stroke him.

"Do it," he whispers, reading my thoughts.

I've come this far, right? So there's no point in being shy. I lean down, bumping my forehead against his taut stomach before I give his shaft a slow lick.

"Fuck. Yeah. Jesus," he breathes. "More."

I open my mouth, slowly sliding the hard knob of his cock-head between my lips, until he lands heavily on my tongue. This is really happening. I grasp the base of his cock in one hand and caress his thigh with my other one.

Roderick's moan makes me bold. I lean in and take him in a little farther, playing with the depth and the suction.

My vivid fantasies, I discover, only got some of the details right. His skin is as hot and smooth as I'd imagined. The fullness of his cock in my mouth feels divine. And Roderick's moan of happiness is just as loud as I'd hoped.

But I'm not very good at this. It's hard to take him deeply into my mouth and still breathe.

"Easy," he says, laying a hand in my hair as I manage to choke myself. "It's not a race. Take a break if you need it."

But I don't want a break. I've wasted so much time already. Years and years. What's more, I recognize the danger of stopping just long enough to let everybody overthink this. Roderick might suddenly remember why he doesn't want to get involved with me.

I relax my throat and adjust my angle. And that works better for me. Bracing my forearm on the rug, I take him as deeply as I dare.

"Oh God. You're a quick study," he gasps, stroking my hair. "Fuuuuuck." His hips writhe happily, and my chest swells with pride. "Why aren't you naked right now?" he pants.

Good question. I pop off him and hastily unbutton my shirt. A fleeting concern about stripping in the living room flashes through me. *Someone might see.* But the orange glow from the fireplace is barely bright enough to show me Roderick's golden body stretched out like a Renaissance painting. And what a sight it is—especially the sheen of his wet cock where I've been sucking him. Just the view makes me want to come.

I shuck off my pants and underwear in a big hurry. Getting naked in the middle of the room feels more bold and adventurous than sleazy.

"That's more like it," he says as I shed the last of my clothes. "God, you're so hot it melts my brain."

Usually, compliments embarrass me. But he punctuates this sentence by rolling toward me, his tongue finding my cock with an accuracy that makes me gasp. His gorgeous mouth takes me in. All I can do is lean back on the rug and breathe through my excitement.

But then I get greedy. I want even more. So I curl toward him, maneuvering so we're both lying on our sides, sixty-nine style. I grasp his hip and tug until his erection enters my mouth.

He hums in response, and I can feel it on my cock.

It's almost too much to handle—the double pleasure of sucking and being sucked. And as if that weren't enough, his hands slide between my legs, stroking my balls, teasing the crack of my ass.

Meanwhile, my mouth is stuffed full of him, and I like the feeling more than I would have ever guessed. Everything about this moment is a revelation.

Roderick shifts his hips and groans, and a drop of briny desire hits my tongue. For some reason, this makes me impossibly horny. I can barely concentrate as he licks and sucks and worships me with his tongue. The blowjob I'm giving gets even sloppier, as I grow ever more desperate for my own release.

"Look out," Roderick suddenly slurs around my dick.

I back off on command. And the moment I do, he moans happily and comes all over my hand and my chest.

And that's all it takes for me, too. I let out a startled gasp and immediately unload several weeks' worth of sexual tension into his perfect mouth. I feel him swallow, and then he moans again.

Sexiest. Sound. *Ever.*

"Damn," I whisper, my head rolling onto his thigh. "Sorry."

He's breathing hard, too. "Holy hell. I can't unclench my toes."

His head thunks onto the floor. We've rolled halfway off the rug. "Wow."

Breathing hard, I try to get some more air into my lungs. I don't really want to come down from this high, but I guess it's inevitable. Roderick rolls out from under me, disengaging. He picks himself up off the floor and pads out of the room without a word.

Resting my head on the rug, I stare up at the ceiling. I'm covered in jizz, and I'm unsettled. Is that it? He's just gone? It makes me wonder if I did something wrong. Is he pissed off that I didn't have time to warn him before I—

Hell. Did I screw up big-time?

If I didn't feel sleazy before, I'm starting to now.

From the kitchen, I hear a sequence of beeps from the oven. Then a faucet flips on somewhere in the house. A moment later, he pads onto the rug and kneels beside me, looking me right in the eyes. "I'm preheating the broiler."

"The broiler?" I echo stupidly. "I don't even know what that is."

Roderick smiles at me. And then, in what feels like yet another miracle, he leans down and presses a slow kiss to my lips. "I need you to get up and follow me." He plucks his underwear off the floor and rises to his feet again.

"Okay?" Maybe he's not mad at me after all?

He steps into his briefs and marches out of the room again, beckoning me. Still feeling stoned, I follow him dumbly into the downstairs bathroom.

"Get in." He points at the big, clawfoot tub, which is beginning to fill with water. "Wait for me."

I look down at the tub, where water streams from the faucet. "Okay?"

"Go on." He gives me a pat on my bare ass. Then he leaves.

I wipe myself up a little before stepping into the tub. When I sit down, the water is wonderfully hot against my cooling skin. I close my eyes and try to make sense of this crazy evening. I haven't taken a bath since I was seven. And why does Roderick want me to?

He reappears a few minutes later. He drops his shorts, turns off the water, and steps carefully into the opposite end of the tub. I can't help but gaze admiringly at his bare body. That V of muscle at his hips almost makes me feel horny all over again.

I'm not sure we're both going to fit into this bath, and I don't understand why he'd want to try.

Roderick lowers himself into the water. There isn't enough space for his legs, so he weaves them between mine. The contact makes my heart jump. Nobody ever touches my naked body. I mean *never*. The brush of his leg hair against mine is seriously unfamiliar. So is the stroke of the arch of his foot against my inner thigh.

Heat rises from my skin, and it's not because of the water. I don't know if I can play it cool when we're face to face in the bright bathroom light. "So...why did you call this meeting?" I ask.

The words come out sounding nonchalant, but I'm freaking out inside, and it has nothing to do with the fact that I just sucked a dick. That was fun, and I'm game to do it again. But now he wants to *talk* to me? I have never felt more naked than I do right now.

"Well," he begins, leaning back, resting his elegant head on the rim of the tub. He looks as comfortable as ever. "In the first place, our oven needs a few minutes to preheat. And I've been wanting to try out the tub for a while. Plus, I think better when I'm submerged."

"With me?"

"Yeah." He gives me a sheepish grin. "It's obvious that we were going to do that again, right? What with you giving me that..." He waves his hand in my general direction. "...brown-eyed smolder you've got going on. And me with insufficient self-control to resist a hunky farm boy."

"*Smolder*?" I don't know much, but I'm sure I've never smoldered.

SARINA BOWEN

"You're just so—" He lets out a sigh. "So irresistible to me. I don't think I can stay out of your bed. Or off your dick. If you want me on it, that is."

I think he's being flip, but I feel my blood stir anyway. "Does that mean you're not going to freak out this time?"

Propping his head in his hand, he studies me. His gaze is warm, but I still feel uncomfortable. Just because I want Roderick, doesn't mean I want to be closely observed.

"Look," he says. "I never meant to break all my own rules tonight, but the truth is I like you way too much. So even though it's a bad idea to jump on your roommate, I'm happier right now than I've been in a long time."

All I can do is sort of stare at him for a long beat. Nobody has ever said anything like that to me before. I made Roderick *happy*, with rough kisses and clumsy hands.

It's more miraculous than my chicken with garlic and herbs, that's for damn sure.

"Say something," he says suddenly. "Or at least smile, damn it. Did I just overstep? Did I freak you out?"

"Fuck no," I say, but it comes out like a growl. "I'm smiling on the inside."

He blinks. And then he tilts his head back and laughs so loudly that it bounces off the tiled bathroom walls.

"What?" I grumble. "I'm serious."

"I *know*." He reins in his laughter and smiles at me. "That's why it's funny. I never met anyone like you. I have zero filter, and you're made of filter. It's like armor. You never take it off."

That's probably true, but it's also irrelevant. "Where do we go from here, though? What happens next?"

"Well, pizza," he says, splashing some water onto his face and then shaking his head like a happy dog. "I went outside in my underwear and rescued it from your truck. I'll pop it into the oven in a minute."

"I meant *after* pizza." Roderick is this bright, shiny thing in my life, and I need to know whether or not to feel hope.

172

"Oh. Well, that depends on you. Bend your knees?"

"What?" It takes me a beat to keep up, but then I do. His legs slide off mine when I lift my knees. And now I'm literally open and vulnerable in this ridiculous position.

But not for long. Roderick gathers up his smaller body and then moves forward into the space between my legs. "We need to eat that pizza," he says, propping his hands on the tub rim on either side of me. "But then we could watch more of our show. Maybe in your bed?"

"Okay," I say quickly as his blue eyes come closer.

"And here I thought tonight was a disaster," he says, leaning down to kiss me.

If this is a disaster, I'll take it all night long.

RODERICK

I think I may have blown Kieran's mind, along with his cock. When I carry a tray into his bedroom after our bath, he's standing by his dresser, looking a little stunned.

"Grab your laptop?" I ask. "It's under my arm."

"Sure." He unsticks himself and grabs it, dropping his towel in his haste.

"Thanks," I say, giving his naked body an appreciative glance. God, the *view*.

I don't know what I was thinking when I'd decided we couldn't fool around. And I'm still not super sure why he's even interested. Kieran should have a guy whose life isn't a dumpster fire. A guy whose car isn't dead, and who can afford to buy groceries.

"Come and eat this while it's warm." I sit down, settling the tray on my lap.

"Whoa." He walks over to take a plate and looks at the pizza like he's never seen it before. "It looks better than it usually does. Maybe this place is upping their game."

"Well... I put some diced red peppers, minced garlic, and pecorino cheese on top before I broiled it. I hope you don't, uh, hate peppers." I really should have asked.

"I don't hate anything," he says, sitting down on the opposite side of the bed.

"Well that's a relief. I'm trying to eat more vegetables and not as many carbs. It's hazardous to be around bread all day."

He takes a bite and chews. He keeps sneaking glances at me, like there's something he can't figure out.

"Is the pizza okay?"

"It's great," he says immediately.

"So then why are you giving me that look?"

He looks down at his plate. "Well, what are the rules?"

"Rules? You mean for me and you?"

"Yeah. The rules. I like to know where I stand."

I set a pizza crust down on my plate and turn to look at him. *I like to know where I stand*, he'd said. As I gaze into his light brown eyes, I realize that it's a simple request, but it's not a demand that I've ever learned to make.

I've gotten too used to living on the edge, never knowing where I stand. At seventeen, I knew I could get kicked out of my parents' house at any moment. Eventually I did. And at nineteen, I learned not to trust anyone, because they might rob you in your sleep.

So it's really no surprise that I spent three years with a man who refused to even acknowledge our relationship. I offered myself to him without reservations, and he treated me like the snack buffet on the club level of a fancy hotel—grazing on my love when it suited him, and ignoring me the rest of the time.

Kieran Shipley waits quietly while my thoughts ping around like caffeinated ping-pong balls. Forty minutes ago he manhandled me into the living room and removed my jeans. But now he's watching me with soft eyes, and I don't even know what to do with all his patience.

"Hot mess, here," I say, holding up a hand. "I'm not very handy with rules. But I'll make some if you want me to. Like I said before, I don't want you to end up hating me." I need to keep my job, and I'd rather not alienate the guy whose house I'm living in.

"Roddy, I'm never going to wind up hating you."

So you say. "What rules were you looking for? Are you worried that I'll invade your space? Too much togetherness?"

"No, uh, the opposite." He shakes his head. "What am I allowed to do. What am I allowed to touch?"

"Oh, honey. I told you that I gave up on trying to stay away from you. Pretty sure there's no part of me you can't have if you want it. What else?"

He likes the sound of that. Those brown eyes look warmer. "Well, you told me you use Grindr sometimes."

"*Oh.*" Now I feel like a tool. I should have guessed what he was thinking about. "No, I haven't had any Grindr hookups in more than three years. I'd only downloaded it because I was curious what it was like in Vermont. I chatted with a few guys just because I was lonely. But I'll delete it tomorrow."

"Okay." He lifts his chin and studies me. "I don't know how these things work. But I don't think I can share."

My needy heart likes the sound of that. "They work however we say they work. And I know your lack of experience embarrasses you a little bit." His eyes flip up and then right back down again. But he gives me a quick nod. "The truth is that we've both probably had the same number of healthy relationships."

"Zero?" He snorts.

"Yeah. That many. So you're smart to bring this up. But I wouldn't live in your house and fool around with you while also fooling around with someone else. That's too complicated, even for me."

"Okay." I get a quick smile.

"On the other hand, I sure don't want to get on your nerves. If you don't want me in your bed, or whatever, you can just say so."

"I want you in my bed, preferably naked," he says immediately. "That's easy. But the other hours of the day are more complicated."

"Because of work," I say slowly. Kieran is in the closet. Or more accurately, he's still experimenting. And the truth is that I don't really need to be the face of Kieran's sexual exploration. "Work is a problem. I guess we'll have to be very discreet."

He nods. "It's private. My family has no clue."

"Right. I understand." But oh, the irony! I promised myself that after all that time helping Brian hide our relationship that I would *never* get myself into this situation again. But here I go.

This is a totally different situation, though. Kieran isn't trying to manipulate me. He's just sowing his first queer oats.

I just have to remember that.

Kieran grows thoughtful again, finishing his dinner in silence. Then I gather our empty plates and stack them on the tray, while he finds the next episode of Silicon Valley on his computer.

When I return to the bed, he's balancing the laptop on his lap, searching for the right viewing angle for both of us. "Can you see this?" he asks. "Wait. Let me try this." He tucks the computer between us on the mattress and fusses with the position. "Maybe the screen is too small for this."

"Kieran, man, let me help. The problem isn't the small screen."

"Then what is?"

I pick up the computer. "Don't take this the wrong way. But your cuddle game is weak."

"My—?"

"Let me show you how this is done. Lift up your left arm." I nudge it upward until it's shoulder height. "Just like that. Now…" I shove a pillow against the wall and then move my ass until I'm snugged against him, tucked under his arm and leaning against his muscular chest. The laptop lands on my knees, and we're close enough that we can both see the screen.

"Oh," he says softly.

"Yeah, see?" I hit Play and relax against him.

For the first few minutes of the show, he doesn't move a muscle or relax. Kieran isn't used to being touched, but I'm a cuddle whore of the highest order, and undeterred by his hesitation. I stretch out against his body, my hand finding one of his muscular thighs beneath the sheet. And I gently sift my fingertips through the soft hairs at the top of his knee while I watch.

Bit by bit he relaxes, too, until one wide palm cups my ass, and his other hand rests snugly on my chest.

And I'm like a happy housecat, drowsing against his bare skin, his chest bouncing against my ear whenever he laughs. This blissful, simple moment is everything I ever wanted. Why does life have to be so fucking complicated, when this right here is so easy?

Snuggling closer, I reach up and stroke his bare chest with light fingers. I'm rewarded with a happy sigh.

"Another?" I ask when the episode ends. I could stay here my whole life.

"Maybe," he says, catching my fingers. "But it's hard to concentrate when you're touching me like that."

"Is it? The problem is that you have no cuddle stamina. We'll have to work on that." I turn in his arms until I can see his warm brown eyes. I can't believe I ever thought I could resist Kieran Shipley. This lonely man needs me almost as badly as I need him. "Maybe that's enough TV, then."

I fumble for the laptop, clicking it shut. I roll my body all the way onto Kieran's, and, without waiting for an invitation, I kiss him.

Long arms wrap around me almost instantly. As he dives into my mouth like he's never tasted anything so good, we sink down against the sheets, hands grasping, bodies shifting, hearts thumping.

And nothing has ever felt so right.

RODERICK

After that, I give Kieran many more chances to improve his cuddling. In fact, we work on it the very next night, after I retrieve my groceries from my broken car.

We cooked that roast, and almost burned the risotto, though, because we got to fooling around on the couch while we waited for the meat to finish cooking. I forgot all about the food as Kieran pushed me down onto the cushions and blew me.

Work. Food. Sex. Cuddle. Sleep. Repeat. I'm living the dream right now. My job is going well. I live in a nice house with a hot man who can't wait to see me every night when he gets home. And we still have Mondays off together. That means sleeping in and waking each other up with various naked activities.

There hasn't been any full-on sex, though, in spite of the hints I've dropped. The sex fairy (that's me, I guess) has left a bottle of lube on the nightstand and some condoms in Kieran's bathroom.

He's taking it slow, though. And that's fine with me. Mostly fine. Except it's midmorning on a Monday, and Kieran is stretched out on the rug in the living room, reading a magazine.

And I'm stretched out on his back, thinking dreamy thoughts of being pounded into the rug. As one does. Lifting my head, I look down at the magazine to see what's keeping Kieran so busy. "You're reading about…" I squint at the page. "Cows?"

"Yup," he says patiently.

I stretch out a little more, as if he were my personal cushion. And then I kiss the back of his neck just once. Okay, twice. But not in an annoying way.

So much has changed since the night my car died, and we barely managed to eat that pizza between make-out sessions. On the other hand, a few things haven't changed at all. A very expensive car repair has left me just as strapped as before. And apparently I'm still a needy fuck. Because here I am pestering Kieran with more kisses to the back of his neck, while the poor man tries to read a farming magazine.

He doesn't really mind, though. In fact, after a moment or two, he drops his head, giving up on the article, and providing me with better access to the sensitive skin under his ear.

"So tell me about these cows," I say between kisses. But what I really mean is *roll over and grab my ass.*

He tells me about the cows instead. "Kyle wants to breed some Angus cross cattle this spring. Up until now we've only done purebred Highland cattle."

"Oh." I don't know squat about the Shipley family business. "Is that a good idea?"

"It's a fine idea," he says. "And I'm kinda stunned that he had it. Kyle isn't much of a businessman. Or maybe he could be if everyone stops telling him what to do. My dad is a dictator. Usually Kyle just agrees with him, to stay on his good side."

"But not this time?" I run a hand shamelessly through his hair. Touching him is my new favorite hobby.

"Well, he wants my support. Which means he wants me to fight his battles for him with my dad." Kieran flips a page in the magazine, and I see an ad for chicken feed.

"*Calcium for great laying.* There's a joke in there somewhere," I quip.

"There's lots of dirty jokes in farming," he agrees. "Not to mention that I grew up outside a town called Hardwick."

I snort. "I noticed that. And I wasn't going to say anything, but that is the gayest sounding town I ever heard." After the joke comes out, I wonder if Kieran will object. He doesn't use the word *gay*, or discuss his sexuality. Or his feelings, for that matter.

But now he turns his head and smiles at me anyway, like he's in on the joke. "I'll bet you don't know how cattle is bred."

"You'd be right about that. But I want to hear it. Are we talking about cow sex now?"

"Yes and no. Our operation is organic, and small. So we breed by putting our bull in the same pasture as the cows. But on a big ranch they do everything artificially."

"Artificially," I repeat slowly, trying to decide what he means. "Now you have me picturing a bunch of cowboys jerking off bulls."

"Well…" Kieran chuckles. He flips to the back of the magazine and shows me a whole page of listings for…

"Does that say *semen*?"

"Oh yeah."

"This farming stuff is freakier than I thought. They *do* jerk off cows?"

"Bulls," he corrects.

"That sounds both dirty, which I appreciate, and dangerous, which I do not. How does that work? Are cow condoms a thing?"

Chuckling, Kieran sets the magazine aside. "It's almost like a condom—but thicker. And the funnel has insulated sides—like a warm water bottle. The heat of it makes the bull ejaculate immediately."

I let out a whoop of laughter. "Are you telling me that bulls are two-pump chumps?"

"More like one pump. And the young ones sometimes get overexcited and jizz on the floor. As soon as they walk into that breeding barn, they know what's going to happen. Except the older ones don't always get it up."

"Then what?" I demand. "Is there a channel on Porn Hub for bulls?"

"Better," Kieran says with a naughty smile. And, wow, there's nothing hotter than Kieran's naughty smile. I see it a lot these days. "When the bull won't get with the program, the rancher does this." He reaches back and runs a hand up my thigh. "Usually does the trick."

"*Oh my fucking god.* There's foreplay?"

"Basically. And bulls are used to doing the deed on their hind feet, right? They mount the cow. But in the breeding barn, they can't use a cow, because they can't take the chance that the bull hits that target. So you'll never believe what they use instead."

"Please tell me it's a big, bovine blow-up doll. With big tits and long eyelashes."

"Nope." Kieran laughs. He's enjoying this story almost as much as I am. "They train a steer who's particularly calm to just stand in front and let the bulls mount him."

"A steer," I repeat. "That's a boy."

"Right—a young, castrated male. A rancher leads the breeding bull into the stall. He rears up onto the other dude's back. The breeder plops the funnel bag over his weenie and he shoots. The whole thing takes less than a minute."

"Get out of town," I gasp, rolling off Kieran so that I can look into those amused, light brown eyes. "You're telling me that bulls are mounting one of their pals to bust a nut?"

"That's right."

"Holy fuck. The gay agenda is alive and well, so long as you're a bull. Why are the evangelicals not up in arms about this?"

"Because." He taps the magazine. "Quality bull semen sells for fifty bucks a pop, and they can harvest him once a week."

"Hot damn. I'm in the wrong line of work. This is like our favorite episode of *Silicon Valley*. How many bulls can I jack off in an hour? Forty, you think?"

Kieran just shakes his head. He knows I'm clowning around to get his attention. And he doesn't even seem to mind.

"Let's practice," I suggest. "On you."

His chuckle is low and deep, and I feel it against my chest. "I would if I could. But I have a call with an admissions officer at Burlington U in ten minutes."

"Oh!" I wrap an arm around him. "Is this it? Did you get into the class you wanted?"

His brow furrows. "Not yet."

"Then what's the call for?" I sit up to give the man some space. He's so tolerant of my clingy nature. He's still gruff and a little hard to read. But he also seems starved for physical affection. And I sure don't mind providing it.

"Well, she's trying to talk me into applying for the undergraduate degree program. She said I'd be eligible for financial aid, and every class I took would be half price or less."

"Winner, winner, chicken dinner!" I clap my hands. "Sounds like a plan. What's the catch?"

"It's more work," he says slowly, and those eyes I love so much grow worried. "I'd have to take two courses at a time instead of one."

"So? Zara already agreed to cut your hours in the new year." Besides, nobody works harder than Kieran. He could slice through two design courses like a sharp knife through butter.

"But they'll *grade* me," he says with a shiver. "I'd have to do well to keep my financial aid. That means taking the tests instead of just listening from the back."

"Oh," I say softly. And now I understand the issue. Kieran had planned to audit these classes the way that he does everything— thoughtfully but silently. If he's taking the courses for credit, he'll have to raise his hand, or even—gasp—contribute to a group project.

"And do I really want to be a twenty-five-year-old freshman?" he asks, sitting up beside me. There's confusion in those lovely brown eyes.

Yes you do, I realize. The question wouldn't be troubling him at all if he didn't understand the benefit.

But I won't push him. My strong, silent-type boyfriend doesn't need someone to order him around. Instead, I ask a couple of crucial questions. "What's the commitment?"

"Two classes, starting in January."

"And how long will they last?"

"Well, the semester goes until May. But a degree would take me eight years at that pace." He laughs. "Can you imagine?"

The thing is that I can. Kieran loves design. He should get the chance to find out what it's like to surround himself with other design nerds. "So you're saying that it's only a four-month trial. If you hate it, you can stop before the strawberries are ripe. And you'd still have the benefit of those two classes."

He opens his mouth to argue with me, and then shuts it again.

"Look, I'm not the kind of guy who's going to tell you how to plan your life, because I'm pretty bad at planning my own. But this is an opportunity, not a problem. I never got to try music school. And I'll probably always wonder what that would have been like. Here's this nice lady who's offering you a shot. Just think about it."

He rubs his forehead. "I just wanted to ease into it."

"Uh-huh." I grin.

"I'm terrible at trying new things."

I reach out a hand and pat his firm chest. "Gotta call bullshit on that. You tried me in bed. And on the rug. And in the shower…"

He snorts. "Fine. Sure. It only took me eight years after I first thought about you."

"Good point," I concede. "And you'll be seven years older than the other freshmen. So you're right on schedule."

Kieran laughs, turning his head to the side in that way that he does. As if laughing were a private matter. And it's just as well, because a full-on smile from him is hotter than the sun.

"Okay. I'll think about it," he mumbles. Then he reaches out and takes my hand. And when his fingers close over mine, I feel like I won a prize. "What are you doing today, anyway?"

"Taking a run. Testing out a recipe for shortbread cookies." His eyes brighten at the mention of cookies. "Trying to decide how many holiday cookies I can bake in the next ten days. I thought we could let people buy in bulk, and pull in some extra cash."

He tilts his head. "If you're not careful, you'll end up making cookies all night, every night."

"That wouldn't be so bad." I shrug. The truth is that I'd rather be indispensable than well-rested.

Everything in my life is going so well right now. My job is working out, and my new man is the nicest guy in the world.

I'm basically just waiting for the other shoe to drop. It always does.

KIERAN

Pratt and Son Advertising Agency is slammed because Christmas is a'coming, and everyone wants to glam up their promo imagery with bows and glitter.

Honestly, it's boring design work. I can't wait until the holidays are over.

"Kieran," Mr. Pratt barks. "Can you redo this Christmas tree? The client doesn't like all the ornaments. They're too busy."

Ornaments? I take the page out of his hand, and what I see there makes me feel ragey. Once again, Deacon has taken my nice, crisp design and mucked it up. "There shouldn't be any ornaments at all. Ask Deacon to delete that layer on the source file."

"He's gone for the day," Mr. Pratt says. "Could you handle it for me? Thanks."

I look down at the pile of other requests on my desk and nearly snap. But I'm distracted from my misery when my phone lights up with a message.

Roderick: *Hey! I think you forgot to defrost that chicken I was supposed to cook. It's still in the freezer? We could get takeout instead!*

That's all it takes to make me forget all my work troubles.

Because Roderick is home and thinking about cooking our supper, and part of me is already there with him.

I don't even recognize my life right now. It's full of hot meals and couch cuddles and blowjobs. We eat together every night now. After dinner, we watch TV on the couch, until Roderick leans in to trace my ear with his tongue, or lifts my T-shirt up to kiss his way across my abs. And then—after we exhaust ourselves —we curl up together in my bed and pass out. He sleeps spread-eagled on the bed, limbs everywhere.

Every morning, when his alarm goes off at some unholy baker's hour, he rolls over and hugs me before getting out of bed. His sleepy hand trails though my hair, and I feel his warm chest against my ribcage as his knee hooks over mine. Clumsy with sleep, I reach over and give him a quick squeeze. He kisses me on the jaw and leaves, but I can still smell his skin on the sheets after he goes.

Having Roderick in my life is like having a fire in the hearth. He warms me even when I can't see him.

A couple years ago I watched my cousin Griffin fall head over heels for Audrey. The two of them were so right for each other that I wasn't even envious. But I thought—*that will never happen to me*. Now I wonder if I was wrong.

Too bad I'm too distracted by my man to defrost a chicken.

Kieran*: I did forget. I'm sorry. I'll buy takeout if you want to order something. Looks like I'll be here for a while. The Christmas rush is on. And Junior fucked off early.*

Roderick*: If I ever meet that guy, I'm going to spit on his bagel.*

Kieran*: Gross. Remind me to stay on your good side.*

Roderick*: He gets paid more than you, and does half the work.*

Half is generous. But I probably shouldn't complain. A job is a job.

Roderick*: I have a radical idea. Let's go out to dinner. It doesn't have to be anywhere fancy. But wouldn't it be fun to let* *other people bring us food? I think we're due a small extravagance. Like that noodle shop in Montpelier.*

I smile at the screen, because Roderick texts like he talks—in idea bursts. And he's still going.

Please?

I'll be your best roommate.

I'll make it worth your while later.

He adds a wink emoji and then an eggplant. And I laugh.

"Kieran!" Mr. Pratt's voice barks. "Can I have those revisions? I have plans tonight and you're just staring at your phone."

I set it down hastily. I never used to goof off on my phone, because I never had a confidante. "Coming right up," I say, grabbing the computer mouse to open the file.

I quickly discover that Deacon didn't save a new file when he gaudied up my Christmas tree, and he didn't make a new layer either. I'll have to start over.

Maybe the old Kieran would have sat here fuming, but this one has had it. "Mr. Pratt," I call, standing up to give him a piece of my mind. Something has got to give. I'm so sick of this.

"Yes, Kieran?"

I'd intended to argue, but instead, I hear myself say, "Would you write me a recommendation? I'm applying for a design program, and there's scholarship money at stake."

He blinks in surprise. Maybe we both do. But I have to make a decision about this—my application is due in ten days, and I can't work here forever.

"Sure, kid," he says eventually. "Sounds like a good opportunity. If you can get me a damn Christmas tree in the next fifteen minutes... I'll make you sound as talented as Van Gogh."

"Yessir." I hustle back to my desk to redesign a Christmas tree.

Still, I find a few seconds to reply to Roderick, holding the phone surreptitiously underneath a file folder.

Kieran: *Let's eat out. Is eight too late?*

Roderick: *I'll be there with bells on.*

But not actual bells.

That sounds awkward.

WTF does that mean, anyway?

Smirking, I hide my phone and hurry through the rest of the day's work. I can't wait to go out for noodles with the guy who makes all the rest of this bullshit worth it.

RODERICK

"This is the best idea I ever had," I say after slurping another noodle into my mouth.

After he takes a sip of broth, Kieran looks at me with an expression of patience and warmth that I've never seen him bestow on anyone else. "We should do this every week, if we think we can afford it."

"Deal," I agree immediately. "Although I wasn't sure you'd come."

He lifts his bushy eyebrows in surprise, "Why not? I like food. And this place doesn't break the saving-for-college budget."

"Well…" I glance around the room, taking in the other diners. At this hour, it's a mix of young professionals. "Someone might look at us and assume we're on a date."

"That doesn't bother me," he says evenly. As if he weren't blowing my mind right now. "I don't care what strangers think."

"*Really.*"

"Nah."

I plop a lovely piece of fatty pork into my mouth and chew, buying myself a moment to think. I used to drive my ex crazy when I'd ask him questions about coming out. *Why not now? Will you ever be ready?* And every time he'd put me off, I'd hear the subtext beneath the excuses: *It's you, Roddy. You're not worth the trouble.*

I still have those emotional scars. Kieran baffles me, but in entirely different ways.

"Well…" I say. "It's just that you haven't told anyone close to you that you're into men."

"Nope," he agrees, sipping his beer. "I also haven't told them that I might try for a college degree. Or that I've started painting again. Everything is on a need-to-know basis."

"But why?" I press, even though I'll probably regret it.

He wipes his mouth on a napkin and then looks down at his bowl. "My family is weird, Roddy. We don't tell each other the things that matter. We only talk about the things that don't. We never share."

"But what would happen if you did?" I whisper, hoping he won't hate me for asking. "I'm not judging you. I'm just trying to understand."

He sits back in his chair. "If I tell all my truths, then it could make other people tell theirs. And some of that stuff is ugly. I really don't need to hear everyone else's secrets. It's better this way."

"You don't want to make them say it out loud? What they'd think about you and me?" I clarify.

"Exactly. It's just a bad idea. Because then it's too real, and I'm stuck laboring on a farm for a man who openly hates me. And if I stop helping, I'm bailing on my mother and my brother."

Well, heck. I have never navigated that particular minefield. My parents' disapproval is more or less in alignment. I take another bite and try to think. "I've met some of your extended family, though, and they seem pretty great."

"They are," he agrees. "And as long as I toe the line, I get to keep the good people in my life. I don't ever have to find out whose side they'd be on if they knew how things really are at my house. And anyway—why I should go first? Nobody else tells the truth. Why me?"

"Because it might set you free?" I say softly.

He makes a face. "It might, or it might not. I could be the guy who broke the truce and blew the whole family sky high."

"It's a risk," I concede. Sometimes I forget that Kieran was living at home when I met him. Independence is still new to him. After a little time passes, he might realize that his father—or whoever—doesn't control him anymore.

"Besides," he says, pushing his empty bowl away. "School might not work out. I might be a shit painter. And you might leave Vermont. Then I would have stuck my neck out for nothing."

My chopsticks pause on the way to my bowl. Because he's right about that last thing. I've made him no promises. I was so careful not to. "The thing is, Kieran?" I take a breath and gather my courage. This usually ends badly. But I'm already used to being the guy who cares too much. "You're the kind of guy who's worth sticking around for. Just so you know."

He gives me a slow blink. "I am?" It doesn't sound like he believes me.

"A hundred percent. So just… Think it over."

The waitress picks that moment to approach our table, ruining the moment. Of course, she does. "Can I bring you boys any dessert? Or another drink?"

We ask for the check, because it's getting late, and neither one of us wants to overspend. Kieran tries to pay, but I insist on splitting it. "I didn't ask you out to dinner to make you pay."

"I know that," he says. "But I really needed a night out, and I didn't even know it. And you just had that car-repair bill."

He's right about the car-repair bill. It was ghastly. And the shop warned me that other issues are lurking on the horizon. But I still won't let him pay. I plunk down my half and close the bill wallet.

"Suit yourself," he says. "We'll just come here again next week, then."

Outside, the storefronts of Montpelier have been decorated with white lights and fake snow, because we don't have the real stuff yet. "I *love* Christmas," I gush.

"Why?"

"What do you mean, *why?* Lights. Carols. Wrapping paper. Christmas cookies."

"Okay—I understand the cookies." He bleeps the locks on his truck. "The rest of it never turns out like it does on TV, though."

Of course he's a hundred percent right. I've never had a Christmas that even came close to fulfilling my Hallmark fantasies. But I can't quit hoping. "Do you think we'll get more snow soon? I haven't had a snowy Christmas in a few years."

Kieran's lips quirk up in a smile. "You'll get your snow, probably. And nobody makes better cookies than you."

As usual, the praise makes me light up inside. "Play your cards right, and you can have all my cookies." Somehow this comes out sounding flirtatious. I have a gift. Kieran's smile only widens. Then he leans in and gives me a long, slow kiss, right here on the street where anyone might see.

I'm stunned, truly. But not too stunned to kiss him back. When it's over, all I can do is gaze up at him in wonder. Did that just happen?

"Roderick," he says gently.

"Huh?"

"You know you drove your own car, right?"

"Um, yup," I stammer. "I'm parked in the municipal lot."

"You want me to walk you over there?" His eyes twinkle.

I shake myself. "Nope, I'm good. See you at home."

"You sure will." The low, hungry tone he uses sends me hurrying off to my car.

Forty minutes later we're in our favorite place—Kieran's bed. He's half on top of me. Kissing me. Grinding his hot body against mine. Everything is wow.

Maybe he's not a talker, but Kieran has other ways of showing me how he feels.

One of his rough hands coasts up my chest, then pins my hand against the mattress. His other hand strokes down, over my abs, onto my groin. He gives my dick a slow stroke that makes me moan. Then his fingers dip down to play with my balls.

I'm loving every minute of it. But we could do even more. "Kieran," I breathe, thrusting into his hand. "Would you ever want to fuck me?" I don't always bottom, but lately I've been dreaming about it.

"Maybe," he grunts before kissing me deeply.

Maybe. What does that mean? Does it mean yes, but not now? Or no, and he'd rather not talk about it? Does he hate the idea of anal? Maybe it's too gay for him.

Although that seems unlikely, because he's presently licking his way down my body and—*ungh*—weighing my cockhead on his tongue. Kieran has been practicing this with the dedication of an athlete who's angling for a spot on the blowjob Olympic team.

And *why* can't I ever just be happy with what I have? A hot, kind man is giving me head. I don't need to take it further. I don't need him to love me.

But I *want* him to, damn it. And I'm scared that I'll always want more than Kieran Shipley can give me.

He lifts his head suddenly. "Where'd you go?"

"Nowhere," I promise. "My squirrel brain just took over for a second."

He gives me a slow smile. "Squirrel brain?"

"Yeah! Don't you have one? When your thoughts chase around in circles and distract you from what's really important? Like a great blowjob?"

"Not so much. No."

"Of course you don't." I flop back onto the pillow. "You probably spend all day thinking sturdy, mountain-man thoughts. All that time you've spent outdoors makes your beard thick and your biceps strong and your head clear. Got it."

He chuckles. "I don't know about that. But—" He leans down and licks the length of my cock. "—when you're here in my bed, you're all I can think about. And after we fall asleep? I dream about you."

Well, *that's* exciting. My squirrel brain doesn't get a chance to react to that, though, because Kieran rubs his thumb across my taint and swallows my cock. Not even a hot mess like me could ruin the moment. I'm too busy fucking his mouth as he sucks and strokes until I'm gripping the sheets, muscles quivering.

I'm not ready for it to end. "Not yet, hunk," I beg, tugging on his hair. "You're too good at that now. I'm going to disgrace myself. Come up here."

He releases me with a smug grin that looks exceptional on his rugged features. He puts a muscular forearm on the bed and scales my body like some kind of flannel-wearing, cider-pressing Vermont superhero. Those powerful shoulders alone are enough to make me pop a woody whenever he walks into the coffee shop kitchen.

He looks me right in the eye before giving me a deep, searing kiss that leaves no space for ambiguity. Kieran doesn't say a lot in words. But each of his kisses tells me just what I needed to hear.

I fumble a hand off the bed and onto the floor where I've strategically placed a bottle of lube, just in case tonight was the night. I flip it open and spill some into my palm. Nudging him until he slides halfway off my body, I grasp his dick in my lubed-up hand and stroke.

"Mother of—" he gasps, startled. "Fuck." For a split second I think he doesn't like it. But then he looks down at my hand around his cock, his eyes flashing, his color deep, and he makes a hungry, broken sound of pleasure.

Oh, hell yes. I stroke faster, craning my neck up to give him my mouth, too.

With a groan, he cups my hand in his, gathering both of us up in his long fingers. Pressing himself up on one hand, he begins thrusting earnestly.

"Ohhhh," I moan under his kiss. "So hot when you do that." I almost can't stand it—the heat and the friction between us, and Kieran's deep, driving grunt every time he thrusts against me. "I'm going to…"

Yup. I'm done. I dig my heels into the mattress and give him all my struggles—every ounce of soul-deep yearning erupts onto his hot body.

And it's beautiful the way he follows me with a happy groan and a long shudder. Then we're just two sticky guys, chests heaving, mouths chafed from aggressive kisses.

His heart thumps messily against mine. And I know I'm falling for him, whether I'm ready or not.

KIERAN

It's Monday again—our day off and my favorite day of the week. We slept in and fooled around, as is our habit. But now we're both up and showered and Rod is standing in the kitchen, proving himself to be a study in contrasts. He's got some loud punk music playing, and he's dancing around yelling along to some lyrics that seem to say "stick it to the man, stick it to the man" over and over again, as he pipes delicate icing onto a gingerbread cookie.

There is nowhere I'd rather be right now.

"Kieran!" he yells over the music. "Look!"

I cross the kitchen and peer over his shoulder at the cookie in front of him. "What the hell is that? A Christmas...polliwog?" That can't be right.

"Dude, it's a *sperm*." He glances at me like maybe I need to get my eyes checked. "I mean, I did a good job on the tail."

"Yes, you did." I chuckle. "But I don't know how many of those you can sell." Lately Roderick is obsessed with getting the Busy Bean's revenue up. He wants to prove his worth.

To me, he already has.

"They're not for Christmas! They're for Audrey's baby shower. She said there was no reason to be boring. There's going to be a cornhole competition with sperm-shaped beanbags."

"Wait—really? I thought she and Zara were just joking."

"Nope!" His laugh is gleeful. "I'm just playing to my audience, working with the baby-making theme."

"So you're feeding everyone a happy-faced sperm. Do sperm smile?"

"Mine do," he says, craning his neck to kiss the corner of my mouth. "I could give you a demonstration." He nuzzles my jaw, and I feel goosebumps rise up on my back.

It turns out that I like being touched. A lot. I've gotten very used to having his hands on my body. I step in close and kiss his neck. He smells like shampoo and vanilla cookies.

My phone rings, and since it's in my shirt pocket, we both hear it. Roderick steps away, and when I look at the screen, I curse. It's my mother, and I have not returned any of her recent calls. Rod turns down the music, and so, of course, now I have to answer.

"Hello?"

"Kieran. I'm so glad I caught you," my mother says. "I was hoping you could come out and cut a Christmas tree for us. You always pick such a good one. And Christmas is almost here."

Oh Lord. Today is one of the few days this week that I'm not scheduled to drive out there. "Kyle could do it, Ma. It'll take him twenty minutes."

"But you *always* cut the Christmas tree," she says. "And I never see you anymore. Your truck pulls up, and you do the chores, and then you leave before dinner. Rexie gets more time with you than I do."

She's right, of course. But why would I want to sit down at that table, where I don't feel welcome, and I haven't since I was a teen? Roderick's eyes flick over to me and they look a little nervous. He's the most observant person I've ever met, but somehow it never feels like an intrusion. *I see you*, his glance says.

"Ma, I'll cut the tree. But I can't stick around. There's a bunch of things I need to do today to get ready for another busy week."

"You'll stand it up in the living room, right?" she presses.

"Sure, so long as Kyle is there to help me."

"Okay," she says, giving a sniff. "It'll have to do."

"Give me like an hour," I tell her. After I disconnect the call, I text my brother to make sure he's available for this little charade.

"Everything okay?" Roderick asks.

"Yeah, you know, just the parents. They're exhausting." He leans over to decorate another cookie, and it gives me an idea. "Hey, Roddy?"

"Yes?"

"I gotta go to my folks' place for a couple hours."

"Oh. Okay." His shoulders droop. "I'll put the roast in while you're gone."

"I was going to ask if you want to come with me. You wanted a Christmas tree, right?"

He straightens up immediately, setting the pastry bag down with a thunk. "Of course I want a tree."

"Then drive out there with me. I'll cut down two, and we'll bring one home. We'll need a stand, though," I say, thinking this over. "And some lights."

"Not a problem," Rod says happily. "The drugstore has all that stuff. This is great! How big a tree do you think will fit in the living room? The ceiling is pretty high."

"Whoa there, fella. Just because we have a twelve foot ceiling doesn't mean we need a monster tree."

"Where do you cut trees around here, anyway?"

"Oh, on our farm," I say. "We have a couple rows of them planted, just for this."

"And they won't mind if one goes missing?" he asks, looking happy.

"They wouldn't dare. Who do you think pruned those fuckers this summer? Get your coat."

"It's the next turn-off," I say an hour later as I wind my truck up the hill toward my parents' place. A light snow has begun to fall.

"Kind of a long drive from the high school," Rod says.

"Yeah, but our land is zoned for Walden, which is a sending town." That's what we call a town that's not big enough to have its own high school. "We had school choice. And all our cousins went to Colebury. So did my parents."

"So it's a tradition to drive twenty miles to school."

"Pretty much. When I was in ninth grade, Kyle drove me. And of course my father had me take the driver's test the week of my birthday."

"Getting my license was like magic," he says, leaning his head against the headrest. "I wanted freedom so fucking bad."

"Same."

Roderick is humming a Christmas carol and looking out the passenger window. "It's pretty up here," he says as the snowflakes fall slowly past us.

"Yeah." But I feel suddenly reluctant to show him this place where I grew up. "It's not like my aunt Ruth's place, though. It's not party central."

"I'm just here to watch you chop down a tree with an ax."

"If I use a hand saw, is that a dealbreaker?"

"Nope!" he says cheerfully. "Just flex for me while you're doing it."

It's all fun and games until I pull up to find Kyle's truck missing. "Oh, hell."

"What's the matter?"

"My brother was supposed to be here to help me get the Christmas tree in the stand. Looks like he flaked out on me."

"I'll help you," Roddy says. "Unless you don't want me to come inside."

"No, it's fine," I say quickly. The truth is that I'd rather he didn't witness the awkward way my family exists near each other. We're like a constellation in the night sky—people associate the stars with one another, but those stars only look like a group. They're really millions of light years apart.

And I don't want to explain why I'm the reason everyone in this house is unhappy.

I park the car over by the tool shed. "Bundle up. We have to walk all the way over there." I point across the meadow.

"No problemo." Roderick puts on his gloves and hops out.

I get a saw out of the shed. As we're crossing the meadow, the farmhouse door opens and shuts. I hear a happy bark. Rexie streaks across the field, ears flying.

"Hey, boy!" I greet him by kneeling down, so he can do his best to push me over and lick my face. "Hey! Who's a good boy."

"Aw!" Rod says, clapping his hands together. "Isn't that adorable? Your dog and I have similar instincts when it comes to you."

I laugh even as my face heats. "You're not allergic to dogs, are you?"

"No, why?"

"I've been toying with the idea of bringing him home with me. But my dad wants to keep him, even though he's my dog."

"Ouch."

"If I didn't work two jobs, I'd've already kidnapped him." I scratch Rexie behind the ears. "My hours are long, though. Maybe Dad is right." Although I suspect he's keeping Rex out of pure stubbornness.

"Is that your Christmas-tree farm?" Rod asks, pointing at a row of nicely shaped Douglas firs.

"That's the spot. Show me the tree you like best. It will only take me a couple minutes to cut it. Carrying it back to the truck is the hard part." We can't bale it up like they do at a store.

"Excellent," Roddy says, rubbing his hands together. "This is like lumberjack porn, but real."

"Lumberjack porn is *not* a thing," I argue. "Nobody would watch that."

"I'd watch the hell out of it," he says simply. "I have a lumberjack kink, apparently."

He's ridiculous. But I still like hearing it.

"Well, this one is taller," Rod says, pacing around the tree at the end of a row. "But that one has the more perfect shape."

"God, just pick one," I grumble. I've already cut a tree for my parents and carried it across the meadow. We could have been done here fifteen minutes ago, but I didn't account for Roderick's over-analysis of Christmas-tree size and shape.

"You're an *artist*," he says, scandalized. "This kind of thing should matter to you."

"Trees aren't supposed to be perfect," I argue. "They grow the way they grow, and they don't care what you think. Pick a favorite?"

Rod does one more circle around one of the trees. "This one," he says. "I have chosen."

"Hallelujah." I drop to my knees, set the saw blade against the trunk, and start cutting.

"Oh baby," he says. "Work it. Work it."

I snort. "Want a turn? The pine sap smells good."

"Nah, I'll just lick it off you later."

I have to stop sawing, because I'm laughing so hard.

Christmas has its moments. Who knew?

RODERICK

When Kieran and I are alone together, he's loose and easy, and he talks more. He talks a lot, actually; he's much more open than he used to be. But the minute we approach his family's farmhouse with the tree, I can almost see the tent flaps go down. He stands the tree up and gives it a little shake, and his face is all business.

The door opens to reveal a middle-aged woman with Kieran's pretty eyes. "That's gorgeous!" she says. "Thank you, honey."

"Sure," Kieran grunts. "Mom, this is Roderick. My roommate."

"Hi, Roderick! So *you're* the roommate!"

"Yup," I say, bobbing my head nervously. "I'm the roommate. In the downstairs room. We have separate bathrooms." I clamp my lips together, trying to shut up, but Kieran's discomfort is contagious.

"Come in, come in!" she says, oblivious. "I made hot cocoa."

"Nice. Thank you, Mrs. Shipley." I follow Kieran inside. His arms are full of Christmas tree.

"Call me Sally!" she says brightly.

This stings a little, if I'm honest. It's my daydream to love a man who will introduce me to his mother. Not as his roommate, but as his partner.

I'd better stop falling for guys who won't do that. You'd think I'd learn.

The Shipley abode is another classic New England farmhouse with white clapboards and those electric candles in the windows. The floors are hardwood, and there's a fire in the fireplace.

It's not cozy, though. And not particularly comfortable. It's the kind of house with old-fashioned furniture and doilies on the tables. The kitchen table is in a claustrophobic little nook. When I look around at the furnishings, I'm struck by how different it is from our house on the Colebury green. Kieran chose a deep, comfortable couch for our living room, modern print pillows, and a plush rug.

Interesting.

Kieran carries the tree through to the living room, where a stern-faced man is sitting in a hardbacked chair. "Hello," he says in a low voice to me. "Kieran, thanks for cutting the tree." He winces, as if it pains him to say this. Or maybe he's just generally in pain.

"No problem," my man says quickly. "Roderick, if you could line this up at the base, I'll jam it down on the spikes."

"Sure." I drop to my knees and align the tree's trunk with the stand's metal ring. "Okay, go for it."

There's a very dirty joke I could make right now about jamming his log down through my ring. And I wonder why men don't introduce me to their moms.

"How's that, Dad? Straight?" Kieran asks.

His mother jumps in. "Two inches toward the window. Good. Now another two inches toward the door."

After a few minutes of fussing, I tighten the screws onto the trunk, while Kieran holds the top in the right spot.

"How's the desk job?" his father asks.

"Fine," Kieran says. "But the hours are long. Partly because of the holidays."

"And partly because they're jerks," I mutter, turning the last screw.

"I don't know about that job," Kieran's dad opines from his chair. "Long drive for low pay. You got *two* dead-end jobs. Can't make a career out of a coffee-shop job."

"*Dad*," Kieran gasps. "Leave it alone."

Luckily, I'm able to gulp back my bark of laughter in time. Because of course I'm trying to build a career from a coffee-shop job. And that goal is at the tippy-top of my list. Well, that and seeing Phish in concert.

When I stand up, my fingers are sticky with pine pitch. "Come, come!" Sally Shipley guides me to the kitchen. "Here's the lava soap. It will get that right off."

I accept this fussing, and also a little cup of weak cocoa and a bland cookie. Kieran wasn't kidding when he said his mom wasn't great in the kitchen. Cocoa is supposed to be dark and sinful. Or maybe that's just me.

Kieran drinks his propped against the counter, unable to hide the fact that he's counting the minutes until he can leave. His dog rises up onto his hind legs to beg from him. "No cookies for you," he says, scratching the dog between the ears.

I would totally give that dog a cookie, but he only has eyes for Kieran.

The kitchen door flies open, and Kyle steps through. "Hey! Sorry! I went to the pharmacy for Dad."

Kieran frowns but doesn't say anything.

"Can I help you put the tree up?" He takes off his coat.

"We did it already," I say. "It was no problem."

Kyle spins and notices me on the kitchen chair. His face creases in confusion. "Okay, thanks. I'll take care of the lights."

"Good plan," Kieran mumbles. "We have to take off."

"Already?" Kyle yelps. "It's your day off. You could stick around. We could watch a movie."

"I can't," Kieran says, setting down his empty cup. "Got a lot of errands to do. And another tree to set up at home."

"So just stay for lunch. Rexie would love it."

Oh, ouch. Kyle fights dirty.

"Nah. Maybe next time," Kieran says unconvincingly. "Gotta roll." He flips on the sink and rinses his cup.

I take the hint and drain the rest of my cocoa.

Sally Shipley bustles in and repeats the offer of lunch. Kieran declines just as quickly, but she follows us out the back door anyway. "Kieran? There's something I need to ask you."

He turns around, a wary look on his face. "Sure, Ma. What is it?"

"It's about the cows. Your brother has this big idea. He wants to do some angus crosses next year."

"Yeah, cool. Why not?" Kieran draws his keys out of his pocket.

"Your father hates the idea," she says. "Highlands are our breed. That's the way we've always done things."

"So? Is the way we do things always so great?"

Sally's mouth forms a hard line. Like she's trying really hard not to say anything. They just stare at each other for a moment, as if continuing some age-old argument through mental jiu-jitsu. "Just talk to Kyle," she says eventually. "Tell him it's not a good time."

"No," Kieran says forcefully. And everyone is surprised. Even Kieran. "Dad wants Kyle to step up around here. We all do. And when he does, his idea gets shot down."

"That's not just an idea," his mother hisses. "Changing our whole breeding program?"

"So he could do a few of them, not the whole herd." Kieran shrugs. "But it won't be me who talks to him. If you and Dad and Kyle need to make a decision, you can all sit down and discuss it like grownups."

"But Kyle listens to you," she tries.

"This is not my job. It's literally his job. I can't be your go-between."

"I see." She folds her arms across her chest. "Fine. Drive safe."

"I will," he says gently. "See you soon."

She looks down at her shoes. "I meant to tell you—we're going to your aunt Ruth's for Christmas. She's invited us all. I'm sure you won't mind that plan."

"Not at all," he says. "Sounds fun."

"Nice to meet you, Roderick," she says, recovering her polite face.

"My pleasure." I give her a small wave.

And then we're out of there. Kieran is silent until we're back in the truck and the engine is running. "Fuck," he says, blowing out a breath. "I'm sorry my father said that thing about dead-end jobs."

"Oh, I don't give a crap," I promise him. "I don't need your dad's permission to like my job."

"I know." He sighs. "But why can't people just keep their traps shut?"

"He's stuck in that chair, counting down to his next pain pill. He can't do his own job, and he feels super irrelevant."

"Damn." Kieran glances at me as he puts the truck into drive. "Accurate. All of it."

"I'm sorry I was such a goofball talking to your mom. I couldn't shut up about the whole roommates thing."

He shrugs. "You were fine. My parents aren't paying attention, anyway. Nobody in that house ever listens."

Except you, I privately add. Kieran listens more than he talks. And that house feels full of minefields. I don't know why, but it's clearly weighing on him. "Your brother didn't bail on you after all," I point out. "So that's something."

"Yeah. True."

"He misses you. Not quite as much as the dog, but…"

Kieran chuckles.

"By the way, Audrey invited me over on Christmas. Is it okay if I come?"

"Sure," he says, perking up. "Of course you can come. Christmas at their place is much more fun than Christmas here." He jerks a thumb over his shoulder. "It's a big party."

"Cool." We wind down the dirt driveway toward the main

road. And I try to think Christmassy thoughts again. Audrey is making ham, with a million side dishes. I offered to make a Bûche du Noël, which is a Christmas cake shaped and frosted to look like a yule log.

Kieran and I can go there together. Except not really *together*, and that's going to eat at me. Even though I understand that Kieran is still just figuring out his sexuality. And I wouldn't ever pressure someone to come out.

The holidays always bring this stuff into high relief. When I was with Brian, he'd fly home to his parents' place in Georgia without me. And I'd stay home alone, or go to the movies with a few LGBT friends that I saw a little less often every passing year.

I love the holidays, but they make me broody. And here I am with a fresh Christmas tree in the back of Kieran's truck, that he cut down just for me. Why can't I just enjoy it?

KIERAN

Two days before Christmas, I have to go to Burlington on our day off. The art school dean wants to give me an interview and a portfolio review before they decide on my application.

So I'm scowling in front of my closet, wondering what the hell a guy wears to something like that. And wondering if I own it.

"Is something wrong?" Roderick asks, entering the room. "You just made a grumpy noise."

I pluck a white shirt out of the closet. "Is this my nicest button down? You don't think I'm supposed to wear a tie do you?"

"No tie," he says lightly, taking the shirt from my hand and holding it up to the light. "This one is fine. But it isn't the one I'd choose."

I take a step back from the closet and close my eyes, like a man condemned. "This is why I was just going to audit a class or two. I never asked to be *interviewed*, for fuck's sake. Or to submit a portfolio."

"It was a terrific portfolio," Rod says, flipping through my shirts.

"But this isn't just about learning now," I argue. "It's paying people to judge me."

"That's one take on it." Rod laughs. "There's a reason nobody uses that as a university slogan."

"Am I a better person if I get a diploma on a piece of paper?"

"No." Rod pulls a shirt from the closet. It's white, with a conservative navy-blue check running through it. "If this fits you, wear this with dark jeans. And tuck it in."

"Jeans?"

"This is Vermont. And nobody is trying to make you into someone you're not, Kieran. The only point of this exercise is to get half price on courses that you already want to take."

"I hate interviews," I grumble, pulling on the shirt.

"You don't say." He snickers. "It isn't a parole hearing, honey. Go in there and smile at the nice lady so she'll give you money for art school."

"Parole hearing." I snort, reaching for my dark jeans. "You have first-hand experience with those?"

"No, but the day is young. Now quit whining and get out of here. You look hot in that shirt, by the way. Be a good boy, and I'll take it off you later."

That's as good a motivation as any. So I go. Reluctantly.

Things start off pretty well with the interviewer. Dean Eloise Rubinstein is a comfortable-looking woman in her mid-sixties. Rod would probably compliment her earrings and chat her up about the art on the walls of her office. But I'm intimidated by the abstract art on the walls and the grand office overlooking the sculpture garden.

"So tell me, Kieran, why do you want to go to art school?"

I've been expecting this question. But that doesn't mean I have a satisfying answer. "Well, that's the thing. I never did apply to art school. You basically talked me into it."

She laughs, which is a good sign, I guess. "Yet, here you are. So how exactly did we arrive here?"

"Right. Well, I've been taking online classes in design. I never tried to become the next great artist. That's not how I look at my designs. But I enjoy making things, and I'd like to make *better* things. And—if it's possible—I would like to find a way to make a living at it."

She nods encouragingly.

The rest comes out in a rush. "So that's why I thought I'd audit some classes. Because you guys know things that I don't."

"See, that's actually a pretty good attitude for starting an art program. And there are more people than you can shake a stick at making a living from their art, either directly or indirectly."

"That's good news."

"When did you first realize you cared about the visual arts?" she asks.

"Oh, I was just that kid who was always drawing," I tell her. "Teachers liked it. They used to tell me I was creative and put my drawings in the middle of the bulletin board. But when I hit my teen years, I stopped drawing in public. I got the message that art wasn't a cool thing for boys to do. And I didn't take any art classes for a really long time."

She flinches. "You're not the first person to sit in this office who had that experience. I worry about all the boys—and girls—who are told not to express themselves this way. So what got you started again?"

"Farming," I say with a chuckle. "My parents needed to list some products for sale from our website. My mother asked me if I could design something that looked professional. So I started noodling with designs. My younger cousin does the art for his family farm, too, and he introduced me to Photoshop. I liked it so much that I dove right in."

"What did you like about it?"

"I liked how practical it was," I admit. "If you make a mistake in paint, it can be hard to fix. But Photoshop lets you undo anything. Copy anything. Try anything. The result is a little less interesting than a painting or a drawing. But I guess I'm an awfully practical guy."

She beams.

"And one day I wondered if I could make extra money doing this fun thing that I'd taken up as a hobby. So I typed 'Photoshop' into a jobs board. That's how I lucked into a design-rendering job at an ad agency. They didn't care that I have no formal training. They thought it was a plus, honestly, because they pay me almost nothing, and I'm still happy to show up every day."

"Ah," she says with a sad smile. "Many young artists are familiar with the problem."

"Sure. So I've made a lot of digital art for them. But I also started painting at home when I have free time. Which is almost never, especially during the holidays. There's no daylight when I'm home from the ad agency, and there's been a lot of overtime in the last month. That's why none of my paintings made it into the portfolio I sent you."

"Okay. And the work in your portfolio was mostly done at the ad agency?" she asks.

"Exactly. I made a lot of notes so you could tell what was mine and what I'd been given to work with." God, it's probably the weirdest portfolio she's ever received. But I only had ten days to pull something together.

"I read your notes," she said slowly. "But maybe you can talk me through how you put one of your pieces together. I like to hear how artists think."

"Well, I'll try." I let out a nervous laugh. I'm sweating, and I hope she can't tell.

The dean opens my portfolio—which is really just a binder from Staples—to a poster I did for the Farmers' Market Association. "This is my favorite piece. Can you tell me where you got the inspiration?"

"Well, sure." I clear my throat. "As I wrote in my note, this was the one time they barely gave me any instructions. The boss basically said, 'You come from a family of farmers. Just see what you can come up with.'"

She smiles. "Are you related to the Shipleys who make cider? That's your family, too?"

My body flashes hot and then cold again, the way it often does when I get this question. "That's one side of the family. They raise apples and dairy. We raise beef. So I've spent a lot of time at farmers' markets."

"And how did you choose this design?"

I look down at my drawing of a red, vintage pickup truck carrying produce. "Well, the first design I made had a purple beet filling the page, with stylized text stacked inside it. It was very bright and contemporary, and I loved it. But the boss said he wanted more variety. It can't represent just one farmer, you know?"

"Sure," she says mildly.

"My grandpa once drove a truck just like this one," I say, pointing at the drawing. "His was black, but it had those curvy vintage wheel wells. I used to sit on the tailgate with him while my grandma sold apples. The truck had a lot of farmers' market cred. And, in the drawing, the truck bed gave me a place to stack some more imagery." There's lots of produce in back, but the sizes aren't true-to-life. There's an enormous melon, a freakishly large ear of corn, an elephantine tomato, and a towering carrot. "I was thinking about those colorful French posters while I drew it. So I gave it a vintage text treatment, too."

"Lovely," she says. "And the logo? I like how the spade and the pitchfork are crossed, like a knife and fork."

"Yeah, I like it too. But that's not my work. I said so in my note."

"Mmh," she says. "So I have another question for you, and it's a little difficult. But just bear with me a second, okay? I received another portfolio, with some overlapping elements." She pulls out a leather folio and flips it open to a page that's marked with a sticky note. Then she turns it toward me.

For a moment, I'm super confused. It's a drawing of a hot-air balloon I did for a festival in Quechee last June. But someone added textured effects to each of the balloon segments. The result is hideous. "What the—?"

But even as the words are leaving my mouth, I realize that I already know who did this. And I'm so aggravated that I stand up suddenly, causing my chair to jerk back a few inches. Feeling like a brute, I sit down just as quickly. Then I take a deep breath and try to speak through my anger. "I sure hope there was a note in that portfolio, too, explaining who drew the balloon before it was attacked by clipart patterns."

Slowly, the dean shakes her head.

I tilt my head back and let out a heavy sigh. I can't believe Deacon Pratt took that balloon, gave it a nasty makeover and submitted it as his own. I can't believe he even wants to go to art school.

Working for the Pratts really is a dead-end job. And—insult to injury—this means my asshole father was right.

"Kieran," the dean says. "Why don't you tell me about the version in your portfolio."

"Sure," I say woodenly. "I drew the version in my portfolio. It's in there because I wanted to include something I'd done in ink on paper. They wanted it to look handmade, so I freehanded it. But you can see it's not the best." I feel deflated, though. This woman is probably suspicious of everything coming out of the Pratt Agency now.

I hate my life.

"I liked your version better," she says gently. "I suppose you can guess where this other one came from."

"Sure." My voice is flat. "There aren't that many suspects."

"Well, I'm sorry to have brought it up. But I needed to know why I received two very similar portfolios."

I sit up a little straighter in my chair. "Are there more like this?"

She nabs the other portfolio off the table and sets it on the floor on her side of the desk. "Yes. But I'm not going to show you. It will only make you angry. It's obvious who is coming up with the ideas, and who is just tarting them up."

A wave of nausea rolls through me. "Crap. This isn't how I wanted this interview to go," I say in a rare burst of candidness.

"I bet. But take a deep breath, okay? You did a nice job explaining your process to me. And I've been admiring that farmers' market poster for two years now."

"Yeah?" I smile in spite of myself.

"Of course. It's cheery. And now I've met the artist, so I like it even more." She flips my portfolio closed, then hands it to me. "It was a pleasure meeting you, Kieran. In a couple of days, you'll receive notification about your application. But if you're accepted, your financial aid award won't arrive for another couple of weeks, okay? I'm asking the financial aid office to squeeze in your application, even though it's past the deadline. I hope that works."

"Me too," I say. "And thank you." I stand up and shake her hand. I make all the right polite noises.

But if that financial aid doesn't come through, this was a waste of time.

"How'd it *go*?" is how Roddy answers his phone.

"It went okay," I say, staring up at an impossibly blue sky. "If they take me, I'm going to go."

"Yaaaas!" he thunders into my ear. "This is so exciting."

I smile, because his voice makes me happy. I still don't know if art school is the right choice for me. But if I get to go home to him every night, it might not matter. "I have to swing through Montpelier on the way home," I tell him now. "What should I pick up for dinner?"

"Let's make a lasagna."

"Sounds good." Cooking anything with Roddy is always good.

"Bring home a couple pounds of ground meat, a box of those flat noodles, and... Got a pen? I have big ideas."

"How about you text your big ideas to me while I drive to the store?"

"An excellent idea, hunk. This is going to be great."

I already know it's true.

KIERAN

On Christmas morning I wake up alone. Music rises from down-stairs, along with the beckoning scents of coffee and frying bacon. It's only seven, and I don't have to be anywhere for once in my life. I could roll over and go back to sleep.

Except bacon.

I get up, shuffle into the bathroom to brush my teeth, and then trundle downstairs. Roderick is making French toast and singing away to Jane's Addiction.

"Hey!" he says, flashing me a quick smile. "Do you have the timing or what? I'm making French toast. Want to help?" He's wearing sweatpants, messy hair, and my oldest flannel shirt. "Have you made this before? It's easy." He glances at me over his shoulder.

"What? No. Show me." I put my arms around his waist and look down at the counter. He's got some bread soaking in a dish full of an eggy mixture.

"It's a great way to use up stale bread. And it's eggier than pancakes, so there's more protein."

"Nice," I say, kissing the back of his neck. This must be why people like Christmas. I get it now.

"I use a little cinnamon in the custard. But that's really it. If you start with good bread, the flavor takes care of itself." He uses both hands to flip one soaked slice of bread into the skillet, where it sizzles. Then he turns his head to speak to me. "Your cuddle game has seriously improved. I'm so impressed. Top marks from the Russian judge."

I laugh into his neck and kiss him again. "I have a Christmas present for you to unwrap."

"Is it in your pants?" He nudges his ass against my crotch, and my body does not fail to take the hint. "I love opening presents," he teases.

"No, it's under the tree."

"Okay, here's what we're going to do. You flip the French toast, and I'm going to grab your present out of my car." He turns around in my arms, kisses me, then slides away to dart outside.

I tap my foot to his loud alt-rock and wonder how my life became so fantastic.

"Oh my God," Roddy says a few minutes later as he drops to his knees in front of our Christmas tree. "Is that what I think it is?"

"Yeah. Some things just can't be wrapped." I take a big bite of French toast. It's terrific—crunchy on the outside with a custardy center.

Meanwhile, Roddy pounces on the guitar case under the tree, untying the bow I lamely strung around one end. "I can't believe you did this! Please tell me you got a good deal on a secondhand instrument."

"I bought it new," I confess. Secondhand for a gift just didn't feel right. "I hope it's the right style."

He lifts the lid. "It's *awesome*. God. So much nicer than my old one. You really shouldn't have done this."

"I wanted to," I say before casually stuffing my face with more breakfast. The fact that he's so excited does unusual things to my heart. He looks, as they say, like a kid on Christmas, as he lifts the guitar out of its case and runs a thumb across the strings.

The deep tones give me a shiver. It really does sound good. I've never been happier to spend four hundred dollars in my life.

Forgetting his breakfast, Roderick fusses with the tuning. And then he launches into a pretty riff, right there on the rug.

I give a low whistle. "I thought you said you weren't very good?"

He shakes his head. "I'm not Nashville good. But I sure like to play. Kieran, seriously, this is just amazing." He lets out a happy little sigh and then carefully tucks the guitar back into its case. "My present for you isn't as fancy."

"I don't need anything at all," I insist. And right that minute it's true. "Eat your breakfast."

"But it's your turn." He pinches a bite of bacon off his plate and pops it into his mouth before ducking out of the room. He returns with a wrapped box and hands it to me. It's still cold from sitting outside in his car.

I rip the paper off and open the box. Inside I find two things: a flannel shirt in a cognac color and a hardcover cookbook by someone named Christopher Kimball. The cover is shiny and new, but there are already a bunch of those sticky flags jutting out of the pages. "Hey, thanks! Did you pick out some recipes for me? But what happened to, 'You can't learn to cook from a book'?"

"Hey—we're still cooking together. But this way you can be in charge of the menu if you want. Christopher Kimball has some Vermont cred, by the way. I flagged a bunch of dishes that we're set up to make. Like, I skipped anything that required a food processor or too much attention."

I run my hand over the cover, imagining all the time we'll spend together cooking. "Thank you. The shirt is nice, too."

"Well, that was a selfish purchase. The flannel speaks to my lumberjack fetish. And that color will look great with your eyes."

"Whatever you say." I laugh, pulling it out of the box. "I just like the fabric."

"Good." He gets up and comes to sit next to me on the couch. "Thank you for that outrageous present. I love it so much."

"I really liked giving it to you," I say, feeling more than a little self-conscious. "Now let's eat this food before it gets cold.

Rod picks up his plate. "I'm going to get some jam for my French toast."

"Wait." I say, pointing at the little jug of syrup I'd brought out here with me. "You like jam better than Vermont's finest?"

Roderick shrugs without meeting my eyes. "Both are good."

"But which do you like better?" I press.

"What does it matter?" he asks, biting another strip of bacon.

"It matters because you feed me all the time, but you won't use the syrup I brought here for both of us."

"I like feeding people. It's my profession. And that stuff is expensive," he says.

"It would be," I concede, "except that Kyle and I made it." I grab a piece of bacon and bite off the salty, wonderful end.

He blinks up at me. "Really? That's neat. My lumberjack. Do you carry around an ax while you tap the trees?"

"You're changing the subject." And I am really terrible at working through something like this. But my breakfast smells really good and Roderick looks so right in my living room. I like having him here, and I need him to know it. "What if I like feeding you, too? Maybe it makes me happy to share groceries."

"It's not personal. I just don't want to owe you. My ex was really weird about it. He made me feel like a slacker."

"Well, I won't," I say abruptly. And then a bunch of nonsense comes tumbling out of my mouth. "And when you won't eat the food I've bought, I really can't tell if we're a team at all. It's like you don't want to give me that satisfaction of helping you."

Roderick flinches. He takes a bite and chews. "Honestly, I really didn't plan to *like* you so much. I wasn't looking for more than a roommate and then a hookup. I thought I'd make you orgasm a few times and send you off to find a boyfriend. But you are irresistible."

"I don't want any other boyfriend." *Just you*.

"Yeah, maybe I'm irresistible, too. If you like hot messes with car trouble and relationship baggage."

"Maybe that's my fetish," I say, cramming another big bite into my mouth.

"It must be." We eat in silence for a couple of minutes.

Roderick sets his plate down and then grabs mine and sets it down, too. He climbs into my lap, straddling me. "Merry Christmas, lumberjack. For someone who claims to hate Christmas, you're pretty good at it."

"It's not so bad," I say, kissing his jaw, then nosing into his hair to take a deep breath. He smells like bacon and all the good things in life. If you'd told me two months ago that I could be so wrapped up in another man's embrace, I would have thought you were crazy. But here I am, holding Roderick on the sofa.

My *boyfriend*. I try that word on in my head. It seems odd, but I like the concept a whole lot. I like making breakfast together in the kitchen and opening presents under our tree. "Can we please make another slice of French toast, with syrup?"

Roderick laughs in my arms. "Sure. But I thought you were about to say—can we please have some sex? I have a one-track mind." He kisses my neck and then slips his hands up under my T-shirt.

"Mmh." The contact with his skin makes me feel electric. "Now that you mention it, I like this idea."

Roddy doesn't argue the point. Instead, he puts his hand down my pants and strokes my thickening cock. His lips move sweetly across my throat. I can't help it—I thrust into his hand.

"Kieran," he says against my skin. "There's one more present I got you for Christmas. But now I'm not sure if I should show it to you."

"Unngh," I groan. "Show me later."

"Well, it's relevant to the topic." He slides a piece of paper out of his shirt pocket and unfolds it. "Look, I got tested again."

I squint at it for a fractional second. "That's good, right?"

"Yeah, I wanted a follow-up, because of the cheater. And I thought…" He clears his throat. "Well, I thought maybe you'd feel better about fucking me if you knew I was healthy. In case that was holding you back."

"Oh." I lean back on the couch and sigh. "That was never holding me back. You're just plain tasty." I run a hand up his chest to prove my point. "But we have a lot of fun the way things are. And sex makes me think of…" It's not easy to say out loud.

"You can just tell me," he says quickly. "Not everybody likes the idea of anal."

"Oh, I like it fine as a concept. But I don't have any game at all. Before…" I pause again. This is super awkward. "I don't think I ever satisfied anyone. Least of all me. And with you—it's not like I'll suddenly know what I'm doing."

Roderick doesn't laugh, although I'm not sure I'd blame him. He strokes a thumb across my stubbly cheek and looks me right in the eyes. "That sounds stressful. I get it. But what if this wasn't an Olympic event? I just want to be that close to you."

"Oh," I say slowly. "I don't suppose there's a book to teach me this, too? You could put flags on the relevant pages."

Now he smiles. "Sounds like a really fun book. Especially if there were illustrations."

"There should be."

Roddy leans down and kisses the corner of my mouth. Just once. "Tell you what—we could do this *mise en place*."

"What?"

"You know when I teach you a new recipe, I arrange all the ingredients so that you can focus on the technique?"

"Yeah," I say warily.

"Come on." He climbs off my lap, then tugs on one of my hands. "Come in here for a second."

I let him lead me into the kitchen. "You fry up the rest of the French toast, because it freezes well, for reheating later." He hands me the spatula. "And come upstairs when you hear Adele." He turns the music back on.

"Adele?" I repeat, a little confused.

"Yeah. It's a ways down the playlist. Meanwhile, I'm going upstairs to prep for you. When Adele starts singing, then you come upstairs. You still don't have to do a thing you don't want to. But just consider it."

Then he turns up the music and turns to leave. "Oh, and make a pot of coffee. For after." Then he goes.

KIERAN

I fry up the rest of the French toast, and do a few dishes. But I can barely concentrate.

Maybe Rod knew what this would do to me. Anticipation is a powerful drug. Even if I'm inexperienced, I'm still curious. And horny as fuck.

What's he doing up there, anyway? He's probably stroking himself, which is enough to make me crazy. But maybe he's also got the lube out. His slicked-up fingers are probably thrusting lazily in and out—

I groan uncomfortably. My flannel pants are tented with arousal. I don't think Adele is anywhere on this playlist. I've heard every other musical artist on three continents already, but Adele is behaving like Kyle right now—late, when I need her most.

Finally, she sings the first line of "Hello." I throw down the dish towel and abandon Adele and the kitchen. I climb the stairs with a thumping heart, slowing my pace as I reach the top. It was only a couple of months ago when I dared Rod to meet me upstairs.

Is it crazy to wonder if his heart was pounding, too? I always assume that he's more confident than I am about almost everything. But it was hard to miss the plea in his eyes when he said, *I want to be that close to you.*

So here I am right outside the room where I may or may not fuck a man for the first time. A man I'm totally falling for. No big deal.

I take a shaky breath and step through the doorway. And then I practically swallow my tongue. Rod lies on one hip, hair damp from a recent shower. His bare, golden skin flexes over rippling muscle as he fucks himself with a toy in one hand, his cock in the other.

Good. Lord. I've never seen anything so erotic. For a moment I stand like a dummy, the music from downstairs still vibrating through my chest.

He turns his head, watching me watch him. "I've *always* liked putting on a show for you. When you look at me like that? So hot, baby."

Suddenly, I'm no longer content to watch. I stalk into the room, removing my shirt as I go.

"Yes," Rod whispers, his eyes hooded. "Show me more."

My skin flashes with heat as I drop my flannel pants. My gaze is fixated on his cock, so hard and flushed against his palm. I want it in my mouth. So I kick my clothes aside, brace one knee on the bed, and knock his hand away.

"Yes, fuck!" He curses when I swallow him down. His fingers weave into my hair and tug. I love it. I will never get tired of this. And after a few minutes sucking his cock, I'm all worked up and basically humping the bed.

"Kieran," Roddy grunts. "I'm close. If you ever wanted to fuck me, now would be a good time." He takes a deep, gasping breath. "Just saying."

That sounds like a damn good idea all of a sudden. I release him with a pop and sit up, face flushed, cock painfully hard.

"Here," Rod says, tossing me the lube. "If you want a condom, I can find one."

I barely hear him. I'm too busy flipping open the tube and

drizzling the liquid onto my unbearably hard dick. When I use my hand to spread it around, Rod licks his lips, his clear eyes fixed on the motion of my hand.

And now I realize that hesitating was stupid. I won't fail at this because I've already won some kind of karmic lottery.

"Now," he grunts, tossing the toy onto the floor, then rolling onto all fours, presenting me with his ass. It's a vulnerable, trusting position, and I don't plan to let him down.

Moving into place, I grasp his hips in my hands. And finally I fit the blunt head of my cock against his hole.

Roddy doesn't want me to go slow. He rocks back, seeking me, his head dropped with expectation. I slide slowly inside the tight grip of his body.

"Fuck yes. Fuck yes," he chants. "More."

I can't rush this, though. It's too amazing. I watch my cock disappear into my boyfriend's tight ass, until I bottom out, stunned by the full-body embrace of our joining, and barely able to breathe through my excitement.

"Baby, you feel amazing," he whispers.

I need a deep, steadying breath before I can move. He feels so fucking good. I pull out slowly, the slickness of the lube making each motion into a sensuous slide. Then I push inside again, tugging his hips back, tightening our connection. Everything is wow. The pleasure is so intense that I can't help picking up the pace.

"Yes. God. Harder. Don't stop," Roderick chatters as we move together. He puts his forearms down on the bed, changing the angle of our connection. "There. Ungh. *God*," he tells the bed. "*Fuck*." He turns his sweaty face to check mine. He must like what he sees, because he closes his eyes and smiles.

I'm such a sucker for that smile. "I need your mouth," I grunt. "Right now."

"Then push me down already," he pants. "Take what you want."

I don't need to be told twice. I roll us onto our sides, wrapping an arm around his waist, pulling his body flush against mine. All that contact makes my body flash hot. My questing mouth clumsily greets his, and we both groan as lips and tongues slide together in sync.

I can't move as much in this position, but it's probably just as well. I already feel like a Fourth of July firecracker with the fuse lit. So I palm Roddy's cock and start stroking, while I slowly fuck him. We're communicating only with breaths and tongues now, but I can tell he's close. I'm *past* close, hanging on from sheer determination. I coast a hand down to give a gentle tug on his balls, while I pump my hips as hard as I dare. And finally it happens. Rod lets out a shout, and then all his muscles tense at once.

Even before I feel him shoot, I'm there—groaning and shuddering and gasping like a runner crossing the finish line.

At last, I sag onto the mattress, feeling rung out and victorious. "Fuck. I love Christmas." I come dangerously close to adding, *I love you, too.* We don't use those words. But I've never felt this way about anyone.

Roddy lies in my arms, breathing hard. "Thank you for trying my latest recipe. I hope we can make it again sometime."

"Oh, this will be in heavy rotation on the menu." I withdraw from him and ease off the bed. "Don't move, okay?" I duck into the bathroom to get a damp cloth for him. And after a quick cleanup, I pull up the comforter when I come back to bed, wrapping an arm around him, because my cuddling game really *has* improved a ton.

"Are you sleepy?" he asks.

"No." But that doesn't mean I want this quiet moment to end.

"What time are we supposed to go to your aunt Ruth's?"

"We're due at three," I say, which is hours from now. Feeling tender toward him, I roll onto his body and kiss him again. I love the feel of his hard body under mine. And I love the way he gazes up at me, smiling. "Did you get enough breakfast?" I seem to remember he didn't eat much of it.

"Yeah, but I didn't get enough coffee." He runs a hand through my hair. "I made a pot and then forgot to drink it when—"

His gaze flicks to the side. He startles and his eyes get wide.

I crane my neck to follow his gaze. But by the time I do that, my cousin Griffin is already turning away from my bedroom door. A beat later, his feet pound down the stairs.

"Oh, shit," Roddy breathes. "Oh my God. Where did he come from?"

That did not just happen. That did *not just happen*.

I leap out of bed, as if that makes any sense at all. As if I could undo the scene that Griff just stumbled upon. I duck into the bathroom and turn on the shower. Not waiting for the water to heat, I step under the cold spray and rinse the sex from my body. It's only fitting that my whole body is covered with goosebumps.

Griffin saw me in bed with Roderick. Holy shit.

I cannot *imagine* what Griff is thinking right now. I didn't see the look on his face. Was it disgust? I shiver, and I don't even know if it's the cold water or the situation.

Less than two minutes later I step out of the shower to find Roderick standing there, fully dressed. He hands me a towel. "Baby, he's still out there," he says quietly. "I can see his truck from the bedroom window. I think he's waiting for you."

"Shit." I have no idea what I'm going to say.

"I'm really sorry," he whispers.

"Not your fault," I grunt.

"I know but…" He groans. "Christmas dinner."

"Yeah." That only makes the whole thing about a hundred times worse. In a couple hours I'm supposed to look my entire extended family in the eye.

And Griff got an eyeful of me naked on top of Roderick. My day went from terrific to horrific in the space of five minutes.

Cursing, I stumble into my jeans and yank on a shirt. I walk downstairs like a man headed for the gallows. When I step into my shoes and open the front door, Griff is sitting at the top of the porch steps, his back to me.

He doesn't turn around, and a little bolt of fear runs down my spine. Besides Kyle, Griff is the person I'm closest to. I can't stand the idea of him turning his back on me.

Then he moves over a bit, making room for me to sit beside him, and I feel just a millimeter better.

I sit down and wait, while Griff studies his hands. Eventually he clears his throat. "Talk," he says. "Is this a new thing?"

That's surprisingly hard to answer. "Yes and no? I don't know. I never dated anyone before now. But, well…" I'm so uncomfortable right now that I wish I could just disappear from this Earth. "I guess it's been a long time coming."

"I had no idea," he says to his shoes. "None. You never said a word."

"No kidding."

"*Why?*" The word is surprisingly harsh. "My sister is bisexual. You *know* we don't care."

"But it's weirder among guys," I say quietly. It sounds like a cop-out.

"Is it? If Dylan was gay, I wouldn't feel differently about him…" Griff puts his head in his hands. "Shit. I'm not trying to make this about me. Never mind. I'm just surprised, that's all. That you'd carry that around and not tell anybody. Is this why you moved out of your house?"

Yes. "Partly. I was just so stuck in a rut at home. Dad and I fight. Kyle doesn't step up, even though he's supposed to run the place with Dad."

Griffin lifts his head and looks me in the eye for the first time. "Does Kyle know about you and the baker? He doesn't, does he?"

I shake my head.

"That one time he was shooting off his mouth about you living with a gay guy. *Jesus.* You must have wanted to strangle Kyle."

"A little," I admit. "But Kyle isn't the big problem, okay?"

"Who is? Your dad?"

"Yeah. It's like…" There's no way I can make Griffin understand, because he doesn't know my other secrets. "I'm not ready to come clean about Roderick, because it's one more thing for Dad to comment on. I don't want to discuss my personal life."

My cousin listens quietly. "Okay. I get it. Sort of. I won't say anything when I go home. Or later today."

"Ugh." Fucking holiday. "Why did you, uh, end up in my bedroom anyway?"

Griffin laughs. "I brought you a dresser. Remember I said I'd ask my mom?"

"Oh. And she just had a dresser lying around?"

"Yeah. Anyway, I loaded it into the truck and also took six pies to the church for their Christmas supper." He points at the church, just across the green. "Two birds, one stone, right? You didn't answer your door, but it was open, and I heard music. Your kitchen has breakfast all over the counters—thanks for that strip of bacon, by the way—and since nobody answered when I called your name, I went upstairs."

It all makes perfect sense. And now my face is burning up again.

"You can bet I won't make that mistake again."

I let out a groan.

"Looking you both in the eye this afternoon will be a little tricky, since I'll be trying not to laugh." He lets out a snicker. "Roderick is coming over, right?"

"Yeah," I say in a low voice. "He has nowhere else to go."

"Oh right—Mom said something about his parents being dicks."

"Aunt Ruth did not use the word *dick*."

"I'm paraphrasing." He grins.

That's the moment I know that Griff and I will be okay. Kyle wouldn't understand, and Dad might treat me like a freak show, but Griffin and I will be fine.

"So let's unload this fucker, okay?" Griff stands up and walks down toward his truck. "If I don't get home soon, Audrey is going to ask what took so long. And I'm going to have to make up some shit about an alien abduction or something so as not to let the world in on your big secret, if you're not willing to tell."

"I am *not* willing to tell." I follow him down to the truck, and he lets down the tailgate.

Griff hops up on the truck and slides the furniture toward me. "Ready?"

"Let's do this. But, uh…" We lift at the same time and I ease the dresser back slowly, giving Griffin a chance to join me on the ground again. "We can't carry this into my room right now."

"Why not?"

"Can't walk in there with you yet. Maybe not ever." The bed is *right* there. I'm still embarrassed.

"It's okay—I'm stopping on the way home for eye bleach," he says.

Then I laugh. The tension inside me breaks, and I keep on laughing.

"Who's going to carry it up the stairs with you?" Griffin huffs as we ease the dresser up onto the porch.

"Roddy," I gasp, still laughing.

"I can't believe the first guy you've ever dated happens to be named *Rod*," Griffin says. "I suppose it could be worse. Dicky, maybe. Or Hammer."

It's very difficult to carry a piece of furniture while laughing. We have to set it down just inside the door, so I can catch my breath.

Before he goes, Griffin wraps an arm around me. It's half-wrestling maneuver, half-hug. "I still get to tease you, punk."

"But not during dinner today."

"Yeah. I saw nothing." He gives me a manly squeeze. "Jokes aside—this is good, though, right? Sometimes we worry about you being kinda solitary. Although, not this morning." He chuckles.

"Yeah, it is good. But it's still private."

"Is it ever going to be public?"

"Doubt it."

"Okay. I sort of get it. See you in a while." He whacks me on the back one more time and lets himself out the front door.

"Thank Ruth for the dresser!" I call after him.

"You can thank her later. Don't bail, because you'll be putting me on the spot."

"Okay," I say before shutting the door.

Although bailing sounds pretty good right now. What the hell have I done?

RODERICK

The whole time Kieran and Griffin are outside, I'm a wreck. First, I pace the living room, hoping to somehow develop X-ray vision so I can see them through the oak front door. When that proves fruitless, I clean up the kitchen instead.

Finally, when I'm back to pacing again, they reappear in the driveway. I see Griffin grab Kieran into a hard hug and pat him on the back several times before releasing him.

Only then can I breathe again. I would never wish a sudden, unplanned outing on anyone. But hugging is a good sign.

I hide in my room when they come inside with the dresser. When Griffin finally leaves, I come bursting out of there. "Are you okay? That was… I'm sorry." I babble. "Do you feel any better after speaking with him?"

"Fuck no," he says, trudging into the living room to flop down on the couch. "What a mess. Griffin isn't going to tell anyone. But he's, like, Mr. Honesty. So I'm basically forcing him to lie to his wife and our entire extended family on my behalf. It's a disaster."

"So *don't* force him?" The words slip out, even though I know it's the wrong time to make this point. Kieran is in shock right now. He's not ready to hear that staying in the closet is a choice.

The horrified look on his face is proof of that. "Roddy, I'm not you."

"I know you're not," I quickly agree. "We're walking different parts of the path."

"That doesn't even begin to cover it," he says. "It doesn't matter how nice Griffin was to me just now. The timing is terrible."

A very familiar panic begins to percolate inside me. "You feel this way right now because you had a scare. But once you have a little while to get used to the idea, you might realize that it's not so terrifying to show people who you really are."

"Not happening," Kieran snaps. "That is not how it works for me."

His sudden anger is so shocking that I spend a long beat trying to figure out how I made him so mad. And I've got nothing. "Look, I know your family is important to you."

"You don't know the first thing about it," he says icily. "Griffin isn't the problem."

"Then tell me what is," I fire back. He only scowls. "I'm not trying to paint some rosy picture for you. I promise you that. But your cousins love you. One of them is bisexual, for fuck's sake. Your dad is kind of a dick already. Is he really going to get any worse if he knows you like men?"

I take a badly needed breath into the silence that follows. I don't know how we got here, arguing about whether or not Kieran can come out. This whole thing is probably my fault. I should have locked the door after I got his Christmas present out of the car. And I shouldn't pressure him. Especially on *Christmas*, for fuck's sake.

"Rod," he says tiredly. "It's almost time to go. I have to go find a nice shirt to wear."

"Make sure it's a really straight-looking one." It's a cruel thing to say, and I know it. So cruel that his eyes widen in shock. He waits for me to explain myself, or at least laugh it off somehow.

But I don't. I just sit back against the couch cushions and close my eyes. "You should go, so you're not late." That's as conciliatory as I can manage to be.

"Are you ready to go?" he asks quietly.

"Yes."

He gets up and climbs the stairs, while I sit on the couch feeling like a complete shit. Kieran had a stressful moment with his cousin, and instead of listening, I threw a tantrum. I pushed him away, because I'm terrified that he's going to end up like Brian—trapped in the closet, with me in there with him.

It's not an idle fear. Kieran clearly isn't ready. This is all new to him.

But not to me, unfortunately. Nothing about this is new at all. And I promised myself I wouldn't end up here again. I *promised*.

Kieran comes back down the stairs a few minutes later, wearing a nice blue button-down shirt that I cannot even compliment because I was already an ass about shirt choices. "We're going together, right?" he asks. "Driving two cars is a waste of gas. And everybody likes to save gas."

I listen to this rambling bit of logic, and it hurts my heart. If I'm going to be in a relationship, it has to be with someone who doesn't need a solid alibi for sharing a ride with me.

And while I know that Kieran isn't ready to come out on Christmas, I can easily picture myself sitting on this same couch *next* Christmas, with the same fancy cake waiting in the kitchen, asking myself how another year has gone by in our secret relationship.

I take a deep breath and do the difficult thing. "Kieran," I say quietly. "I'm not in the right head space to go with you today. Can you take the cake I made and just tell anyone who asks that I need to catch up on my sleep? Or that I have a headache?" It's not even a lie. I can feel a headache blooming behind my eyes.

"What? You said you were coming. Everyone will be there."

That's the problem, isn't it? I've been trying to make a life for myself in Vermont. But every single person I know in this town is related to Kieran, either by blood or through my job. I've done it again. I've painted myself into a corner by falling for a man who requires me to hide how I feel.

This is all my fault. But it's still going to hurt both of us.

"I shouldn't have agreed to go," I say as gently as possible. "I don't want to spend the day pretending that you and I are just roomies who split the heating bill. Not on Christmas."

"Oh," he says, and then frowns. "But this morning you said you were excited to go."

"Yeah," I admit.

"What did I do wrong?"

I try on several answers to that question, and they all sound petty. *You won't hold my hand under the dinner table. After two whole months of exploring your sexuality, you're not ready to change your life.* "It's not you, it's me," is what I come up with. "I've faked my way through many social gatherings before. I just can't do it today."

His forehead wrinkles, and I'm sure he wants to argue the point. But in the end, he says, "Okay." And then he turns around and walks toward the backdoor, where his coat is waiting on a hook.

I follow him with the cake I made, so he won't forget it.

"If you change your mind…"

I nod quickly as I hand over the cake. We blink at each other for a second. It's the first awkward moment between us in a really long time.

Then he goes. I stand there in the back hall, listening to the sound of his truck's engine warming up. After a minute he backs down the driveway and leaves. Still, I don't move. I wait until the engine sound has completely died away. I don't know what I was waiting for, anyway. I was definitely not waiting for Kieran to stop the truck, walk back into this house, and grab me into a hug.

I was not waiting for him to say, *I'm sorry you're sad*, and *I love you*. It's definitely too soon for that second thing, if not the first.

But now that he's really gone, I'm faced with a whole empty day. I'm probably going to spend part of it binging TV shows on Kieran's computer.

First, I need to give myself a task to feel good about. I start cleaning. The bathrooms are first. Then I vacuum the living room and clean out the refrigerator. I turn on some music.

My dining options are pretty limited, given the fact that I thought I'd be eating Audrey's cooking today. So that's a little depressing. But I pour myself a mug of coffee and decide I'll worry about food later.

The house smells like cleaning products and determination a few hours later when I see a man walk up the driveway. He looks familiar, but I can't quite place him. He approaches the backdoor, and I spot his collar. He's the same priest whom I briefly met at the Shipleys' party back in the fall. The one who said that my parents were his parishioners.

I feel a sudden, soul-deep chill. Did something happen today? To the Shipleys? Or—wait—to my parents? I yank open the door.

When the priest smiles at me, I feel a powerful wave of relief. "Roderick?" he says cheerfully. He's carrying a covered dish in his hands. "Sorry to drop by unannounced. But I brought you something, and I wondered if we could have a quick chat."

"Well...sure?" I'm still a little confused, but I gesture him inside. "I have coffee, if you want a cup. But that's about it. It's been a busy month of seasonal baking, and I took the day off from that."

"I would love a cup of coffee!" He wipes his shoes on the mat that I bought at Goodwill for three dollars. "And I know just what you mean. Christmas Day is peak season for me. I give more than one service, and then I drive around visiting a lot of people. In the evening, we throw a communal dinner."

"Right. I heard about that." The damned dinner is the reason Griffin showed up at our door today, starting all the trouble. See? Church is dangerous. I knew it all along.

And isn't it weird that the priest is paying me a friendly visit? Is he here to proselytize? Or could he be, like, a creepy priest?

"I swung by the Shipleys' an hour ago," he says, tossing his coat onto Kieran's empty hook.

"You really do get around." I lead him toward the kitchen and take a clean coffee cup out of the cabinet.

"Well, Audrey's cooking is pretty spectacular. A man's got to eat, even on the busiest day of the year. And then I heard that you were feeling a little under the weather, so I brought you a plate on my way back into town." He lifts the lid on the dish he's holding, and I see a thick slice of spiced ham, a wedge of potato and cheese gratin, a selection of vegetables and a polenta-looking dish that I might need to taste to properly identify.

"Wow." What an incredible kindness. The scent of a home-cooked meal rushes up at me. And—this is mortifying—my eyes get hot. "Thank you." I take the dish from his hands and look away.

"Hey now," Father Peters says softly. "Christmas is a glorious day for half my parishioners. And the hardest day of the year for the other half."

"Only half? Shit," I curse. To a priest. "Sorry."

He shakes his head. "Don't be sorry. Put that in the microwave for sixty seconds and get a fork. I've eaten my weight in that ham already. You really don't want to miss it." Then he takes the empty coffee mug I've fetched for him and fills it from the carafe himself.

And that's how I end up eating Christmas dinner with a priest. "Is this stuffing flavored with water chestnuts?"

"I think so," he says. "And cranberries. How's your headache?"

"Miraculously recovered. I just wasn't up to crashing a big family dinner today. I wasn't in the mood."

"I see," he says, sipping his coffee. "And no last-minute invitations were forthcoming from your own family?"

"They don't even have my phone number," I point out. "But I don't dwell on it. Not at all. I hadn't even thought of them today." Or I wouldn't have, anyway, if I hadn't fought with Kieran. But home alone in this empty house, I managed to think about everyone I ever tried to make love me. My parents. Brian. Kieran. The whole lot.

That's what happens when you dive too deeply into your own misery.

"It isn't right," Father Peters says quietly. "I inquired about you to them."

The fork pauses on its way to my mouth. "You don't have to do that. In fact, it's easier on me if you don't."

"All I did was invite the conversation. I told your parents that my door was open to them if they wanted to discuss their relationship with their son."

"How would that even work?" I ask carefully. "The Catholic church does not approve of me."

He tips his head side to side, as if weighing the idea. "Technically speaking, the Catholic church disapproves of actions, not people. Although most of the congregants who walk through my door have done some things that the church dislikes. Birth control, for example. Or divorce. But that doesn't matter to me. I am not a walking rule book. And I don't disapprove of you at all. And I don't judge you, either. That's not my job. My job is to love you as one of God's most sacred creations. And I am very good at my job."

My fucking eyes fill with tears. "I'm having kind of a hard day," I say by explanation.

"I can see that. But so am I, because I'm expecting two hundred people for dinner in forty minutes. So I need to do something."

"Go, go," I say waving him toward the door. "I'll be fine."

"Sure you will be. But I meant that I need to ask you a favor. Would you come and help me serve two hundred meals for a couple hours? You may not approve of the rolls. We buy them frozen. But we could use an extra set of hands. And it seems like you already cleaned your house from top to bottom, so…"

I laugh. "This was all one big recruiting mission? You are *slick*."

"No, I'm innocent." He spreads his hands and smiles at me.

"But we are always shorthanded. And you've finished your supper."

I look down at my plate and see that he's right. I've hoovered the entire meal in a short period of time. The meal that this man brought me when he suspected I was sitting home alone today. "I'm very handy in the kitchen," I admit. "But I won't come if you think my parents will show up. I don't have the stomach for that tonight."

"Well, I don't have a tracking device on their car. But I have never seen your parents at one of our community dinners. They're Sunday-only Catholics, as far as I can tell."

I realize that I have no earthly idea how my parents spend Christmas. And that makes me feel a little blue once again.

"Come on, Roderick. It's right across the green," Father Peters says. "You could throw a rock and hit the church."

"That sounds like vandalism," I say, lifting my now-empty plate off the coffee table.

"I don't mean literally," he scoffs. "The church disapproves of that. It's in the rule book."

"I'm sure it is."

Five minutes later I'm locking the door and then heading down the driveway with the priest.

"So, is there any particular reason why today was especially hard?" he asks.

"Well, sure. I really like Vermont, but I'm not sure I can stay."

"Why is that? Seems like you have a good job with people who care about you."

"A fair point," I grumble. "But see—I like people. And I need people in my life. That's a good thing, right?"

"I've always thought so."

"But it has a dark side. Before I came here, I was with a guy who wasn't a very good guy. But I stuck with him anyway, because I don't like to be alone. Then I came to Vermont, and I started dating a good guy. No—a *great* guy. But he's not ready."

"Ready for—?"

"For *me*. I'm kind of a lot to handle. I have a lot to give, but he isn't ready to receive everything I want to offer him. And it doesn't look like he's going to be ready anytime soon. So unless I want to put my life on hold for the foreseeable future, I probably need to leave. This is a small town, and I don't want to put pressure on him. But it's just so *depressing*. I feel like I'm going to be bumping around from guy to guy like a drunk pinball for the rest of my pathetic little life. When all I want is to find the right man and be *very* good to him."

I need a big, gulping breath of air after all that word vomit. I can't believe I just emptied my heart to a Catholic priest, of all people. But he's a really good listener. He's probably trained for that.

"That does sound heartbreaking," he says as we round the corner toward his church. "But the self-awareness you have about this problem is a precious thing. Not all of my parishioners can see their troubles as clearly as you can."

"I'm not always this lucid," I promise him. "I stayed with that other rat for three *years*."

"And how long have you given this new guy?"

"Not long," I hedge. "But it feels so familiar. I know he's going to let me down. So I feel like I should just get it over with, and save us both the anguish."

"Hmm," he says. "And how would he feel if you did that?"

"Sad," I say without hesitation. "But maybe relieved."

"Uh-huh. Maybe before you deprive the greater Colebury area of those sourdough pretzels, you should find out for sure."

I snort. "I sense a conflict of interest here."

"It's minor," he says with a wave of his hand. "I won't let it affect my judgment. My counsel is that you should take a breath. You're afraid to put pressure on your man. But you're putting the most pressure on yourself tonight. You wouldn't rush a sour-dough, would you?"

I shake my head. "That's how you ruin things."

"Step back, take a breath, leave the kitchen, Roderick. But don't leave town, or you'll always wonder what might have been."

Exhaling, I look up to see people streaming into the church. But Father Peters doesn't rush. He slows his pace on the sidewalk, just in case we're not finished yet.

"Thank you," I say in a low voice. "I'll try. But even if it all works out, I could never get married in your church anyway, right?" I'm pretty conflicted about stepping over that threshold, even to serve dinner.

"Right," he says brightly. "But that doesn't mean I wouldn't come to your wedding. I could cheer you on from the front row. What kind of cake do you think you'd serve? Just hypothetically?"

"You are *not* what I expected," I say with a laugh.

"Good. Now let's wash up and serve some ham and inferior rolls."

KIERAN

"Are you okay?" my cousin May asks me as she deals out another hand of poker. "You're quiet, even for you."

"Yeah," I say. And that's all I say.

May shakes her head and deals two cards face up. "Then ante up."

"Oh. Sorry." I push a couple chips to the center of the table and try to focus on my cards.

I'm not, in fact, okay. I left things completely unsettled between me and Roddy. He should be here with us playing poker. He should have been here for Aunt Ruth's pie, and for the game of capture-the-flag we played outside in the dark.

At least he got a good supper. It was Audrey's idea to send him a plate with Father Peters, since the church is right across the green from our house.

It should have been me who brought it to him, though. Not that I was willing to say so out loud.

Roddy is right, of course. We have a problem, and it seems to have no solution. Before now, I never noticed how much pretending I do just to get through the day. There are conversations I don't enter, because they'd be too revealing. ("Which model is the hottest?") The way I listen more than I talk—even with my closest family members—is a habit I picked up so long ago that I wouldn't know how to break it.

And there's no way for me to suddenly be more like Rod—someone who dares the world to love him just the way he is.

I don't like my odds. I really don't.

Meanwhile, I wish he were here. I miss him like crazy. But I am not about to let everyone in this room know that we're lovers. That's just not happening. And I don't know how to make Roddy understand why I can't.

It's not that I'm ashamed of him. I'm not afraid to be gay. But my privacy is basically my life's work. And fitting in with the rest of the Shipley clan has never been easy for me. Setting myself apart on purpose would feel like peeling off my skin.

"You in or not?" Grandpa asks suddenly. "It's ten to call. Expensive hand, boy. But you still can't take all day deciding."

I glance at the cards on the table, and then at the cards in my hand. I push two chips onto the table almost before I notice that I've got three of a kind. "Okay. Sorry."

Everyone frowns at me simultaneously. "Fricking Kieran," Kyle says with a sigh. "You can't tell when he's bluffing, because he always has that same expression."

"The original poker face," my cousin Dylan agrees.

They're right. Because I'm always bluffing.

Always.

At eight o'clock, it's finally time to leave. I say goodnight to all the Tuxbury Shipleys, and congratulate my grandpa on his poker wins. "I'll get you next time, you old coot."

"Sure you will," he scoffs. "Bring more cash next time."

"Will do." Then I say goodbye to my parents, as my father walks slowly and painfully toward their car.

At last, I hurry towards my truck, eager to go home and see how Roddy is doing.

"Kieran? Can I ask you a favor?" my brother calls.

Uh-oh. "What is it?"

"Well, I know it's kinda late, and it's kinda Christmas. But I was hoping you could come home with me for a couple of hours and replace the hinges on the barnyard gate."

"What? Why?"

He rubs the back of his neck. "Dad hit the gate with the tractor this morning. His mobility is still pretty bad."

"Even for driving? Shit." I glance toward my parents' car and see my mother at the wheel. If he let her drive, it must be bad.

"Yeah." Kyle sighs. "He wanted to fix it with me tomorrow. But if we fixed it without him, we could pass it off as a Christmas gift. I kinda don't think he should be lifting anything. And we'll need to manhandle that gate."

"Sure," I agree. It won't be fun in the dark. But farming always throws you these challenges at the most awkward times. "Let's go."

It's eleven p.m. before I can head home. But the gate is fixed. And Kyle and I strategized about how to keep Dad busy until he's healed enough to work comfortably.

"I told him it was a good time to fix that baler connection that's been acting up. He can tinker with that thing while he's sitting down."

"Maybe," I'd hedged. "Or maybe he just needs another few weeks off." The truth is that there aren't a lot of desk jobs on a farm, except for keeping the books and ordering seed.

"You try telling him that," Kyle had muttered.

The house is completely dark when I get home, except for the Christmas tree in the living room window. This morning I was so excited to give Roddy his gift. And then we had epic sex. Inside the walls of this house, my life is exactly how I want it to be. Keeping my joy behind walls is something I'm used to, but

Roddy isn't. And I'm the jerk who's asking him to do it indefinitely.

I enter the house quietly, dropping my coat on the rack, and putting a piece of pie I brought home for Roddy in the fridge. I stop by the living room to turn off the tree before I go to bed, and that's where I find him, curled up on the sofa, his sleeping bag over his body, his head on a pillow. Instead of my bed—the bed I've come to consider *our* bed—he's tucked himself in on the couch.

I feel sick. All I can do is stand here, frozen, wondering what's happened to us. Is this it? Have I lost him already?

My worried gaze takes in two empty bottles of wine on the table. But then I notice that there are three wine glasses and a soda bottle, too. And a mostly eaten bowl of popcorn.

I want to wake him up and ask a hundred questions. Who was here? How are you? Why aren't you upstairs in our bed?

But instead, I turn off the Christmas-tree lights and climb the stairs alone.

Things don't improve the next day. At all. Roderick goes to work before I get up. When we're working the coffee counter together during the morning rush, I ask him if his evening was okay.

"It was surprisingly nice," he says, then gives me a sheepish smile. "I served two hundred helpings of ham and got drunk with the priest, Sophie, and Jude the mechanic."

"Jude doesn't drink," I say stupidly.

"Right." He nods. "But he didn't mind that we did."

"Oh, you mean after the community supper," I say slowly. And now I understand. Father Peters is a top-notch recruiter of idle hands. "That's cool." Except I spent all of yesterday worrying about poor Roderick alone at home. Meanwhile, he was getting wasted with new friends.

"Father Peters is nothing like I'd expect him to be," Roderick says, frothing a pitcher of milk. "He's a good time."

"Can we talk?" I ask suddenly.

Roderick looks up at the line of people in front of us and raises an eyebrow at me. As if to say, *Is this really the time?*

It isn't, of course. But later, when I go looking for Roderick on his break, I find him standing outside the kitchen door on his phone, ordering a twin-sized bed from the mattress store.

That evening after work, I watch, depressed, as the same delivery guys who brought my mattress set up Roddy's in his downstairs room. I feel blindsided, and after they leave, I stand in his doorway and blurt, "Why are you doing this?"

He's silent a moment, busy unwrapping his new sheets. Then he drops them on the mattress, turns around, and sits on the edge of the bed. "We need a little distance, I think."

"Why? One minute everything was great, and the next minute you're like a stranger again."

"That's not true," he says, fiddling with the piping on the edge of his new mattress. "But we have a problem. And the problem is that I love you." He looks up, gutting me with his sad expression. "And I know you also care about me. But I'm not in the right place in my life to have a secret relationship with you."

I love you. The words reverberate through my chest as I stay there in the doorway, struggling with what to say.

"—And you're not in the right place in your life to come out. It isn't anybody's fault. It's just true."

"But maybe I will be someday." Not that it's easy to picture.

"See, I know you mean that. You're one of the most honest people I know." He folds his arms in close, as if trying to warm himself, and it seems like there are five miles between us, instead of five feet. "But I refuse to put pressure on you. And I refuse to ignore what I need, too. What if there's some guy out there who's ready to be my other half?"

Ouch. Times a million. The thought of him meeting someone

else tears me to shreds. But I'm suddenly too angry to give him the satisfaction of saying so.

"It's not your fault that I've been down this road before," he says. "But I cannot make the same mistakes again."

"But I'm *not* your jerkoff of an ex."

His smile is sad. "Nope. You're a hundred times more worthy. And thank you for reminding me that I don't have to shop at Jerks Are Us anymore. Even so, I'm going to look around for another apartment, Kieran. It will take me a while, because Jude says my car needs even more work, and cash is always tight. But it's better if I live somewhere else. Wouldn't you agree?"

"No," I grumble. "You don't have to move out." That would make it final.

"Look, I am not trying to upset you. But there's one more thing I have to say. I'm not sure I feel right about keeping this." He stands up and moves to the corner of his room, where the guitar I gave him is balanced against the wall. "Maybe you want to return it."

"*No.* Just no. I wanted you to have it and I still do. I want—" I break off again, because talking was never my strong suit. I'm failing at it right now, anyway. Nothing I say is getting through. "I want a lot of things. But I don't want that back. Keep it. Sell it. Whatever you have to do."

And then I leave the house and eat a takeout sandwich in my truck, because I'm too upset to be at home while Roderick plans a new life without me.

KIERAN

Usually I drive to work at the ad agency straight from the bakery. But today I make a quick detour up the hill, where I swing by the house and check the mailbox. University classes start in four days, and I've been waiting for my financial aid award to arrive. I've already been admitted to the program, but it doesn't mean much if I can't afford to enroll.

When I pull down the mailbox's metal door, I find a grocery-store flyer and a single fat envelope. Right here—behind the wheel, with the engine idling—I tear open the envelope and read the enclosed letter.

Dear Mr. Shipley, we are pleased to offer you the following tuition assistance package. This greeting is followed by a grant number that looks awfully generous, plus a student loan for two thousand dollars. The result is that I'll have to pay upfront... Seven hundred and two dollars per course.

I read it twice more. The number remains entirely affordable, and I let out a whoop.

My first thought is: It worked! I can totally afford to become the oldest freshman on campus.

My second thought is: I can't wait to tell Roddy.

And then—splat—I fall back down to Earth. Because Roderick and I aren't a couple anymore.

It's been over a week since Christmas. He's spent every night downstairs in his new bed. While I've spent every night alone and upset.

He's trying hard to be my friend. At work, he'll bring me a bagel. Or one of the slices of pizza he's been testing. His smile says, *I'm sorry.*

But I don't know how to go back to being friends. So I avoid him. My subconscious hasn't gotten the message, though. Every time I hear something funny, or I read something interesting, my first impulse is to share it with him.

He's already looking around for another apartment. I heard him making a phone call last night, inquiring about a room for rent on a farm in Tuxbury.

"That would be a terrible commute," I couldn't help pointing out.

"I know," he'd said quietly. "And they found a tenant already. But the price was right."

The price is right here, I'd wanted to argue. But we've had that discussion a few times already, and he's still determined to put some distance between us.

I get it. He isn't willing to put himself back into the closet, and I can't see a way out of mine. Sometimes I lie awake in my lonely bed and imagine things are different. That I'm some other guy who can make his own rules.

Meanwhile, it's killing me to have him so close, but to only be friends. My heart can't stop hoping for more.

So I don't call him with the good news about my financial aid package. He'd be happy for me, but I refuse to be that needy. I'm back to being a loner, and it feels very familiar to me. I've kept my deepest thoughts and my personal victories to myself for twenty-five years. What's one more?

To celebrate, I turn on the radio as I pull away from the curb.

The truck's cab fills with the music from the country station that Roddy hates. Now I can listen to it whenever I want.

When I get to Burlington, I find that everyone at the office is in a crappy mood. "You're late," Mr. Pratt barks as I take my seat. "You said you were going to start work at twelve thirty."

"Yeah, *next* week," I remind him. That's when the schedule shifts. That's when classes start, and when I've cut my Busy Bean hours.

He frowns down at me, possibly because he's not used to me ever arguing with him. But I'm not taking any more crap from the Pratt family, I've decided. Not after the fiasco of Deacon's portfolio.

"Look," Pratt says. "We need to get these logo drafts ready for the client's eyes before four o'clock. I have a conference call."

"Sure," I say coolly as I log in to the computer. "What changes am I making?"

"Deacon has my notes," he says before heading back to his office.

Well, that's going to slow things down. With a sigh, I cross the room to find Deacon in his dickweasel office. It's taken extraordinary restraint on my behalf not to bring up Deacon's treachery on his art-school portfolio. But the Pratts haven't mentioned his application to me, and if I say anything, I could get the dean in hot water. That's really not the way I want to start things off with the college.

So I say nothing. Mr. Pratt wrote me a recommendation, as promised. And it must have been decent. I can only guess that he pressured his son to apply, too. I wonder if he was rejected.

Since I'd like to keep my job, I guess I won't ask.

"Hi there." I lean against the doorframe. "Your dad said you had some notes on the Mayer Farm labels?"

"His notes are here." He points me toward a sheet of paper in his father's careful script. "He wants you to try some different typefaces."

"Okay, sure." That sounds easy.

"But I don't like these cows you drew."

My blood pressure jumps. *You think you can do better?* The words are on the tip of my tongue, but I bite them back. "What about the cows?"

"Those splotches look dopey. I was thinking we need something more like this." He wakes up his computer monitor to show me two drawings from a stock-art site.

I let out a bark of laughter when I see them. "Oh, man. Not happening."

"Think again," he says with typical defiance. "This is the direction I'm taking it."

This jerk. "Okay, the first problem is that those are bulls. This art is for a dairy farm, and you can't get milk from a bull."

His chin jerks toward the screen. His mouth gets tight, but he doesn't acknowledge the mistake.

"The second problem is that the Mayers raise Randall cattle. It's a specialty breed. And just because you think the patterning on their faces looks 'dopey'—" I use air quotes. "—doesn't mean you get to repopulate their herd."

His lip curls, and I know he's not going to back down. "Just do half the sketches the way I'm asking for, and the client can decide."

And, yup, that's when I sort of snap. "Seriously? You're going to waste my time just so you don't have to admit that you didn't do your homework?"

"When you're here, your time is my time," he says in a low voice. "So just do what we pay you for."

"Your *father* pays me," I say, digging in. "He mostly pays me to clean up your messes. But a check's a check."

"You arrogant prick. Get the fuck out of this office and do your JOB!" Deacon shouts.

Well, fuck. I should have seen that coming. With my face reddening, and my pulse ragged, I turn around and walk back to my desk. I *never* argue with him, because there's really no point. And it only leads to more of his bullshit.

The truth is not always an option. Nobody knows that better than me. So why did I just step in that? Helen, the receptionist, is sneaking nervous glances at me.

Sure enough, Mr. Pratt steps out of his office a minute later, phone pressed to his ear. "What the heck is going on?" he stage-whispers. "I'm on a *call*."

Whatever. Even if a client heard Deacon yell *fuck* in the background, the world won't end. But this time I'm smart enough not to argue. In fact, I say nothing at all. I simply shrug and pull up the Mayer Farm files where I've hidden them—so Deacon can't tweak my work. And I squint at Mr. Pratt's notes about the typeface.

"What's the problem?" he whispers from the doorway.

"I don't have a problem," I say carefully. "I'm changing the typeface now."

"And the cows!" Deacon yells.

"Not the cows," I say in a low voice. "There is nothing wrong with these cows."

Apparently Deacon's only life skill is supersonic hearing, though. Because he comes storming out of his office. Never mind his father's call. He's out for blood. His face is red and getting redder. Spit starts flying as he shouts. "I *asked* you to change the cows. And you will *do it*."

"You asked for a change the client would never approve," I say in a low voice. "So I'm going to prioritize the typeface."

"It's *not your call*," he says through a clenched jaw, as his father stands there just observing this ridiculousness, his phone pressed to his ear. "You don't make the decisions around here."

"I make plenty of decisions when I make art," I point out. "We all do. And as an owner of cattle, maybe this is one moment when my opinion is especially useful."

"Bullshit. You think you're such an artist. With your new design classes and your faggot boyfriend."

My head actually jerks backward like I've been slapped. "*What* did you say?"

"You heard me," Deacon rages. "Get off your high horse and do the thing we hired you to do. You're still an hourly employee after all."

I look down at my hands where they're gripping the armrests of my chair. My heart is thumping loudly, but I am not about to let this go. "Just because you're the owner's son," I say, lifting my chin to look him in the eye. "Does not mean you have the right to use a slur. Do you kiss your mother with that mouth?"

And then I stand up—all six feet and one inch of me. Now I'm looking down at Deacon, who's clearly stirred himself into a rage.

His father slides his infernal phone into his pocket. So much for his super-important call. "Boys, this has gotten way out of hand."

"Is that what you'd call it?" Each of my words sounds like ice chipping.

"Let's have everyone go back to his corner and cool down. Deadlines are stressful," Mr. Pratt says, in a tone of voice that implies he's the sane one here.

But he isn't. "I can't hear the word *faggot* and then pretend it's just a little deadline stress that's turned Deacon into a raging homophobe."

"You're not even gay," Mr. Pratt says. And then his eyes widen, as if he's realized that maybe he missed something. "Are you?"

"Maybe I am, but that's none of your business," I say coolly. "And now you've both gone too far." I feel surprisingly calm as I open the desk drawer and retrieve my truck keys and my phone. I glance around the desk and spot only one other thing that belongs to me—a pencil cup that Roderick bought for a quarter on one of his thrift shop runs, because *artists need pencil cups*.

I pick up the pencil cup and grab my jacket off the back of the chair.

"Where are you going?" Mr. Pratt's voice is worried. "The cow art is due at four."

"You'd better get busy, then. Here's a tip—google 'Randall cattle.' It's Vermont's only heritage breed. I quit."

"What?" Mr. Pratt yelps. "But we have some work for the farmers' market association, too."

"Deacon can draw it, whatever it is. His portfolio needs a few new images. Originals, this time." Man, it felt good to say that. "And my last check had better not be short, or I'll contact the department of labor."

Yup. That felt good, too.

"Kieran, wait!" Mr. Pratt calls as I head for the door. "Deacon will apologize!"

"Save it for the next guy," I say. "Poor slob is going to need it."

I leave in a blaze of glory. At least, that's how it feels.

Quitting this job was not on my to-do list, but it should have been. Mr. Pratt used my skills without ever treating me like I had any. And his son is just a first-rate asshole. They deserve each other.

Now what? my truck asks as I sit there letting the engine warm. It's only three o'clock on a weekday. Setting aside the fact that I'm suddenly underemployed, I have a few empty hours all to myself. That never happens.

And I really want to talk to Roderick. Right this minute. Giving in to this craving, I pull out my phone and hit his number. He should be finishing up at the bakery right now.

"Hello? Kieran?" he answers on the second ring. "Everything okay?"

"Yeah," I grunt, suddenly shy. What did I think I was going to say to him, anyway?

"I thought maybe you had car trouble." He chuckles. "Or does that only happen to me?"

"It's more like life trouble," I say, because the sound of his laughter in my ear is so nice that I feel a pain in the center of my chest. "I just quit my job at Pratts'."

"What? Why?"

"Because I just had all I could take of Deacon Pratt. He made it easy, though, by calling me a faggot."

"Oh *honey*," he gasps. "I'm so sorry. Are you okay?"

I think it over for a moment and realize that I really am. The interaction was more shocking than hurtful. "Honestly, it was just a wakeup call. I don't care what he thinks of me. But I can't work for someone who says that."

"No, you can't," Roddy agrees emphatically. "Why did he say it, anyway? Random slur? Lucky guess?"

It's funny, but until now I'd forgotten to even wonder. "I think he must have seen us somewhere. Whatever. It doesn't really matter. I walked out, and you should have seen their faces."

"You amaze me," he says softly. "Congratulations. But I'm sorry you're out of a job."

"Yeah." I let out an awkward chuckle. "I didn't think that through. I need a nighttime job now, seeing how I also got my financial aid package today. So I'm definitely starting school next week."

"You did? Congratulations! This is so exciting."

"Thank you." I clear my throat. "So anyway, I'm free right now. And we haven't cooked together in a while. What if I went to the grocery store and got us something to make?" Maybe I sound pathetic right now, but it's worth it. I don't want to be alone tonight. My life is completely up in the air. But the only thing I really care about is how much I miss him.

"Sure," he says softly. "In fact, swing by the house and pick me up. We'll shop together."

"Okay, yeah." My heart gives a happy kick. "I'm on my way."

Then I hang up before he can change his mind.

RODERICK

Here I go again, breaking my own rules. Spending time with Kieran isn't the problem. He had a crazy, shocking afternoon, and I am here for him. The problem is the hope that's fizzing through me as I climb into his truck and see his bashful smile. There's no denying how we feel about each other.

Maybe he'll become the kind of man who's not afraid, my poor little heart says.

"So what are we cooking?" he asks as we pull away from the curb.

"I'm not sure yet. Let's see what looks good. How do you feel about fish?"

He shrugs. "If you're cooking it, I'll probably like it."

Oh, Kieran. He kills me sometimes.

The truck does a careful circumnavigation of the town green and then points toward the commercial strip. It's a gray, cold day, but the truck is warm. There's country music on the radio again, because I apparently have a thing for guys who like twangy guitar and heartbreak. But I'm in a sentimental mood, so I don't even change the channel.

Kieran's phone rings in the cup holder. "Man, that's loud," he says. "Could you silence it?"

"Sure." I grab the phone. "It's your mother."

"I'll get 'er later."

"Are you going to tell your family you're enrolling in the art school?" I ask.

"Nope," he says. "I already know what my father would say. I'll save us both the aggravation."

And now I'm sorry I asked. The phone rings a second time. "It's her again."

"Hmm. Well, maybe I'll call her before we go into the store. Just turn the ringer off?"

I'm doing that when Kieran makes a startled noise. "Did you hear that?"

It takes me a second to figure out that he's talking about a story on the radio. The announcer is saying, "Country star Brian Aimsley made this announcement onstage in Tampa last night."

And then I hear my ex's voice. "I know it will surprise a lot of my fans to hear that I'm attracted to both men and women. But it's just part of who I am."

Wait. What?

"And I'm telling my story now, because there might be some fans out there who are struggling with their sexual identity. And I want them to know that it's okay to be yourself."

"*Christ.*" I feel a hot rush of anger, and I squeeze my eyes shut as Kieran pulls into a parking spot.

"Hey, that's crazy!" He pops the parking break. "I can't believe he's bisexual. It's pretty cool to just announce it like that."

I make an angry, gagging sound. "No *way*. Somebody forced his hand. I'd bet you any amount of money that the story was just about to break anyway. In fact—" I grab Kieran's phone again and unlock it. Then I hastily google Brian Aimsley and watch the screen fill with news stories. I scroll for a second, and then, *boom*. "Look. It was a gossip rag." I shove the phone in Kieran's hand, so he can see the story. "Somebody had pictures."

At least they aren't of me.

Shit. They aren't, are they?

"Oh my *God*." Kieran takes a sharp breath.

I go cold inside. "What's wrong?"

"It's my dad."

"What?" For a moment, my mind serves up a strange image of Brian Aimsley making out with Kieran's dad. But then I realize Kieran is staring at his texts. I lean over to read whatever it is that's turning his face a gray color.

Kyle: *You have to come to the hospital in Montpelier. Dad had an accident. It's bad. He might not make it.*

He drops the phone in his lap and grips the steering wheel. "Shit," he whispers. "I have to go to Montpelier."

"Okay," I say, taking a breath, and trying to think through my whiplash. "Breathe. And how about you let me drive? That way you can talk to him while we're on the way."

"Yeah. Okay." He unbuckles his seatbelt. "Sorry."

"Don't be sorry." I dash around the front of the truck, past the store that we didn't make it into. Then I climb into the driver's seat and adjust the seat a few inches forward, because Kieran has the long legs of a giant. "Buckle up. Let's go."

During the twenty-minute ride, Kieran speaks with both his mother and his brother. From the one-sided conversation, and snatches of Kyle's voice, I can piece together most of the crucial information.

Kieran's dad was alone in one of their outbuildings, trying to fix some piece of equipment. But he isn't very mobile these days, and some kind of spinning tool caught the loop on the end of a wrench he was holding.

The wrench became a spinning, high-speed weapon, and it slashed Mr. Shipley several times before he got free of it.

"He lost a lot of blood," I hear Kyle say. "It's bad. It's so bad."

"You keep saying that," Kieran grinds out. "Why was he screwing around with the PTO shaft?"

"Because he does whatever the fuck he wants!" Kyle shouts. "He doesn't listen to me. This isn't my fault. Mom and I were out at the feed store."

"I didn't say it was your fault," Kieran says quickly. "Who found him? Mom?"

"Rexie," Kyle says. "Rexie saved his life. The minute I got out of the truck, there's Rexie barking his head off. I knew something was wrong. I dropped everything and ran after him."

Kieran hangs up the phone before we reach the hospital. He drops it like it's burning him, and then he leans back in the seat and closes his eyes. "I can't believe this is happening," he mumbles. "This might kill him."

"I'm sorry, babe," I whisper.

"And I feel—" There's a long pause before he speaks again. "*Freaked*. I guess that's the right word. We never got along. Never. He doesn't even like me. But I don't want him to die in a farming accident."

"Hey." I reach out and grab his hand. "Your relationship is complicated. I get it."

"Complicated is not the half of it," he says.

"Don't think about that right now," I try. "Just get through this. Get your mother through this. Who else shall we call?" I pull into the hospital parking lot and start looking for a parking space. It has to be big, because I don't know how to park a pickup truck.

"We should call my aunt Ruth," he says. "She'll know what to do."

"And Father Peters," I add. Now that I spend time every week with a Catholic priest, I finally understand what they're for.

"Yeah. Him too. Thanks."

———

We find Kieran's family quickly, but then we all sit for hours in the waiting room, with no news.

Mr. Shipley is in surgery. Kyle looks red-eyed and sad. Kieran's mom looks white with fear. There's blood on her clothes, at least until Ruth Shipley arrives with fresh clothes to put on.

When I summoned Ruth Shipley, I apparently summoned the entire Shipley clan. Griffin and Audrey are here. Strangers keep glancing at Audrey, wondering if she's here to have her baby, I think. That's how round she is. Dylan is here, too, along with Grandpa Shipley.

Zara dropped off sandwiches that nobody is eating.

Kieran sits hunched in a chair. When I bring him a soda, he drinks it without noticing. Griffin and his other cousins stop by to speak to him in hushed tones, and Kieran nods at their kind words. But he seems to have retreated into himself.

Father Peters sits beside Kyle, an arm around his shoulder, while Kyle tries to hold it together.

Finally—seventy-two years after we arrive—a nurse manager comes out to brief the family. "He's still in surgery, but that will be over soon," she says. "He lost a lot of blood, but his vitals seem to be stabilizing."

"That's good, right?" Kieran's mom asks.

"It's a positive sign," the nurse says gently. "It will still be a while before the surgeon can come out to explain the procedure."

"Okay," Kieran's mother says shakily. "He has a rare blood type."

"Yes, he does," the nurse agrees. "We had to ask the Red Cross to transfer some more units. It's coming, just in case he needs it."

"I'm B negative," Kyle says, raising a hand. "Can I donate? My mother is B positive, so she can't. But maybe my brother can."

Kieran stiffens beside me, and I feel a chill roll down my spine, because I have a bad feeling about the turn of this conversation. Whether he knows it or not, Kieran is now an "MSM," or a man who's had sex with men. It makes you ineligible to donate blood.

Oh *shit*.

"Well, you can absolutely donate, if you feel like you want to make that contribution," the nurse says. "We can take both of you right now. And if you're not the right blood type, another patient will benefit."

Kyle shoots out of his chair. "Nah, I'm a good match. I wrote a paper about this in bio class. I swear it was my only good grade that year because I thought testing blood was cool."

Oh Kyle, I think wistfully. *Don't ever change. It's a shame we're never going to be in-laws.*

"Let's go, Kieran," he says.

Everyone watches Kieran give his head a slow shake. "I can't."

"Sure you can," Kyle says. "At least try."

"I'm O neg!" Audrey says, rising out of her chair, her big pregnant belly leading the way. "I'm a hundred percent match for anyone, so I'll go."

"I'm sorry," the Nurse says, shaking her head. "There are rules against pregnant women giving blood."

"Oh, geez." Audrey says. "I'm not allowed to do anything."

"Thank God," Griffin says.

"Let's go, Kieran," Kyle says. "You're probably a match."

He shakes his head, and my heart drops. This could be the most awkward coming out in the history of ever. *Don't do it*, I beg, even though I've wanted him to do this very thing for months.

"What? Why?" Kyle thunders. "Dad would do it for you."

"I'm not a match," Kieran says quietly.

His mother gasps. Her eyes are round and worried.

And now I'm really confused.

Kieran looks up at his mom, seeming to snap out of his trance. "You want me to walk in there and pretend? My blood type is AB. I already know."

"You can't be AB," Kyle argues. "Mom and Dad are both B. That's impossible."

And that's when it finally dawns on me. Kieran isn't talking about the homophobic regulations at all. One of his parents is not his bio parent. He knows this. But Kyle has no idea.

"Kieran," his mother sobs. "*Wait.* How did you…"

"I took that class, too." At that, he stands up and walks out of the room, while more than a dozen pairs of eyes follow him.

Meanwhile, the nurse has turned as white as her shoes. "My goodness," is all she says.

"Hey, try me," Griffin says, rising. "I'm the patient's nephew." He puts an arm around a stunned Kyle. "If you want to donate blood, I'll go with you."

"But—" Kyle's eyes are fixed on the doorway where Kieran disappeared.

"You can talk to him later," Griff says, leading Kyle away before the moment gets any freakier.

"Excuse me," I whisper, standing, although nobody is paying me any mind. "I'm just going to…"

Then I gallop after Kieran.

Luckily, Kieran isn't hard to find. He's right outside the sliding door of the hospital. "Do you have a cigarette?" he asks me when I arrive at his side.

"No way. Let's not poison our lungs over this," I say, startled.

"Fine." He tucks his chin against his chest.

I move to stand next to him, so we're both holding up the wall together. And, very surreptitiously, I reach a pinky finger out and hook it over his. "Are you okay?"

"Not really."

"That was your real secret, right? The thing that made everything else hard."

"Yeah." His finger hooks around mine.

I look up at the wintry sky, but I'm really seeing all those faces in the waiting room, staring at Kieran as he drops this bomb—that somehow he's not his father's biological son. He didn't say why, but if it's such a big secret, the reason must be something shameful.

"I should have just gone with Kyle, right?" he says. "Maybe

263

the hospital wouldn't have said anything. My whole life I've dreaded this." He looks up at me with red eyes, and it's as if I can see right through him.

He'd said his family had secrets, but I hadn't really understood. "You've been sitting on this a long time, then? That couldn't have been easy."

"It wasn't my secret to tell," he croaks. "I was just supposed to pretend I don't know the things I know. So my parents could save face."

"That's exhausting."

"Sure, but..." He swallows. "The reward was staying in the group, you know? My cousins aren't even my cousins, for fuck's sake."

Oh. "Of *course* they are," I say fiercely. And then I step into Kieran's personal space and hug him. And he wraps his arms around me and puts his chin on my shoulder.

It feels so good and so necessary that I feel like crying. It's just hitting me why Kieran is so obsessed with his secrecy. He's been clinging to it all his life.

"I'm sorry," Kieran says. "All this drama. We were just supposed to be grocery shopping."

"With you, it's never just grocery shopping," I whisper. "I'd go anywhere with you. And I'd do anything for you." If only he'd let me. I take a big breath, and then I do the difficult thing and step back from this man I love, so that he can maintain the facade that we're just buddies.

He's too emotional right now to protect himself. So I will do that for him.

"Besides," I say, giving his shoulders a quick squeeze before I step back to my spot against the wall. "The Shipleys are never boring."

He gives me a crooked, grateful smile. Then he reaches his hand out and grabs mine. All five fingers this time. "Roddy, I don't want to be alone."

"None of us do. And you aren't, you know." I've seen the

Shipley wolf pack in action. I'd bet cash money that a month from now they're watching sportsball together just like always.

"No," he argues. "I mean that I need *you*. If you move out, it will kill me. I want us to be together."

"*Honey*." My heart thumps in my chest. "I am a hundred percent available for this discussion. But we need to get through this outrageous day before you make any more life-changing pronouncements." If Kieran ever decides to tell his family about us, I want him to do it with a clear head, so he doesn't regret it later. And nobody should come out to his family while his father lies bleeding on an operating table. "One family crisis at a time, please."

"You don't believe me."

"I do," I say calmly. "But you shouldn't march into that waiting room in front of your terrified extended family and yell, 'Guess what, Shipley clan! This ass is so gay!'"

Kieran gives me a sideways glance. "If that's what you needed, I'd do it," he says in that serious voice of his. "I'd even toss around some glitter around if you dared me."

I turn to look into his gorgeous eyes, and we stare at each other for half a second before bursting out in loud, inappropriate laughter—the kind that happens when you're having a top-ten stressful day, and the tension just needs somewhere to go. Kieran's face creases into hilarity, and I actually see tears in his eyes as he leans against the brick wall and laughs.

And I'm just as bad. Every time I think I can stop giggling, I picture Kieran tossing a handful of glitter and...

Yup. Laughing again.

We keep it up until the hospital doors slide open, expelling an elderly couple who give us a stare. Only then can we dial it back. Kieran squeezes my hand as we catch our breath.

I hold his tightly, too. I drop it as the doors slide open again to reveal a very pissed-off Kyle Shipley, with Griffin bringing up the rear. They're both wearing Red Cross stickers on their flannel shirts.

"There you are," Kyle says, breathless. "What the *hell* just happened?"

"Easy," Griffin says, a hand on Kyle's shoulder. "Maybe Kieran doesn't want to talk about it."

"Yeah? Well, *not* talking about it doesn't work so well, does it? We play this weird game of telephone at our house. Our father prefers me and our mother loves Kieran best and everyone is tense and weird from dawn till dusk. And my whole life nobody would ever say why. And you—" He pokes a finger into his brother's chest. "You always assume I can't tell. Like I'm deaf and blind."

Kieran looks uneasy. "Well, you have the privilege of pretending everything is fine."

"The *privilege*," Kyle scoffs. "Like I can't tell when Dad is angry and Mom is stressed. I act the way I act because someone has to be the rodeo clown. Would *you* step up and run that shit show if you were always kept in the dark like me?"

Kieran puts his hands on top of his head and sighs. "No. I guess I wouldn't."

"I notice plenty, okay? Like you're in love with your roommate, for example."

"What?" Kieran blinks.

Griffin smiles. And I clamp a hand over my mouth.

"You heard me," Kyle bellows. "I see things. I know things. Not that anyone ever bothers to bring me up to speed. What happened back there, anyway? I mean, I was there when you were born. How the hell are you not—" Kyle catches himself before he finishes the sentence. "I'm sorry. I don't even know what to say to you right now."

"I do," Griff says quietly. With one of his lumberjack arms, he steers Kyle away from his brother. Then he grabs Kieran into a tight hug. "Love you, brother. Whatever bullshit happened before you were born wouldn't change that."

Kieran gulps audibly, and my eyes feel hot all of a sudden.

"Love. You. Too," Kieran grunts, although this display of verbal emotion almost kills him.

"Okay. Okay," Kyle says from the sidelines. "As usual, Griff is better at this than any of us. And here I am yelling at you." He sighs. "I'm sorry."

Griffin steps back, then whacks Kyle on the shoulder. "It's a hard day. Take a breath. And maybe it isn't Kieran's job to explain your parents' past."

"Good point," I say, even though nobody asked me.

The hospital doors open up again, and Grandpa Shipley appears. "He's out of surgery!" the old man yells. "And stable!"

All three Shipley cousins sag with relief. "Finally," Kyle says, and then gallops toward the doors.

Griffin squints at Kieran. "You going to be okay?"

"Yeah," he says hoarsely. "But I do not want to go back in there right now."

"Your dad won't be awake, or seeing people for a while," Griffin says. "Take a breather." He gives Kieran's shoulder one more squeeze, claps me on the back, and walks away.

Grandpa walks slowly toward where we're standing on the sidewalk. He stops in front of us, tears in his eyes. "I thought I'd lost him. A man shouldn't bury both of his sons. That's not how it's supposed to work."

"You're right, Grandpa," Kieran says.

"My sons aren't perfect people," he goes on to say. "Did you know your father was a difficult, angry teenager? Never listened to a thing I said."

Kieran's eyes widen. "No?"

Grandpa shakes his head. "I love every stubborn hair on his head, though. And yours, too. I always will. Blood type doesn't mean shit, boy. You know what does?"

Speechless, Kieran shakes his head.

"Who shows up at the hospital when you cut yourself up in a dumbass farming accident. *That's* what matters." At that, the man turns away and limps toward the doors again.

KIERAN

Roderick takes over after we get the news that my dad's out of surgery.

First, he figures out that the hospital will allow two people at once to see Dad in the ICU. Mom and Grandpa have that honor.

"So I'm taking you home," he says. "It's cold out here, and you're shivering."

I hadn't noticed. But I let him steer me to the truck, where I get into the passenger seat and let him drive me home.

Then he makes me a grilled cheese sandwich, because when you live with a baker there's always bread. But I eat it without tasting it.

"Come on," he says afterward. "You look beat. Let's watch an episode."

Numb, I follow him to the sofa for the first time in way too long. He sits at one end. And instead of sitting down beside him, I lie down with my head in his lap, shamelessly asking for affection that I don't actually deserve.

Roddy doesn't hesitate, though. He puts a hand on my head, sifting his fingers through my hair. It feels so good that my eyelids get heavy.

"Thank you," I say sleepily.

"It's okay," he whispers. "Everything is really okay."

"I love you," I try. It isn't nearly as hard to say as I thought it would be. "I love you so much." Actually, it does hurt to say it. But it aches in a good way. Like sore muscles after a good workout. It aches like progress.

Roddy leans down and places a soft kiss on my temple. "I know," he says. "I love you, too. Now just relax."

I must fall asleep, because the next thing I know, I'm waking up on the sofa, my head on a pillow, and Roddy is opening the back door to someone.

"Is he here?" my mother's voice asks without preamble.

"Yes, but he's *sleeping*," Roderick says.

"But I need to speak to him."

Before I can tell them I'm awake, I hear Roddy let fly with a response. "Oh, so *now* you want to talk to him? Because it's convenient for you, and you drove all the way into town to have a conversation that's years overdue?"

"But—"

"You know what, lady? That's the very definition of conditional love. On your terms, right? Well, I say come back *later*."

"Roddy," I bark, my voice hoarse from disuse. "I'm up."

"He's awake," my mother growls. Even though I can't see her, I know she just pushed past him into the house.

I sit up, and the room slowly rights itself. I feel sluggish, but surprisingly calm. Today's disasters were inevitable. And even though all those eyes on me in the hospital waiting room gave me a case of emotional sunburn, I also feel relief.

Griffin was right when he said that it wasn't my job to explain it. It shouldn't be my burden. But it has been, for ten years.

My mother loses some of her bluster between the backdoor and the living room, though. Because her head appears at the doorframe before the rest of her. "Kieran, are you awake?"

"Yeah, Mom. Come in."

"Your roommate doesn't seem to like me very much," she sniffs.

"Boyfriend," I correct, standing up.

Her mouth hinges open. "What?"

"Boyfriend." I yawn deeply. "Hang on a sec. Sit down." I wave a hand at the couch and then leave the room to look for Roderick.

I find him standing in the kitchen with Zara, who has Nicole on her hip.

"Hey," I greet them. "When did you sneak in?"

"Just a second ago, right after your mother. I brought you a lasagna, because Audrey told me about your dad's accident."

"Oh, wow. Thank you." I guess I'm having that kind of day—with drama of such magnitude that the neighbor brings you a casserole.

"Seems like Roddy needs a piece, too, because he looks a little worked up."

"I'm sorry I yelled at your mom," he says, rubbing the back of his neck. "I have some, uh, parent issues I'm working through."

"Hey, it was kind of hot."

His surprised smile is so cute that I have to step closer and give him a quick kiss. "Thank you for being my chauffeur and bouncer today. And heat up that lasagna. We're going to need it."

When I step back, Zara is blinking at us. "Something tells me I missed a few other developments."

"You have no idea," Roddy says cheerfully.

"Cool, cool," Zara says. "Just let me know if we need to shuffle the schedule tomorrow to let Kieran visit the hospital. You know where to find me."

"Nazagna," Nicole says. "Eat."

"Ah, Mama's girl," Zara says. "Let's get home and find you a snack."

"Cookie?" she asks, hopefully. The sight of her two neighbors kissing does not faze her at *all*. It didn't seem to faze Zara, either, now that I think about it.

"We'll see." My boss rolls her eyes. "Night, guys. Reheat it with the foil on top."

"Thanks, boss!" Roddy says. "See you in the morning."

She departs, leaving Roddy and me alone in the kitchen. I glance toward the living room, dropping my voice to a whisper. "I have to go back in there, don't I?"

"I tried." His eyes sparkle. "But I'll bring you a glass of an adult beverage. For courage."

"Would you?"

"Sure. And remember—you didn't create this problem."

"Uh-huh," I say, only I've spent my whole life believing otherwise. I created the problem just by showing up twenty-five years ago.

He gives me a gentle shove, and I walk toward the living room where my mother waits.

I find her on the sofa, her head in her hands. "I've always dreaded this conversation," she says.

"That must be why we never had it," I point out.

She looks up. "I couldn't ever figure out how. I was protecting you. And I was protecting your father. How did you figure out that you're not biologically his son? Was it really in a biology class?"

I shake my head. "Nah. I overheard a conversation outside of church. One of my teachers was gossiping with a friend. I was in a tree above them so that none of the old ladies would pinch my cheeks or ask me about school." I used to hate the coffee hour because I didn't like making small talk with adults. Sue me. "They were talking about families who had 'oops' babies." I make finger quotes. "And the other woman said, 'Well you know, Bert Shipley had the ultimate *oops* baby. He wasn't even the father.'"

As I watch, all the blood drains from my mother's face. "Oh my God."

"Yeah." I swallow hard, because I can still hear the sound of their laughter. "I still wasn't ready to believe it was me. But then they mentioned Father Craig."

Father Craig was a very popular priest who left Colebury right before I was born. Years later, I used to hear people wonder aloud why he'd left. I think I might be the reason why.

271

"Jeez." My mother wipes her eyes. "How did they know?"

I shake my head. "You think I jumped out of the tree to ask?"

"No, of course not." She sniffs. "So you heard it from a couple of church *gossips* that I had an affair with a priest."

"Yeah. Basically."

The women had said as much. I'd known immediately that it was true. Because whenever my parents had their very worst fights, my father used to end the conflict by yelling, "Just don't seek solace with the *priest*." I'd never understood why he'd say that. Until the day I finally did.

"How old were you?" my mother asks quietly.

"Fourteen."

"That must have been shocking. I wish you could have told me."

"How was I supposed to ask questions about it? And I wasn't sure I wanted to know."

"Baby, I'm sorry," she says, as tears track down her face. "Even now it isn't easy for me to explain. I did a terrible thing. When I got pregnant, I told your father everything. I offered to give him a divorce. But…"

Roderick walks into the room with a box of tissues, sets them down on the coffee table, and walks out again.

My mother grabs one and mops the tears from her face. "Your father decided he didn't want a divorce. He didn't want Kyle passed back and forth between us. So we went to counseling. He decided he wanted to be your father, too. And that we would go on as we were before."

Ouch. "How did that work out?"

"We tried, Kieran. You know there's tension."

I snort loudly.

"The thing that you don't understand is that we loved each other. We had a good marriage before I ruined it, and your dad wanted to try to get that back. But once the trust was gone, it was really difficult."

I take a deep breath and let it out. There doesn't seem to be enough oxygen in the world today.

"Your father loves you, Kieran. I believe that with all my heart."

"That is wishful thinking," I insist.

"When you were smaller, you two were close," she says. "He treated you just like he treated little Kyle. But when you were a teenager, you didn't have as much in common. That's when you two stopped getting along. And—" She puts her hands together in the prayer position. "I hope that isn't my fault, too. If you stopped seeing yourself as your father's child, it probably affected your relationship with him."

"Yeah, maybe." But I know she's right. I was so angry with my ugly secret. I'd spent a lot of time wishing it weren't true.

"Sorry guys," Roderick says, entering the room again. "It's time for a margarita. And the lasagna will be warm soon."

I look up at him in relief. The conversation was getting heavier than I could bear. "Margaritas?" I ask, glancing at the tray he's carrying. He's filled it with three glasses and a pitcher of iced liquid. We never make mixed drinks.

"Well, tequila will always remind me of you, so I bought us a bottle a while back and then forgot to drink it." He sets the tray on the coffee table. "Mrs. Shipley, would you like a margarita?"

My mother looks between the two of us like she's trying to untangle a puzzle. "Sure," she says a beat too late. "Just a half glass, though, because I'll be driving."

"I can do that." He pours her a modest drink and hands her the glass. "Kieran?"

"Hell, yes. Thank you."

"Anytime." He looks up from what he's doing, and our gazes lock. He gives me a smile so warm that I can't imagine why I wasn't willing to do anything he asked of me. Roddy is everything. I'm so lucky to have him in my life.

When my mother leaves, I'm so wiped out that I can hardly keep my eyes open.

"Come on," Roddy says. "Upstairs."

I follow him on command. I'd follow him anywhere.

He supervises while I brush my teeth and wash up. Then he literally tucks me into bed, pulling the comforter up to my neck. "Here," he says, plugging in my phone on the bedside table. "If there's any news about your dad, you'll hear it."

"Thank you," I mumble, my eyelids heavy. "You can stay upstairs tonight? If you want to." *Please.*

"I'll be back," he promises. "Sleep, okay?"

I'm not sure if I answer him or not. Sleep takes me, either way.

———

The next thing I know, Roddy is reaching over me in bed, grabbing my phone. The screen illuminates the dark room with a notification.

My sleepy mind is sluggish. My only thought is *Roddy is here.*

"What time is it?" I croak as I start to wake up for real.

"Three thirty. The message is from your mom. She says that your dad woke up. He's talking."

"That's good, right?" I rub my eyes.

"Yeah. Very good." Roddy puts the phone face down again, plunging the room back into darkness. "That's all she wrote, though." He runs a hand down my arm, clasping my hand. "My alarm goes off in an hour and a half. We should sleep."

I can't, though. Roddy is here, where he belongs, and I'm distracted by his nearness. I just lie quietly for a while, wondering what it all means. There's a really awkward conversation with my father in my future. Everyone knows our darkest family secret.

So, what's one more secret? I'll come out to my family—the ones who haven't already heard, anyway. I feel deeply uncomfortable knowing that I'll be the topic of discussion for weeks to come. But if it means I have Roddy by my side, it's all worth it.

"I missed you," he whispers suddenly in the dark.

That's all the encouragement I need. I roll onto my side to get closer to him. "I missed you, too. Like, a ridiculous amount."

He runs a finger down my nose. "I'm sorry. I was trying so hard not to make all the same mistakes."

"You aren't, though. I'm ready now. So don't you dare find some new reason why we can't be together."

"I won't. I swear. I just didn't want to pressure you. It couldn't be me who pushed you over the edge."

"It wasn't."

"True." He rolls up onto an elbow, bringing us nose to nose. "I'm not going to find any more reasons to keep us apart. I wasn't very good at it, anyway. I forced myself to get out of the house and make some new friends. But I spent a lot of time wishing you were there with me."

"Don't move out," I beg.

"Okay," he whispers. "Now, do you think you can go back to sleep?"

"Not so much." I slide a hand under his T-shirt. "But why would you want me to?" His taut stomach is warm and firm under my hand.

"Fair point," he says, grasping the hem of his shirt and then struggling to lift it off over his head. "You feel like showing me how much you missed me? Because I'm in the mood to give you a personal demonstration."

"Yeah. Same." My words are short, but I have reverence in my heart as I lean down to kiss his shoulder. And then his chest. The familiar, soapy fresh scent of his skin is so good that it makes my eyes sting.

"Kieran," he whispers. "I need you so much that it scares me. I wasn't looking for this when I came to Vermont."

"Don't be scared," I murmur against his skin. "I'm not going anywhere." I lift my chin to find his eyes in the dark. And I finally take the biggest leap. "I love you, and I need you, too. I can do what you need me to do."

Roddy grasps my face in his hands. "You already are."

We inch closer, neither of us wanting to break the moment. But I need to kiss him so badly. So I do it. I lean in and take his mouth with mine. He wraps his arm around me and pulls me in, returning my kiss with the same urgency that's driving mine.

And when Rod's alarm goes off an hour later, we're tangled up together, mouths swollen from kisses and hearts full.

KIERAN

The next morning is just as awkward and weird as I suspected it would be.

When I show up at the coffee shop in time for my shift, Zara and Audrey are there. They both seem to pounce on me. "Kieran! You didn't have to come in today," Zara cries.

"Sit, sit," Audrey says, waving me toward a table.

"Hey, I'm fine," I insist. "And I quit my job at the ad agency yesterday, so I wasn't about to lose these hours. I'll probably have to find another afternoon job now."

"Don't worry about any of that yet," Zara says. "How's your dad?"

"According to my text messages, he slept all night. I'll go see him later."

Roderick emerges from behind the counter to set a plate down in front of me. I look down to find a fresh bagel with cream cheese and smoked salmon. He gives me a wink and heads back to the counter without a word.

Audrey and Zara watch me with big eyes.

"What?" I ask, uncomfortable with their attention.

"Nothing," they chorus.

"Uh-huh," I grunt. "Go on. Ask your questions."

Audrey puts on her best *who me* face. "I'm not nosy."

"You are the nosiest person I've ever met," I counter.

"Well, I *try* to rein it in," she says with a sniff. "But Zara said you *kissed* Roderick right in front of her. And I missed the whole thing."

"What if Zara was just putting you on?" Roderick suggests from behind the espresso machine.

"Just answer yes or no," Audrey says. "Is he really your boyfriend? I'm having a little trouble believing it."

I never wanted to be the center of attention, but now that I am, I might as well have some fun with it. "What would you say if I told you that Griffin already knows the answer?"

"*No.*" Audrey's eyes widen again. "Before *me?* How is that even possible?"

"Well…" That's when my bravado runs out. Because I really don't want to explain that super-awkward moment from Christmas morning. "Roddy?" I call. "Help!"

"Aw, you call him Roddy!" Audrey squeals. "That is the cutest thing ever."

"So do you!" I point out.

"It's more adorable when you do it. Say it again. Wait, let me get a video." She unlocks her phone.

"No!" I yelp.

Laughing, Roderick reappears. He sets an espresso next to my bagel plate. "What's the problem?"

"Come here a second, please. Closer," I beckon. Since I'm not a fan of explaining my feelings, this just seems easier. When he's near enough, I grab him by the T-shirt and pull him down for a lip touch. "Thank you for the bagel and the coffee."

"Anytime." Smiling, he gives my shoulder a squeeze before disappearing into the kitchen.

"Oh *man*," Audrey says with a dreamy sigh. "I ship it."

"You—what?"

"She's a fan," Zara says from the counter. "Audrey, leave that boy alone. You can go home, too. This wasn't supposed to be your shift."

"But I'm here now." She swings her feet onto an empty chair and rubs her belly. "I'll only go home if you guys promise to come to Thursday dinner next week."

"What's on the menu?" Roderick calls from the back. "Kieran needs an incentive to be dragged out to Tuxbury and gawked at."

"There will be no gawking," she says with a sniff. "But there will be buttermilk-fried chicken, creamy potato salad, spicy Asian pickles, and corn fritters."

"Oh man," I breathe. "The gawking might even be worth it."

Everybody laughs.

Around noon, my dad is moved into a regular hospital room and is allowed a couple more visitors. "I should go up there," I say, dreading it. How is my father going to feel about me now that his secret is out?

"We'll go together," Roderick suggests. "We can get noodles afterwards."

All the noodles in the world won't make it easier. But I head to the hospital anyway, with Roderick at my side.

When we approach my dad's room, we see my mother standing at Dad's bedside. She notices us and joins us in the hallway, closing the door behind her. She looks exhausted.

"Sally," Roderick says. "Don't take this the wrong way. But when is the last time you slept?"

"I don't remember," she says.

"Let me take you home, Ma," Kyle says, appearing in the hallway with a cup of coffee. "I've been saying that for hours."

"Okay," she says. "Thank you. Let me get my coat."

While she's fetching it, Kyle puts a hand on my shoulder. "You okay?"

"Sure," I grunt. "Why?"

He shrugs. "Because this is stressful as hell. Is he taking good care of you?" Kyle nods toward Roderick.

"Well, yeah. But I'm all right."

Kyle crosses his arms and frowns. "I'm sorry I was a tool yesterday." He turns to Roderick. "And I'm sorry if I was a tool to you at any point."

"I've met bigger tools," Roderick says curtly. "But this macho big-brother thing you're working today is kind of hot."

"Roddy." I sigh.

He snickers. "Sorry. I'm more inappropriate when I'm nervous."

Kyle flashes him a quick grin. "Okay. Whatever. I'm taking Mom home now."

"You want help tomorrow?" I ask him.

He shakes his head. "No, it's okay. I got it. Go on." He points at Dad's room. "You take over here. He's been asking for you."

"Okay," I say as my stomach rolls.

I can't avoid it any longer. I step into the room alone. My father is lying on his back, his eyes shut, his face pale. There are bandages visible on his chest, and he seems frail, older than a man in his early fifties.

I've spent plenty of time irritated at my dad, but until now, I never spent much time wondering what it would be like to *lose* my dad. And I'm not ready. I sit down heavily in a chair and try to hold myself together.

His eyes flicker open, and he turns his chin to see who's there. "Kieran," he says tiredly. "Are you okay?"

"Yeah," I say, my voice cracking. "Sure."

He closes his eyes again. "That's how we always do it, right? We say we're okay no matter what."

"Yeah," I agree. "We do."

"Your mother told me everything. I can't believe how we failed you. In a tree at church? That is *not* how I wanted you to hear the truth."

"I wasn't supposed to hear it at all, right?"

His eyes flip open again. They're a dark brown color that the Shipleys all share. "I'm sorry. That was a mistake. If I could go back in time and find a better way, I would. You were such an angry teenager, and I struggled with it."

"I know."

"I understand now that you probably thought I loved your brother more. He was easier for me to understand, though. I had no idea what you were going through—that it was my fault you were so angry."

My throat is closing up now. "Water under the bridge," I croak.

"Secrets burn you," he whispers. "I didn't understand that when I was young. Don't make the same mistake, if you can help it."

"I'm trying," I say, fighting off tears. "I swear."

He swallows hard. "Good."

"I have a boyfriend. You met him," I blurt out. "Roderick. Maybe that seems weird to you, but it doesn't to me."

"Okay," he says. "I'm sure I can get used to the idea. Thank you for telling me."

I gulp back tears. "You're welcome."

"Hey, my wallet is in that drawer." He nods toward the table beside the bed. "There's a picture in there. Pull it out for me."

Grateful for something to do, I open the drawer and fish out my dad's ancient leather wallet. Inside there are slots for two photos. One is a picture of Kyle, circa first grade. And the other one is a photo I've never seen before. I'm maybe one year old. My dad is holding me, and I've got my small hand on his face. And he's smiling so widely at me. The way a man smiles at his little boy.

"It wasn't always difficult," he says. "Let's both try to remember that."

"Okay," I say, my voice breaking.

"You take that one," he says. "I have the same photo on my bureau at home. Show it to your boyfriend, so he knows what a cute baby you were."

I slip the picture out of the plastic sleeve. My relationship with Dad is heavy. But the photo is light in the palm of my hand.

When I finally come out of Dad's hospital room, I find Roderick and Father Peters on adjacent waiting room chairs, their heads bent together in deep discussion.

"Hey," I croak. "What are you two scheming about?"

"Tacos and enchiladas!" Father Peters says. "We're trying to figure out which one is easier to serve to two hundred people." He jumps to his feet. "How is your father?"

"He's all right for a guy with severe lacerations and no spleen."

"Ah. I'll visit him in a moment. How are you holding up?"

"Fine." I take a deep breath. "Better, actually."

"Good." He claps me on the shoulder. "I'm going to ask you a question, but I don't expect an answer right away."

"Okay?" That sounds ominous.

"Do you want me to find your biological father? Your mother told me about him this morning. I've never met the man, but I'm sure I could track him down. If that ever becomes important to you, just say the word."

"I don't think so," I say abruptly. "But thanks."

He gives me a quick hug. "You call me if you need anything. My door is always open to you. Both of you," he says, including Roderick. And then he strides out of the waiting room.

"Whoa," Roddy says, rising to his feet. "Would you ever want to meet your sperm donor?"

I've wondered about him, for sure. But the man got a parishioner pregnant and then made himself scarce. "Parents are difficult. I think I already have all the parents I can handle."

"Aw. They sure are." Roderick wraps his arms around me and gives me my second hug in as many minutes. "Are you ready to go out for noodles with me?"

"More than ready," I admit. And I give him a tight hug back.

RODERICK

Let it be said that Audrey makes terrific fried chicken. It's crispy and juicy and even a little spicy. I'm in heaven as I sit elbow to elbow with my man, eating this terrific food.

And I'm pleased to report that during the blessing, Kieran did hold hands with me under the table. I never thought this day would come. But here we are.

Kieran was a little quiet on the ride to Tuxbury. He hates attention. And tonight is the first time he's seen all his extended family at once. But now he's communing with his dinner and spreading butter on a piece of cornbread that I made for tonight's feast.

There have been several not-so-subtle glances toward this end of the table, but—lucky for Kieran—it's not us they're looking at. In a bizarre twist of events, we're not tonight's biggest story. Not even close.

Grandpa Shipley invited a guest for dinner. A *woman*. Her name is Lydia. She's seventy-nine years old, and she's eating her fried chicken daintily with a knife and fork.

The Shipleys are mesmerized. Every one of them.

"So, Lydia," Ruth says sweetly. "You're new in town?"

"I was new in town when FDR was president," she says. "But my family traveled extensively. My father was in the army."

"We met in high school!" Grandpa says, reaching for another piece of my cornbread. "I thought I might ask her to marry me, but she moved away again. If she hadn't, you all might be different people."

Lydia sets down her fork and turns to him. "That is a creepy thing to say to your lovely family. And you don't even know if I would have said yes."

Grandpa blinks. "I'm sorry, Miss Lydia. You're right. I shouldn't presume."

Every Shipley jaw hits the floor.

He doesn't notice, though. He uses his knife to swipe a pat of butter, which he applies in a thick layer to the cornbread. "Roderick, this is fabulous stuff. You can come back any time."

"Thank you, sir. Good to know."

"Do you make this for my grandson?" he asks, giving me a pointed look.

"Well, I make lots of things. But I don't think I've made the cornbread at home."

"Hrmf," he says through a bite. "Well, you should. It's delicious. And that boy works hard."

"Indeed," I agree, although I feel as if I've been cast in the role of a fifties housewife, somehow.

"He doesn't know how to cook," Grandpa continues.

"Actually—" I start to argue.

"If he *did* know how to cook, I'd've been invited for dinner already at your new house in Colebury."

My jaw snaps shut.

Kieran gives me an amused glance. "You know, Grandpa, we were *just* thinking you should come over for dinner sometime. Weren't we?" He nudges my knee under the table.

"Oh, definitely," I say, nudging his back.

"Do you drink?" Grandpa asks me next. This is starting to sound like a job interview.

"Occasionally," I admit.

"Do you play poker?"

"Ease up, Grandpa," Kieran says. "Roddy was invited here to dinner. Not to an interrogation."

"I know how to play poker," I answer anyway. "But I'm not very good at it."

"Excellent!" Grandpa says. "See, I knew you were good company. We'll have a little game later. Low stakes. Nothing to worry about."

"Yessir."

Kieran just shakes his head and serves himself another spoonful of potato salad.

———

"That wasn't so bad, right?" I ask on the way home.

"A walk in the park for me," Kieran says as he accelerates on the highway. "You got all the hard questions."

"They weren't so hard. Your grandpa is amusing."

"That he is."

"Can I play some loud music on your phone?"

"Knock yourself out."

I put on an old Phish album and rock out. I'm so into it that I don't notice the car parked in front of our house, or the man sitting on the front porch in the January chill. Not until Kieran points him out, anyway. "Who is that?"

"Oh, fuck," I whisper as the man stands up and crosses the yard toward us. "That's B-Brian," I stammer, fumbling to turn the music off.

I cannot *believe* my ex is here in Vermont. He must have some other business in Colebury, Vermont. Because the farthest he ever went out of his way for me before was to swing through a drive-thru Starbucks on his way home from the studio.

Kieran freezes with one foot out of the truck, and one foot still in. "Roddy? That guy looks like Brian *Aimsley*."

"Yep." If Kieran gets all starstruck I will vomit up all the good food I ate tonight. I get out of the truck, feeling wary.

"You're Brian Aimsley," Kieran says, walking slowly toward my ex. His voice is hushed with surprise.

"Yeah." My ex gives him a big smile. "You're a fan?"

My heart takes a dive toward my shoes.

Kieran stops, and his fingers tease the scruff on his chin. "You know, I *was* a fan. Until about two seconds ago. You're the guy who cheated on Roddy? You're the guy who froze Roddy's credit cards?"

Brian's smile fades. "Well, I was angry. That was just an over-reaction."

"Uh-huh," Kieran says in that low-key way of his. "Did you know your overreaction had Roddy sleeping in his *car*? In the snow."

To his credit, Brian looks mildly horrified. "Baby?" he says, turning in my direction. "I'm so sorry. I know we fought. But I'm here now. I came out for you. I can finally be your man."

"No you can't," I say firmly. "I have a better one now. One who listens when I talk."

Now Brian looks nervous. "I know you're angry. But I had a lot I needed to work out for myself. And I did that hard work, and now I'm here for you. I brought your guitar and everything."

"I have a better one of those, too."

It's rare to see Brian looking so unsure of himself, and I hate myself for enjoying it. "Look," he tries. "I got a hotel room. How about we go talk?"

"How about you get off our lawn?" Kieran argues. "Before I call the cops." He takes a couple of menacing strides in Brian's direction. "You're not welcome here. Roddy doesn't need any more of your gaslighting." He turns to me. "Wait, *is* there anything you need from this guy?"

I start to shake my head, but then I realize there is. "Well, just one thing."

"What's that?" Brian asks, looking hopeful.

"An unqualified apology." I've been waiting for that for a long time.

"Oh." He frowns. "Okay. Here goes. Look, I'm sorry—"

"That'll do," Kieran says. "Won't it?"

"Yeah," I say with a laugh. "That covers it."

"But *baby*—"

And now Kieran has had enough. "Get gone," he says, taking another step.

Brian takes one back. "I'm at the High Hill Inn!" he says, moving back a few more steps as Kieran continues to herd him from our yard. "Text me!"

Yeah, sure. I've already deleted his number.

Kieran doesn't lay a finger on Brian, he just keeps stalking toward him. Brian would never risk his guitar hands to fight for me, so he climbs into his rental car and slams the door.

The taillights glow red as he drives away.

"Jesus," Kieran says, after he walks back to me. He covers his eyes with his hands. "I lost it a little there. I hope you didn't really want a lengthy apology, because I might have ruined that."

"No problemo," I say. "Good riddance."

"I'm glad he left so easily. I don't want to go to jail for punching a country music star. But the man really had it coming."

"Yeah, I'm really glad you won't be going to jail," I say, even though the evilest part of me would *really* like to see Brian get punched in the kisser. "Jail is bad bad bad."

"What a *tool*."

"Yup," I agree.

"*Brian Aimsley*. No wonder you don't like country music. You never said a word."

"It's a matter of principle. And I have principles, even if he doesn't."

"I almost can't wrap my head around it." Kieran shakes his head. "Must have been an interesting couple of years. Bet you saw some pretty glam things."

"Sometimes the glam was fun," I admit, reaching out for his hand. "But you spoil me more than he ever did."

"How? We still don't even have a dining room table or chairs."

"You spoil me in the ways that really matter." I take Kieran's other hand in mine. I've got both of them now. Our street is quiet, because it's nine thirty on a weeknight in January. The stars are bright overhead, and the moon is rising to light up the snow. I feel like I'm a million miles from Nashville, and I love it here. "You spoil me by being real. I used to daydream that I'd find a guy who looks at me the way you're looking at me right now."

"How's that?" he asks, humor in his brown eyes.

"Like you're all in, no matter what happens."

"I am. That's true." He leans down and kisses my cheekbone. "Come inside and I'll show you how all in I can be." Then he kisses me for real.

We're still going at it a minute later when Zara opens her front door. "Get a room, you two!" She cackles and shuts the door.

It's good advice. So we do.

TWO YEARS LATER

KIERAN

"Look at that kid." Roddy nudges me under the table. "That's ballsy."

I turn my head and spot a blond kid, maybe twelve years old, riding a unicycle up the brick street, weaving in and out of the Church Street patrons. "Huh," I say. "Nice reflexes."

Roddy and I are just finishing dinner at an outdoor table at a Burlington noodle shop. Say what you will about our tiny state, but Burlington—population 42,000—is a great destination on a summer night. The marketplace is closed off to cars, so customers spill from the bars and restaurants onto the brick street. The outdoor tables are full of diners. It's a nice place for dinner, and also great for people-watching.

Burlington is the closest thing we have to a real city, and it's worth an hour's drive from Colebury. I've been coming here two days a week for the last two years for school. That's going pretty well—I've liked all my classes, and I've been tapping the alumni network to find freelance design jobs.

I'm on summer break, though, so Roddy and I are here just for the hell of it.

Cash is still tight, but date night happens anyway. Roddy loves to get out, and I love to make him happy. I still pick up Busy Bean shifts sometimes just for pocket money.

At the moment, my date is slyly tucking his credit card into a bill wallet that I never saw arrive at our table. "Sweetheart, did you just trick me into watching a kid on a unicycle so you could grab the check?"

He gives me a cheeky grin. "I'm just using all the resources available to me."

"But you bought last time," I argue.

He shrugs. "Can I ask you a serious question? Why do we do this?"

"Why do we argue about the check? Because you're a conniving troublemaker."

He hands the bill wallet off to the waitress before turning back to me with a thoughtful expression. "Why do we have separate accounts at all? Why don't we just make a joint bank account and stop dividing all the bills in half? Isn't it time?"

Whoa. I pick up my beer and drain it, readying my arguments. *We can't do that.* Well, really we could. *It's too complicated…* Eh. It would actually be simpler.

When you get right down to it, I really have only one true objection. "But I don't make as much money as you do. How will I know if I'm paying my way?"

He shakes his head at me. "You pay your way every day. That's the point. I don't really care if your bank deposits aren't as regular as mine." Since Roddy has continued to grow in usefulness to Zara's and Audrey's various businesses, his paycheck is rock solid.

Mine ebb and flow with my freelance business, and school takes up a lot of my time. "I'm broke sometimes," I point out.

"Yeah, and I remember how that feels." He shrugs. "But it's only a temporary condition. Nobody works harder than you. And we share everything else. The groceries. The heat. The cable bill. I love you, Kieran. We're only going to share more things, right? Why not the bank account?"

He's right—there's no rational reason. But I'm struggling with this idea.

"Just think about it," he says. "In the meantime, I have plans to get you drunk right now."

"You do? At home?"

He shakes his head. "Remember when you told me there weren't any gay bars in Vermont?"

"Yeah. Why?"

"There's a brand-new one up the street, and I think we should check it out."

"Wait, really?"

"Really. We don't have to go now, but I heard there's live music tonight."

"Yeah? Okay. That's an easier decision. Although you're probably right about the bank-account thing, too."

He grins. "Of course I am."

"We both know I'd go anywhere with you, or do anything you asked me to. Sometimes I just need a minute to get used to the idea."

"You don't say."

I give him a gentle kick under the table. "Be grateful. And now tell me about this new place," I demand. "How'd you hear about it?"

"On VPR. It's called Vino and Veritas. One side is an LGBTQ friendly bar, specializing in wine. Or what I'd call a gay bar. And the other side is an inclusive bookstore."

"Huh. Isn't that kind of a strange combo?" But let's face it, I rarely leave Vermont. And I've never been near a gay bar. "And what makes a gay bookstore gay?" I have to ask.

"Oh, not much," he admits. "The difference probably comes down to this—the LGBTQ books are in the front of the store instead of in back. And there will probably be rainbows all over the kids' section."

"Fair enough. And the bar?"

"Eye candy and a comfortable space. Those are the parameters."

"I like it already."

"See? You're a cheap date," Roderick says, reaching over to squeeze my thigh.

"Get a few drinks in me, and I'll be even cheaper."

"I like the sound of that," Roddy says. "Let's do this."

RODERICK

We stroll up the marketplace a few minutes later. "See? There's the place." I point at a large brick building with a Vino and Veritas sign in neon outside. And then I reach for Kieran's hand.

Holding Kieran's hand is something I do as often as possible. Although my reason for doing so right now is a little shallow. Maybe Kieran hasn't been to a gay bar before, but I have. And anyone with eyes will be checking out my guy the moment we set foot in that place.

"Place looks nice," he says, oblivious to my machinations. "And you were right about one thing—there are lots of rainbows in the window on the bookstore. But check it out—farming books, too."

He's right. One of the window displays is dedicated to chicken farming. Go figure.

When we reach the door, Kieran holds it open for me. Inside, the bar is to the left and the bookstore to the right. The store is just closing, though, so we'll have to check that out another time.

But the bar is just heating up. The tables and stools are maybe three quarters full. There's a guy on the stage playing his guitar and singing, with a bass player and a percussionist accompanying him.

I like the place already.

I scan the room and then nudge Kieran toward two open seats at the end of the bar. As soon as I sit down, a very hot, tattooed bartender slides a drink menu between us. "Evening, boys. Is this your first time to Vino and Veritas?"

"Why, yes it is," Kieran says quietly. "What do you recommend?"

"Depends what you're in the mood for. Our wine list is second to none. We have Goldenpour on tap, as well as a full selection of other Vermont craft beers. There's also Shipley cider and…" The tattooed hottie frowns at my boyfriend. "Now, hang on. You're a Shipley, right? You look familiar. I went to high school in Colebury for a year."

"Oh, of course," Kieran says slowly. I'm getting the feeling that he doesn't quite remember the guy, but he doesn't want to sound impolite. "How've you been?"

And now that I'm paying attention, this dude's face does look familiar. "I went there for two years, too, and I think maybe you were in my class. Is your name Tanner? And didn't you have a brother?"

Kieran shoots me a look of relief, happy that one of us knew the guy's name.

"Yeah." A smile appears on his rugged face and then disappears just as quickly. "My brother and I didn't have the best attendance record, though. Water under the bridge, right?" He offers me his hand to shake. "And you're—?"

"Roderick Waites." We shake.

"What can I get you both to drink?" Tanner asks when all the introductions are through.

"How's this Prosecco?" I tap the menu. "Is it on the dry side, or sweet?"

"It's, uh…" Tanner scowls. "Okay—confession time. I'm a great bar manager but I'm new to wine. So why don't I pour you a glass on the house, and you can tell me how to describe it."

"That's a deal I can't refuse." I can only have one drink, though, since I'm the driver tonight.

Tanner pours me a glass of bubbly, and taps a beer for Kieran. He serves a few more customers, while I taste the wine and look around. "So this is the Vermont edition of a gay bar. Fascinating. Not much leather. Lots of technical fabrics. Rugged. Kinda on the wholesome side. It's a lot like how I'd picture a gay bar in Iceland."

Kieran glances around. "Nice place."

"Absolutely." The singer does a unique, acoustic cover of an old Cranberries song, and I dig it.

"That could be you up there," Kieran says suddenly. "On your guitar. You'd sound amazing."

"Nah." I swat that idea away. "I only play for you. I like music, but I'm not ambitious about it. I'd rather sit next to you than be up on the stage."

He gives me a warm look that's only interrupted when Tanner returns. "Okay, Colebury contingent, let's have those tasting notes." He taps a notepad with a pen. "Save me from my ignorance."

I take a taste of the wine and hold it on my tongue. Then I hold up the glass. "The color is straw-yellow with hints of green. The nose is fragrant with notes of citron and honey."

Tanner blinks. "Something tells me you've done this before."

"I went to culinary school."

"Around here?" he asks.

I shake my head. "Nashville. Long story. I stayed away from Colebury for eight years."

"Huh." Tanner rubs his chin. "I got away from this place, too. But it called me back."

"I guess it called me, too," I admit.

"Some of us never left," Kieran says, resting his burly elbow on the bar.

"How's Colebury holding up?" Tanner asks. "There's some new bars, right?"

"Yeah, two of them," Kieran says. "The Gin Mill and Speakeasy. Plus the coffee shop where Roddy runs the kitchen."

"Nice. You guys still in touch with anyone from high school?" Tanner asks.

"Just him." I point at Kieran. "Not that we knew each other back then."

"Not, uh, well, anyway," Kieran says, flashing me a secretive smile. He glances at Tanner again. "Do you still have friends in Colebury?"

"Not so much, because I only lived there one year. But there's a Facebook group for every graduation year. My brother sent it to me. See?" He puts his phone down on the bar in front of me. "Two hundred members."

"Huh," I say. "High school wasn't a great time for me, so I don't have much urge to relive it. Except…" I squint down at the phone. "Is that—?" I stop myself just in time. Because it's not cool to bring up your old hookups with your boyfriend sitting beside you.

It's too late, though. Kieran has leaned over to squint at Tanner's phone. "Jared Harvey," he says. "What's he up to?"

"Soccer player, right?" Tanner says. "The only thing I remember about him is that he was hot."

I chuckle nervously. "Never mind—"

Tanner taps on Jared's picture, oblivious to my discomfort. "He lives in Barre, but he teaches at Colebury High School. Huh. Some people couldn't get enough of that place, I guess. Oh—" He sets the phone on the bar again. "Here. My beer delivery is here. 'Scuse me, boys." Tanner slides off to intercept another staff member.

Kieran and I exchange an amused glance. Then he looks down at Tanner's phone. "Don't you want to know what subject Jared teaches?"

"Nah." The truth is I never think about Jared Harvey. That was ten years ago already. And we had nothing in common and barely ever spoke to each other. All he wanted from me was some hasty physical release. And all I wanted from him was sex and rebellion.

Kieran slides the phone over and scrolls the page. Then he lets out a loud, startled bark of laughter. "Oh my God."

"What?"

Kieran tips his shaggy head back and laughs. "He's the phys ed teacher."

"What? *No.*"

"It's true!" Kieran laughs harder. "He just couldn't stay away from that gym. Too many memories."

"You're kidding." I lean over the phone and let out a snort the moment I see the photo of adult Jared in his Colebury spirit-wear, a whistle around his neck. "I can't believe it."

"I'm telling you." Kieran nudges me with his knee. "You leave a big impression on anyone who meets you. Huge."

"Oh stop."

"It's true." Kieran wraps an arm around me and hugs me even as the music gets louder. "I'm a lucky guy, Roddy." He kisses me quickly on the side of my face. "Under those bleachers was only the start."

"It wasn't even my best work," I say, soaking up Kieran's affection. "When we go home later, I'll show you all my new tricks."

"I'm counting on it," he says.

And I know I'm a lucky guy, too.

T H E
E N D

Made in the USA
Las Vegas, NV
28 June 2022

50818536R00167